Lois Mateus Peters
Tallgrass Farm
Harrodsburg, KY 40330

TRICK
OF THE
EYE

TRICK
OF THE
EYE

JANE
STANTON
HITCHCOCK

miramax books

ISBN 0-7394-3619-8

For my mother

CHAPTER

1

The sign on my door reads, TROMPE L'OEIL, INC. For a reasonable price I will paint a variety of illusory images on any compatible surface. I paint "faux" finishes—faux marbre, faux bois, faux tortoiseshell, faux bamboo—as well as architectural effects—niches, columns, windows, doors. I can fill a room with animals, birds, and people, with swags, ribbons, and clouds. My object is to arrest and amuse my viewers by leading them away from reality and making them look twice, if only for an instant, at the beauty of illusion.

Mine is a narrow and exacting occupation, best executed calmly. I don't slap paint on untreated canvases the size of bedsheets. I don't try to find myself through art, nor do I wait for inspiration. I don't look for glory or immortality. I'm a craftsman, and each day I try to do a craftsman's job. I've made my peace with anonymity. I'm content without being happy.

My name is Faith Crowell. I'm thirty-nine years old and am, to use a word which appeals to a perverse streak in me that favors things archaic and anachronistic, a spinster. I've never been to the altar, though once I came so close I bought a wedding dress. But that's another story. There have been times when, walking home to an empty apartment in the twilight, I've thought about that time, thought about how different my life would have been had I married. Once inside my little home, however, surrounded by the chintz, the cat, and the bric-a-brac that are often the accoutrements of single women living alone in large cities, I feel quite fortunate. I cook a light meal, enjoy a glass of wine, and read, until I drift off with my dreams.

I'm up by seven. I don't need an alarm clock, for habit is the best alarm there is. I have a light breakfast, bathe, dress, and put a plate of food down for my cat. I'm on my way to the studio no later than eight-fifteen.

My studio is on the third floor of an unassuming, rent-controlled brownstone ten blocks from my apartment. I enjoy walking there in the morning when passersby seem filled with purpose and energy. I see the same faces again and again—the shopkeepers, sanitation workers, commuters. We sometimes recognize one another and exchange a friendly nod without words, which suits me perfectly.

I share the building with several tenants, most of whom I rarely see. Should I pass one of them on the stairs, I make it a point to greet him or her cordially. As New York City is not the sort of place where people drop in to borrow sugar or have a cup of coffee, contact with my neighbors is minimal—which is also fine with me.

I live in the city because that's where my work is, but I could just as easily live in the country, and plan to do so one day. It's a way of looking forward to something. I have a limited life, defined by my work and a few friends. I'm more solitary than most, but judging from the appalling amount of neurosis and unrest in the world, I consider myself well-off.

Once, some years ago, I began waking up frequently in the middle of the night for no apparent reason. Hot fingers of panic kneaded away at my insides as I dwelt on the futility of life—mine, in particular. I'd get out of bed, pace the room, stalk my mirror in the half-light, wondering who that wild-eyed creature streaked with fear really was. Come morning, I'd feel as old as death. My technique suffered. Business went downhill. Finally, I had to stop working altogether. The nervous, so-called "artistic temperament" has no place in trompe l'oeil.

This slump was deep but temporary. After a time, I managed to pull myself together. I stopped expecting too much from life. I began to think of my time on this earth as one leg of a long journey, and view myself as a person in transit. I began to accept life's odd turns and disappointments as the seasoned traveler accepts the surprises and inconveniences which are an inevitable part of any trip.

I resumed painting. To my astonishment, my technique had not suffered but improved. There was new depth to my work. Others noticed it, too. Soon, commissions abounded. Now my little trompe l'oeil business is a great success, capitalizing as it does on the fashion of making things appear to be what they are not.

My clients aren't in the habit of visiting my studio. Most of my commissions are arranged over the telephone by a decorator. I was therefore surprised when I answered the downstairs buzzer on an unseasonably warm day in April and heard the voice over the intercom say: "Frances Griffin to see Miss Crowell."

Everyone who knew anything about connoisseurship had heard of Frances Griffin. She and her late husband, Holt Griffin, had been great collectors when there was an abundance of important pictures and furniture available to collect. The Griffin Collection was one of the very best, assembled in the decades just before and after the Second World War when masterpieces were frequently on the international market, before export rules became more stringent. After Holt Griffin died, Frances Griffin gave many of their paintings to museums, including the finest Titian in private hands. The Griffins and their collection were well-known to anyone with the slightest interest in art.

Holt Griffin was the scion of an old, rich New York family who, unlike most of his kind, had gone on to distinguish himself on his own, in a long diplomatic career. The money, I happened to know, came originally from the manufacture of manhole covers, and then was poured into real estate. In the late 1800s, Elias Holt, the great-grandfather of Holt Griffin, had founded an ironworks, the chief product of which were the heavy gray metal disks used to cap the sewers of New York. I know this because I tend to know these kinds of details—dainty, irrelevant bits of gossip which serve no purpose whatsoever and are exquisitely extraneous to everyday life.

Though Holt Griffin had supplied the money, it was Frances Griffin, the woman climbing my three flights of stairs at that very moment, who had the eye. Everyone acknowledged her to be the guiding hand behind the acquisitions. She was one of those legendary figures of style and taste whose name evokes awe, even in the most privileged circles. I didn't know much else about her except that having been a great collector and hostess, she was now a recluse, known for her aversion to parties, publicity, and people.

I stepped out into the dingy hallway and saw a figure climbing the stairs—a slim, impeccably dressed woman with a girlish manner and a sprightly walk. Her eyes were clear and inquisitive, set in a grainy but handsome face. I knew she must have been around seventy or seventy-five years old, but she didn't look it. She was very well-preserved and had the air many rich people have of not being wholly real. Her perfection of dress, her aura of contained graciousness combined with her seeming obliviousness to the hallway's unappetizing details—the broken stairs, chipping paint, and acrid smell—made her seem like a polished actress playing a part.

"How do you do?" Mrs. Griffin said, extending a tapered, discreetly manicured hand to me as she reached the landing. "I'm Frances Griffin."

"It's a great pleasure, to meet you, Mrs. Griffin. I'm Faith Crowell," I replied, aware that my voice had deferentially lowered an octave.

She was wearing an elegant pale green wool suit with a matching hat, carrying white kid gloves and a black patent leather bag. Her feet, noticeably small, were encased in plain patent leather pumps with low heels. A gold pin in the shape of a fish, studded with green and pink peridots, was jauntily affixed to the right side of her jacket.

I invited her into my studio and offered her a cup of tea,

which she graciously accepted. We sat, rather stiffly, on two of the twelve gilt ballroom chairs I had scheduled to faux bamboo that week.

"I have heard, Miss Crowell," she began in a voice tinged with a patrician mid-Atlantic accent, "that you are very good at what you do."

I thanked her. As I am not a believer in false modesty, I replied that I was indeed proud of my work. She squinted while opening her purse, extracting from it a pair of glasses which she put on. She looked around the studio.

"Yes," she said, focusing on several pieces I had either finished or was in the process of finishing—a bureau, a mirror, a small mantelpiece—"I can see that you're good."

She peered at me over the top of her glasses.

"The trick is to lighten reality, isn't it?" she observed.

"In life and in art," I said, smiling.

She chuckled.

"Your work is very painterly. I especially like the faux marbre. That piece," she said, indicating the small mantelpiece. "It's lovely the way you've done it. I like faux marbre in any case, don't you? It's much less ponderous than the real thing. Real marble can be so cold in a room."

"Yes, I agree. Though people still pay a lot of money for it."

"Real tortoiseshell, on the other hand, is lovely and warm," she said. "But you can't get it anymore."

"Faux tortoiseshell is very difficult to do well. If I'm not careful it all winds up looking like some awful leopard skin."

"You've done it very well there." She nodded to the red-and-black faux tortoiseshell mirror drying against the wall.

"Thank you. I just finished it yesterday. Third try. It's not too bad now."

"There's always been a market for the faux—whether we could get the real thing or not."

"That's why I'm in business, I suppose."

"So many real things are impossible to come by these days. Lots of the things we once took for granted are gone," she

sighed. "You do have a lovely, light touch . . . Yes, lovely . . ."
She glanced around the room another time. "I'd like you to
come and do some work for me at The Haven."

Like a queen issuing a royal command, she did not hesitate
at all when speaking to me. She seemed to understand the power
of her request, and to know what an honor it was considered
to work for her. Many would have done it, simply to get a
glimpse of the legendary house on Long Island which had never
been photographed for a book or displayed in the pages of the
fashionable decorating magazines.

"I'm honored," I said. "Of course I'd love to work for you."

Smiling at me as if she'd expected no other response, she
removed her glasses, folded them carefully, and put them back
into her purse.

"It's quite a large job. You'll have to be there full-time for
some months."

"Oh dear, I don't know if I can do that."

She went on as though she hadn't heard me.

"It's a ballroom. I built it for my daughter's coming-out
party many years ago. I want to redo it, to see it again, fresh.
It's never too late to see things fresh."

Though she spoke casually, I couldn't help sensing a certain
intensity beneath the surface of her conversation. She toyed
with the patent leather strap of her handbag, twisting it around
her fingers. She stared hard at me every so often as if she were
trying to recall something, or memorize me, or see deeper into
me. It felt odd.

"I'd have to give up all my other work. That's a bit
tricky."

"Why don't you come round and see me tomorrow? I'll
show you what I want done. Then you can make your decision."

"Mrs. Griffin," I began slowly, "I'm very flattered by your
offer. May I ask you—how did you happen to pick me?"

She hesitated for a moment.

"Well, I heard about you from a couple of friends of
mine."

She named two of my richest and grandest clients. I was

always amazed how small this world of the extraordinarily rich was, like a private country incorporating all nationalities. The titanically rich, like royalty, all seemed to know one another, or know of one another, no matter where they were from. And because many of them led their lives in the fairly constant pursuit of luxury, pleasure, and material possessions, they passed the finest craftsmen and the finest dealers and the finest designers, florists, and chefs along to one another like precious objects in an elaborate, ongoing potlatch festival. I had no illusions about my place in their world. In their world, an artisan was a commodity.

"Also," she continued, "it seems we both share a passion for Paolo Veronese. I read a fine article you wrote on the Villa Barbaro. It was very well written, and appreciative of an artist I adore."

She alluded to a piece I had written some years ago for an obscure art journal, *Chiaroscuro*, on the celebrated Villa Barbaro in Maser, near Venice. Paolo Veronese's whimsical trompe l'oeil mural there was a great favorite of mine. The revelation that she'd read my article appealed to my vanity.

"I'm so pleased you liked the piece. I love that villa. I remember the first time I stood in the great hall and looked up at that marvelous gallery of pets and birds and people staring down on me from their painted balcony. They were so bewitching I almost swore they were real."

"My daughter," she said suddenly. "My daughter was very enthusiastic—like you."

I let the comment go.

"You'll come and see me tomorrow?" she asked, poised on the edge of her chair.

"Of course I will, though I have to think seriously of what your wonderful offer means in terms of my life."

She glanced once more around my cluttered, airless studio.

"Well," she said in a rather imperious tone, "it would certainly mean a change."

With that, she rose from her chair. I walked her to the door.

"Please forgive me for being so hesitant," I said, opening the door for her. "It's just that since I spend my life painting over surfaces, I've gotten used to examining them very carefully. Perhaps too carefully."

"Well, you think about it."

"I'll walk you downstairs."

"Oh, no thank you. I can see myself out. I'll expect you tomorrow, then, at, say, four o'clock? We'll have some tea. Here are the directions."

She handed me a printed card with a drawing of the house on one side and a map on the other. I didn't let on that I already knew where the house was.

With that, she left.

That night I walked home in an uncharacteristic funk, feeling apprehensive, as though Frances Griffin were Fate's harbinger. I honestly didn't want to interrupt my routine by accepting such a commission. On the other hand, the chance to work with this extraordinary woman was a great professional opportunity. And, I confess, I did feel the lure of her glamour.

Long ago I made peace with the fact that mine was a well-ordered, uneventful life, grisaille as opposed to color-plated. I'd come to understand the difference between the climates of loneliness and of solitude: The former was oppressive and humid, the latter cool and invigorating. I abhorred the popular view that people who live alone and work alone remain isolated from life's great experiences. For me, the key to appreciating life was imagination. Without it, even a privileged life could be dull. With it, one could make a feast of straws.

Fortunately for me, my art was more of a craft and therefore less volatile, a friend as opposed to a lover. My moments of loneliness were, I suspect, less intense than those of my more creative colleagues, though, of course, I'd had my share. I felt one such moment creeping up on me now. I knew I needed to talk to someone.

There was only one thing to do. I bought two artichokes, an extra veal chop, and a tarte tatin from the local French bakery, and telephoned my dear friend, Harry Pitt, on the likely chance he would be free for dinner. He was.

Harry Pitt, like me, led a reclusive life, preferring to spend time in the company of his books, pictures, and Mr. Spencer, his miniature schnauzer, rather than with people. Harry was in his seventies and a bachelor. In his heyday, he'd been a noted art dealer, esthete, and an escort of fashionable women of a certain age when they were, as one wag delicately put it, "between men."

He was nearly bald now, and rotund, having led the high life at splendid luncheon and dinner parties. He was a repository of superfluous information about superfluous people, which, of course, made him wonderful company for me. He knew about things like Mrs. Augustus Blodgett's couture shroud, and the Prince de Greve's penchant for paying boys in the slums of Rio to have their teeth extracted so that they could better perform fellatio on him.

Harry knew everything about everyone in society, and he enjoyed regaling me with the salacious tales of "social life's rich pageant," as he dubbed it. I'd passed many a hilarious evening with Harry while he sat perched like a pasha on the tasseled silk pillows of his couch, fingering the long white silk scarf around his neck, smoking a cigarette in a black lacquer holder, pontificating about society as it had once been and as it was now. He'd spent most of his life singing for his supper in the company of the rich and celebrated and, for some reason, had come to the conclusion that the majority of people will behave badly sooner or later given the opportunity.

"One is far safer with possessions and pets," he used to say. "With them, at least, one always knows exactly where one stands, and the repairs are cheaper."

As we ate our supper, I told him about my encounter with Frances Griffin.

"Frances Griffin . . . Frances Griffin . . ." He repeated the name, rolling the r's, savoring it in his mouth as if it were an excellent claret.

"What an interesting woman," he said. "A woman of great complexity and depth. And a visual genius. Of course you know the story about her and the fireplace?"

"No," I replied, intrigued.

"Oh, well, it's a marvelous story, and absolutely true. I know—knew—the architect. He's dead."

"Harry, you never disappoint me."

I sat back and prepared to listen to one of Harry's anecdotes. He was my Marco Polo, coming home from exotic lands with tales of wealth and princes. As he spoke, he cut his veal chop meticulously with his knife and fork, careful to eat the American way—that is, putting down his knife and switching his fork from his left hand to his right before ingesting the slice. He called it one of his more time-consuming affectations.

"It seems that after she built that wonderful house, The Haven—to which you, lucky soul, have been invited tomorrow—she was walking through it with the architect on the day it was finished to make sure everything was absolutely correct. When she got to the living room, she stopped dead, looked around, and said, 'There's something wrong here.' The poor, dear architect froze in his tracks and stammered something. History hasn't recorded those immortal lines, but it's safe to say he was worried. She, meanwhile, turned around slowly once or twice, then finally said, 'The fireplace. It's off-center, is it not?' And so my friend, the architect, who also had a rather good eye, looked at the thing and said no he didn't think it was off-center. He thought it looked absolutely right. The upshot of it was, they got a ruler and measured the damn thing. And by God, the fireplace was indeed about, oh, nine inches or a foot off the dead center of the room.

"So Mrs. Griffin, having made her point, said, 'Please fix it.' At which juncture, my friend the architect said, 'Mrs. Griffin, I promise you, you won't notice it when the room's all decorated.' 'Oh, but I will,' she assured him. So then he said, 'But Mrs. Griffin, you don't understand. I can't fix the fireplace without tearing down all five floors.' To which, according not only to legend but to my friend the architect who was there and to whom she said it, Frances Griffin replied, 'I didn't ask you *how* you were going to do it.'

"She then walked straight out the door, and he proceeded to tear down the entire house and rebuild it—at her expense —with the fireplace dead center. Two years later, she walked into the house again, pronounced it perfect, and moved in. Now if that ain't a modern-day 'Princess and the Pea' story, I don't know what is!"

"Astonishing."

"She's a pathological perfectionist," Harry continued. "Brilliant at proportion. Famous for going into people's gardens and rooms and telling them exactly how to replant the rosebushes or rearrange the furniture. And the thing is, she's always right. She has such a great eye that she actually once went into a museum and told them they had a fake Greuze painting on display. It caused such an uproar you can't believe it. But, by God, fake it was!"

"Where did she learn it all?"

"You can't learn what she knows. Her sense of taste and proportion are like perfect pitch—you either have it or you don't. But she's very informed. She has bothered to learn things. She has curatorial knowledge of old master art and eighteenth-century furniture."

"Where's she from?" I inquired.

"No idea. She wasn't anybody one knew," Harry sniffed. "I believe prior to her marriage, she was a rather murky figure on the social horizon. Of course, she cleared up brilliantly when she married Holt Griffin. Someone once told me she claimed her father was a diplomat. One suspects the most diplomatic thing he ever did was to fade from view before anyone could call his daughter a liar."

We both chuckled. Harry began building a little pyramid with discarded artichoke leaves. He went on:

"I remember seeing pictures of her. She certainly wasn't beautiful but she had great style. And apparently she was marvelous company, wonderful fun. Somehow she managed to break into the top drawer and pull out the very sought-after Mr. Griffin—outraging every single dreary ex-debutante around. Caused quite a scandal at the time. It amuses me to think how they all kowtow to her now."

"She has something, there's no doubt about it," I said. "Even meeting her once there's a kind of mystery about her. I bet she was very sexy in her time."

"Weren't we all?" Harry said, toppling the artichoke pyramid with his fork.

"Well, of course," he went on, "the great rumor was that Holt Griffin was just about gay—sort of teetering on the edge of gay—when she managed to ensnare him with certain exotic sexual wiles. It was thought that she enabled him not to go over the top, as it were. She was always being compared to the Duchess of Windsor in that respect. You know—cocaine on the genitals, Cleopatra's Grip, all that sort of thing."

"Cleopatra's Grip?" I said innocently, forking in a bite of veal.

"Contraction of the vaginal muscles so that the penis has the sensation of being massaged," he replied without apparent interest. "It's an effective exercise known to courtesans and, I imagine, to a few other enterprising ladies. But, to tell you the truth, I don't believe any of it. I think he just fell in love with her. She was fascinating and fun. Compared to all those ghastly little socialites he was used to, she must have seemed like a breath of fresh air. And she took care of him like a medieval chatelaine. The 'on dit' was that she painstakingly researched everything about him before actually meeting him—what his habits were, his favorite wines, liquor, food, hobbies, interests, books, sexual proclivities, etcetera. That way when he finally did meet her, she made him feel as if he were returning to the womb, so to speak."

"How do you know all this?" I asked.

"Oh, it was rather well-known. Nobody could believe she got him, so there was all sorts of speculation as to how she managed to do it. You know how people are—they like to get to the root cause of everything and then trash it. The truth of the matter is men like Holt Griffin need to be catered to. They're not interested in neurotic upper-class girls who are constantly complaining, disappointed with life, who won't put out when they don't feel like it, and who wind up drinking too much because they think they've been shortchanged. Men like Holt Griffin want professional pleasers. That's what Frances Griffin is—or was: a professional pleaser."

"This is certainly a different picture than I expected. I thought she was supposed to be so grand."

"She *is*, my dear. She's the grandest," Harry proclaimed. "Don't think people aren't grand just because they have a dubious past. Dubious pasts make people grander. Think of what they've had to overcome. These silly little asses who think they're grand because they're born into some sort of Junior League nightmare—don't make me laugh. Frances Griffin is grand in the old style—tough and independent, self-made. She's grand like an Amazon."

"Did you know her personally, Harry?"

"Oh well, she's not the sort of woman the likes of me knows personally," he mused. "I knew her rather impersonally though. I met her years ago. She came into my shop and bought an extraordinary Riesener commode on the spot. She bargained with me. She was a very shrewd bargainer but not—how shall I say it?—offensive about it. It was one of the best pieces I've ever had, that commode. Unquestionably. One of the best pieces anyone's ever had, I suspect. I knew she had to have it. She told me she liked my taste. I remember she asked me to look for a few things for her at auction. And I did. We found one or two. All marvelous quality.

"That's the thing about coming from nowhere and having to invent yourself," Harry observed. "You know the difference between the real and the fake because you've had to sort it out so carefully in yourself. Well, *some* people have. Others never learn. Anyway, *she* knew. I would have given my right arm to see the inside of one of her houses, but no such luck. I actually thought of going along with the moving men when they delivered the commode. But I decided it was too tacky."

"I'll take Polaroids tomorrow, Harry," I said, teasing.

"God forbid!" Harry cried. "Anyway I'm getting too blind to see 'em. I'm getting blind, you know."

I patted him on the cheek. He reminded me of a droopy hound.

"I wish I were getting deaf instead," he said. "I've heard quite enough in my life. But I still love to look at things. God how I love a beautiful object. Love going to museums and galleries. Damn it!" He took off his glasses and rubbed the bridge of his nose with his thumb and forefinger. He seemed weary and exasperated.

I got up from the table and cleared our places. I brought in the tarte tatin and cut Harry a large slice, which he attacked with gusto.

"My favorite! You good girl."

I lit a cigarette and sat back in my chair, watching Harry eat.

"So, she got what she wanted," I said. "It's nice when people do that."

"She's had a tragic life really."

"What do you mean? Sounds good to me."

"Well, all that terrible business about the daughter."

"What about the daughter?"

"Do you mean to say you don't know? I thought everybody knew. The daughter, called Cassandra—don't you love it? Only the rich think they can name their children things like Cordelia and Electra and Cassandra without consequence. They feel exempt all around."

"What's the matter with her?" I asked.

"She's dead for one thing."

"Really? Oh dear. How did that happen?"

"I can't believe you don't know this story," he said, sounding very pleased, and looking more animated. Gossip always seemed to invigorate him.

"Cassandra Griffin was stabbed in her room by an unknown intruder over fifteen years ago."

"No!" I gasped.

"To this day they don't know who did it," Harry said. "Never solved the case."

"My God, how horrible."

"*Horrible* isn't the word. It happened right in The Haven. It's a wonder old Frances can still live there. I don't think I could live in a house where my child was stabbed to death. How about you?" Harry inquired somewhat facetiously.

"God, people's lives . . ."

"It was a huge scandal for a while, but for some reason it died down very quickly and one never heard about it again. I suppose out of deference to the family."

"And how long ago did this happen?"

"Fifteen, sixteen years ago. Holt Griffin was still at the U.N. Ambassador or some such thing. I'm surprised you never heard about it. It was really quite something. I suppose you were too young."

"I was in a fog in those days," I said, thinking back. "How old was she—the daughter?"

"About twenty-five, twenty-six. Somewhere around there," Harry replied.

"So she'd be about my age now. A little older."

"Hmmm."

"What a nightmare. And they never solved the case? That seems extraordinary," I said.

"Does, doesn't it? I'm sure there are endless things we don't know about it."

I saw Harry eyeing the tarte tatin.

"More?" I offered.

"Just a sliver, thanks."

I cut him another large slice. This time, he ingested it slowly, picking the apples from the top, saving the crust to eat with his fingers.

"Good, this crust. Like a cookie," he said. "I never taste things properly until the second time around."

"How do people ever recover from something like that? It's ghastly enough to lose a child through illness or accident, but murder . . . She was an only child?"

"The only one," Harry said.

"Mrs. Griffin told me she wanted me to paint the ballroom she'd built for her daughter's coming-out party. And then she said I reminded her of her daughter."

"Really?" Harry seemed interested. "I believe the daughter was very wild. That was the rumor anyway. She married some gigolo type after a rather checkered career."

"Well, she said I did."

"Maybe you look like her."

"Poor thing." I shrugged.

"No getting down on yourself tonight, please, Faith," Harry said, patting my hand. "Well," he continued, "it doesn't always pay to have money, does it?"

I reflected for a moment on Frances Griffin's visit to me that afternoon.

"You know it's funny really," I said. "I never would have imagined in a million years that the woman who came to see me today was the woman you describe. It changes the color of the whole encounter. I'm much more curious about everything now. What do you suppose she really wants?"

"You'll just have to go and find out."

"God, Harry—I'd have to give up all my other work."

Harry pinned me with his eyes.

"Don't be a fool, Faith. You've got to work for her if she wants you to. It's like working for royalty. Better. She knows more. It's that kind of an opportunity, don't you see? Her name is a great provenance. You'll be able to write your own ticket after that."

"I write my own ticket now," I said proudly.

"Yes, but you'll be able to write it for the Concorde."

Brush jumped up on the dining table and began pawing Harry's sleeve. Harry stroked his dipping back. I tried to shoo him away.

"Leave him be," Harry said. "He's just hungry for a little affection, aren't you, Brushie?"

"How old is Mr. Spencer now?"

"About a hundred and twelve. He's toothless, ruthless, and useless, but I adore the little bugger. You must come and have dinner with us next time. He'd love to see you."

Dinner at Harry's apartment was always impossibly chaotic. There were at least three different sauces for everything. In his zeal, he often got them confused. I remember once we had an otherwise delicious leg of lamb topped off with a caramel sauce he mistook for the gravy.

"I wouldn't worry about your other business, if I were you," Harry said. "You'll have plenty of business after you work for her."

"Do I want to be cooped up in the same house for months?"

"We're not exactly talking about a hovel, dear. The Haven is one of *the* great houses of the world. And you're going to make it greater. Frankly, Faith, I think a change would do you good. You're much too insular. It's as though you've packed it in already. I didn't pack it in until I was much older than you."

"Have you packed it in, Harry?"

"Oh well, you know . . ."

He leaned back and put a cigarette in his holder. He was so heavy I thought the poor little Regency chair would break. He picked up the silver lighter in the shape of a monkey he'd given me for my birthday some years back. He flicked the tail. A flaming tongue shot out. He lit the cigarette.

"Want some words of wisdom from an asthmatic old gentleman?" he said, tilting his head backward, exhaling a fine plume of smoke into the air. I nodded.

"I've only regretted the paintings I did not buy, the trips I did not take, the people I did not love. That is to say, I've only ever regretted the things I didn't do—never the ones I did," he said with an air of authority. "One's only real regret in life is the failure to act."

I thought about this for a long moment, wondering if, in

my own case, it was true. The longer I reflected on my life, the more gray and pallid the canvas became. In the distant past, there had been a sudden burst of color—a brilliant red associated with my one great love affair—but even that had faded to a watery pink with the passage of time. Had there been, I wondered, moments when I should have done things I had not done, loved people I had not loved?

I'd always known exactly where I was going. There'd rarely been a question that I was doing the wrong thing or that there was another path to consider. My feet, except during my great love affair, had always been firmly planted on the ground. I'd always walked straight ahead without qualms. Straight ahead to my grave, I thought.

"It all ends so fast, Faith," Harry said. "Much faster than you can imagine when you're your age. Suddenly you feel the whole thing sort of grinding to a halt and you look back and think, was that my life or someone else's? You can't really grasp it. It all seems like a dream. I suppose that's why old people talk about the past so much, because they're trying to figure out what it was that actually happened to them. And, of course, what it was is Life, capital L."

Harry's sardonic little chuckle turned into a brief hacking cough. I made him drink some water, which soothed him. The two of us then lapsed into a reflective silence in which we each stared off into space at nothing in particular. Harry cleared his throat once or twice.

"Faith, dear, I must leave you now," he said wearily, hauling himself out of his chair. "Thanks for the vittles. Very delicious."

"Take the rest of the tarte tatin. I can't finish it."

"No, dear, I'm on a diet." He glanced at his watch. "Oh heavens, look at the time. Mr. Spencer will be extremely irritated with me. He'll have undoubtedly peed all over everything in the house by now."

I walked Harry to the door. The slightest exercise made him short of breath.

"Will you be all right, Harry?"

"I hope not. Getting too old. Time for the final bid."

I kissed him on the cheek.

"You know, Faith, dear, I've always told you from the first time we met that you were destined for great things. This is the beginning."

"Good night, my dear friend."

"Do it," Harry said, taking both my hands in his. "Promise me you will?"

"All right. I promise."

2

The next day I drove out to The Haven. It was located on the North Shore of Long Island where great estates had sprung up at the turn of the century through the Second World War. Most of those grand, rambling properties had long since been cut up or had highways plowed through their hearts, victims of time, neglect, and progress. But a few were still intact, presiding like disapproving dowagers over the dreary twentieth-century landscape of gas stations, fast-food chains, and shopping malls.

The house itself was not visible from the road. I drove around the perimeter searching for an entrance. The vast property was surrounded by a crumbling stone wall covered with vines, overlooked by graceful old shade trees. It was a wonderful wall, European in character, the sort of wall one might come across while driving through the chateau country in France. Weeds lapped up against its base in scruffy little waves. Moss dripped from its cracks. Yet there was something oddly studied about the wall's ragged appearance, as if it had been ravaged by design rather than time. Its imperfections seemed to occur at aesthetically pleasing intervals. I came to the conclusion that it was not simply a wall, but a man-made ruin enhanced by orchestrated neglect.

Finally I found the entrance to the estate. It was modest,

nothing more than a gap in the wall flanked by two stone pillars, one of which had carved on it in discreet block lettering THE HAVEN. I drove up the white gravel driveway, snaking through a densely wooded area at the end of which was a vast clearing. Suddenly, the sun broke through, shining down on the huge emerald lawns unfurling on either side of the driveway. The landscape became increasingly formal as the great lawns shattered into kaleidoscopic gardens filled with brilliantly colored flowers and whimsically cut topiary trees.

One more turn and the main house appeared in front of me, glowing in the afternoon sun. I pulled into a small cobblestone courtyard and got out of the car. The temperature had dropped considerably. It was one of those restless, crisp-edged spring days that remind me of the fall. Treetops were shimmying around in the brief gusts of wind. There was a light scent of lilacs.

As I walked toward the house, it seemed to become richer in texture and more intimate. Constructed out of blocks of pale yellow stone in the manner of a French chateau, The Haven was one of the most beautifully proportioned buildings I'd ever seen. Though large, its luxury was in the detail rather than the scale. It was a precious jewel of a house, worthy of a legendary lady retired to the country.

I was just about to lift the bronze lion knocker when the door opened and a white-haired man in a black butler's uniform emerged from the gloom and bade me enter.

"Miss Crowell?" he said.

"Yes."

"Mrs. Griffin is expecting you. Won't you come this way, please?"

I stepped out of the bright sunlight into the cool, dark entrance hall, squinting to adjust my eyes to the change of light.

Overhead, a nosegay of lights twinkled atop a tole chandelier in the shape of a Montgolfier balloon. The floor was a checkerboard of black-and-white marble. The marble was old and smooth, the squares small and uneven, most likely transplanted from some ancient French chateau. The walls were glazed a pale grayish blue. A charming Canaletto painting of Venice hung over a magnificent eighteenth-century commode. I wondered if that was the Riesener commode Harry had sold her.

I followed the butler down the hall past several pictures, lively country scenes, all of the finest quality, discreetly lit. Our footsteps echoed as we walked. He showed me into a red library facing a garden and asked me if I cared for something to drink. I declined. He announced that Mrs. Griffin would be down shortly and left.

I sat down on the couch and looked around. Over the mantelpiece was a Delacroix painting of a young Moorish tribesman holding the reins of a black stallion. There was a superb collection of bronze horses resting on a mahogany side table. Hanging on the one wall devoid of bookcases was a glass display case filled with faded horse show ribbons. The case was surrounded by an artfully arranged selection of riding crops and hunting whips. In the fireplace, logs were stacked and set with paper, ready to be lit. The room smelled slightly of burnt wood. Bunches of bright garden flowers arranged in silver trophy cups had been placed here and there. There was a small, well-stocked bar on a butler's tray in one corner. A variety of magazines having to do with riding and the outdoors had been neatly placed on the coffee table. It was a room where the twin themes of money and luxury played unobtrusively, like faint background music, a room whose comforts seeped deeper into one's consciousness the longer one remained in it.

I was settling into the peace and quiet, marveling at the understatement of great wealth, when my attention was arrested by the lone photograph in the room, a formal black-and-white portrait of a young woman wearing a white satin dress. She was neither beautiful nor plain, but teetering on the edge of both. She had an uneasy expression, as if she'd been told by the photographer more than once to smile. She reminded me of myself in some ways: the narrowness of her face, the almond-shaped eyes, the awkwardness—or perhaps it was the shyness

—she conveyed in her expression. Aspects of her were quite striking, in particular her long, graceful neck and sloping shoulders shown to full advantage by the dress's scooped-out neckline. Her dark hair was arranged in a neat chignon. She wore a delicate pearl-and-diamond choker. I suspected that her face, like my own, was prettier in motion when it could be better informed by character and intelligence. Still, the photograph was quite lovely, having the soft romantic quality of another era. I thought she must be Cassandra.

It gave me an odd feeling to think that this young woman, so innocent and pristine in her white dress, so privileged and seemingly immune to the violence of the world, was dead and buried, murdered in such a gruesome way. I suddenly pictured blood spurting over the picture. I quickly turned away.

I got up to look over the books all lined up neatly in their brass bookcases. Antique and leather-bound, in no particular order, and most of them sets, they looked to me like the kinds of books purchased by the yard for their bindings rather than their content. I was about to pull one of them out when a small bug-eyed dog with streaming white hair scampered into the room and began dancing around my leg, scratching at it with his miniscule paws.

"Down, Pom-Pom! Down!" cried a voice at the door.

I looked up. Mrs. Griffin stood in the doorway, wearing a simple cream silk dress. The little dog continued digging around me, her command having had no effect whatsoever.

"Pom-Pom! Get down this instant!"

"It's all right. I love animals," I said.

I bent down to stroke the creature's head, which was barely discernible under a bouquet of white hair.

"I apologize for Pom-Pom," Mrs. Griffin said. "He's a puppy and he's just hopeless. I suppose it's my fault. I'm so bad at training things."

"He probably smells my cat," I replied. "Do you smell my cat, you little guy?"

I stood up as Mrs. Griffin approached. We shook hands.

"My dear, your hands are so cold!" she exclaimed.

" 'Cold hands, warm heart,' as the saying goes," I said lightly.

"Sometimes one is better off the other way around," she replied with a slight smile.

She has some humor, I thought.

"You have a cat," she went on. "Actually, I prefer cats. They're so much quieter. And aesthetically far more appealing, don't you think? The way they move. That sort of sleek indifference. But, unfortunately, I'm allergic to them."

Mrs. Griffin sat down and motioned me to follow suit.

"Come here, you horrid little dog," she said, scooping up the fluffy white ball from the floor and placing it alongside her on the couch.

"What kind of dog is he?"

"A Pomeranian. Hence Pom-Pom. Very unoriginal, I know. People say it's good to get a dog for company though. I'm trying it out. Your cat is called?"

"Brush."

"Brush," she repeated. "What a nice, neat name. Does it have a big, bushy tail?"

"No. He's just an old alley cat, I'm afraid. I found him on the street outside my studio one day and took him in."

"Isn't it awful when one sees stray animals lost on the street. I think it's even sadder than seeing stray people," she sighed.

"I don't know about that, but animals do seem so little and helpless. Brush was just a baby when I found him. He was crying he was so hungry."

"Oh, please," she said, raising her hand in protest, "I can't bear to hear about it. The older I get, the more I can't bear hearing about sad things. And, of course, the irony is, the older one gets, the more sad things one hears about."

She glanced at the photograph on the table.

"My daughter loved cats."

"Is that your daughter?" I asked, already knowing the answer.

"Yes. Cassandra. Cassa we always called her. I told you that you reminded me of her. You see, there's quite a likeness."

She picked up the photograph and stared at it as she spoke.

"It was taken for her coming-out party. It's not a very good picture of her. She was actually much prettier than that, even though she never made a single effort with her looks. She loathed having her picture taken. You can see that, can't you? She used to go on and on about the aborigines believing that photographs stole the soul of the subject. Given the state of the modern world, they may have a point."

She put the photograph back on the table.

I didn't know whether to let on that I was aware of Cassandra's tragic history. I wondered if Mrs. Griffin simply took it for granted that people knew. Of course I hadn't known about it until Harry told me, so I felt a certain awkwardness in bringing it up. One walked a fine line with people like Mrs. Griffin who were very private and very public at the same time. I didn't want to risk offending her or having her think I was prying, nor did I wish to open an old wound. I decided the best course of action was to change the subject.

"This is a wonderful room," I said.

Decoration was usually safe territory with the rich, but the comment seemed to take her by surprise.

"Is it?" she said with a slightly bewildered look. "I haven't been in here in ages, and if you ask me it's getting a bit seedy. I should have it redone."

"Who won all the ribbons?"

"Oh, Cassa. She loved to ride. She gave it up though. God, this room smells of damp. What's the weather like? I haven't been outside today."

"It's lovely. A bit chilly. Feels like fall."

"I should go outside," she said, as though the idea taxed her. "But I don't really like going outside anymore. I have to force myself. When you get older you have to force yourself to do things. Shall we have a little tour?"

She got up from the couch. Pom-Pom jumped down.

"I always think he's going to break his neck when he does that. I shall give you away if you wee-wee anywhere," Mrs. Griffin said, shaking her finger at the little dog.

I followed her out of the room. Pom-Pom scampered behind us, slipping like a skate on the marble floor. We walked down the hall toward a large pair of French doors. Mrs. Griffin pulled down on their long bronze knobs. They opened majestically, and she walked into the room. I followed her inside.

"The living room," she announced, flicking several switches inside a concealed panel on the wall near the entrance.

The space lit up like a stage set. It was a charming, ethereal room, full of light and color, intimate despite the grandeur, filled with astonishing art and antiques. Three sets of French doors opened out onto a small garden sheltered by a wisteria arbor. Pale yellow silk curtains wafted back and forth in the gentle breeze. Again, the aroma of lilacs, stronger than before. The effect was transporting.

There were so many wonderful objects and paintings and pieces of furniture, I hardly knew what to look at first. Mrs. Griffin let me poke around a bit until I became entranced by a little escritoire inlaid with flowered porcelain plaques tucked away in one corner of the room.

"You like it?" she said. "It belonged to Marie Antoinette."

"It's just remarkable, a joy. The workmanship!"

I ran my hand over the delicate ormolu mountings and the intricate marquetry, marveling at the style and the craftsmanship.

"Yes, it's rather charming, isn't it? I must say one never tires of great quality. Here's a little surprise for you—look."

Mrs. Griffin pressed one of the porcelain plaques with her fingertip. A small drawer, heretofore concealed, sprang out from the veneer.

"Oh!" I exclaimed. "How ingenious."

"These are two of Marie Antoinette's letters," Mrs. Griffin said, handing me a slim packet tied with a red silk ribbon. "We found them inside when we discovered the drawer. No one knew they were there. Unfortunately, they're not of great interest.

One's to her dressmaker, Rose Bertin. And the other's just a scribble to a friend. Pity so much was destroyed in the Revolution."

I held the packet gingerly in my hand, trying to picture the ill-fated queen seated at this exquisite piece of furniture, dashing off these little notes. It was odd to think of such a treasure being a part of everyday life, for Marie Antoinette, for Frances Griffin. I had become used to brushing up against history. It was a fringe benefit of working for rich people of taste. Nevertheless, the beauty of certain antiques and pictures, combined with their connection to great figures and events, never ceased to thrill me.

Handing the packet of letters back to Mrs. Griffin, I happened to notice a small, strange painting hanging directly behind her. A prosaic little still life of no particular merit, obviously modern, it seemed absurdly out of place among all the other brilliant pictures. Mrs. Griffin noticed it had captured my attention.

"Cassa painted that," she said.

She replaced the letters in their secret drawer and shut it.

"Very nice," I murmured without conviction.

"Well, not really, but for a ten-year-old, it's not terrible."

"Really?" I said, looking at it with renewed interest. "She was only ten when she painted it?"

"Ten or eleven. Holt and I were very impressed. But then, Cassa could do so many things. Too many. She took all her talent for granted, I'm afraid. It's better when people have to struggle for what they achieve. They appreciate it more."

I followed Mrs. Griffin out of the living room and around the rest of the house. She showed me every room. All the rooms had a theme: the Indian Room, the Chinese Room, the Chippendale Room, the Room of Glass Bells, the Blue Room, the Tapestry Room, the Rose Room, and on and on and on. Mrs. Griffin seemed to take pleasure in explaining the genesis of each one, of what had inspired her to create it—whether it had been a wonderful piece of furniture she'd found on her travels, or a painting, or just a feeling she'd had about the room itself. She described herself sitting alone in certain rooms for hours until a scheme came to her.

"I'm very sensitive to space," she said. "I know when a space is filled correctly and when it's not. Rooms are just like people, with their own quirks and personalities. What I can't stand is lack of proportion in a room, or in a person, for that matter. Lack of proportion is as grating on my nerves as fingernails scraping a blackboard."

I remembered the story of the fireplace.

By the end of the tour I was completely disoriented. The house, which appeared so ordered and classical from the outside, was actually a labyrinth of corridors and unexpected chambers. Though individually perfect, none of the rooms related to one another in any way. They were all different sizes and shapes, constructed to fit the period or motif in which they had been decorated. It was as if Mrs. Griffin, unable to make up her mind in which style she was most comfortable, had decided to try them all. A change of atmosphere was as readily available as a change of clothes.

"I wanted a house for my travels and fantasies," Frances Griffin said, as she poured the tea that was waiting for us on a silver tray in the living room. "A room for the journeys of my life. That's what this house is, you know, a trunk of old costumes—costume rooms. I don't go in them very often. But I'm glad they're there. They remind me of the past. The *good* past."

She stressed the word *good*, as if there had been a bad past as well.

"Yes, I suppose it's nice to keep rooms as souvenirs," I said, quite amused at the extravagance of such a notion.

"My husband and I went everywhere together," she continued. "I said to him years ago when we were first married that we'd have to have a place where we could collect our whole life around us. So we built this house. It's taken a lifetime to fill it up. It's way too big for me now. I really ought to move. But it's difficult to move away from one's whole life."

"Where's the ballroom?" I inquired.

"Oh, it's completely separate, a little pavilion across the

garden. I'll show it to you later. We'll finish our tea first, shall we? Tell me a little about yourself. Where did you grow up?"

"In New York City," I replied. "I was born there."

"And what did your father do?"

"He disappeared," I said, laughing slightly.

Mrs. Griffin didn't share the joke.

"Actually," I continued more soberly, "he was a doctor, but I never really knew him. He and my mother were divorced when I was very young."

"And your mother—did she work?"

"She taught music in a small private school," I said.

"How difficult for her, bringing you up all by herself."

"Yes, I think it was."

"You're an only child?"

"Yes."

"Like my daughter," she sighed. "So difficult being an only child, don't you think?"

"It's difficult being anything really." I smiled.

"Were you happy?"

It was an unexpected question.

"I didn't think about it," I replied.

"Do you think about it now?" she said, eyeing me.

I thought for a moment. Her questions were so strange. She seemed to be searching for something.

"Actually, I think happiness becomes more of a decision as one gets older. I think at some point you just decide you're going to be happy with what you've got."

"That's all very well," she said. "But what about longing and regret? Where do we put them—in storage?"

She looked away at nothing in particular. We remained silent for a long moment.

"This is delicious tea."

"Oh, do you like it? I'm so pleased," she said, snapping out of the trance she was in. "I have it specially blended in London. Shall we go and have a look at the ballroom? It's just across the way."

"This house is like the Thousand and One Nights," I said as we walked through the garden. "It keeps having more stories to tell."

Mrs. Griffin ignored my nervous remark, maintaining the detached air of a tour guide.

"There used to be a proper arbor all along here," she said, using her hands to point out the way. "For Cassa's coming-out party, I put a thousand candles on the path and decorated all the trees and trellises with fresh flowers and ribbons and lanterns. I wanted it to be an enchanted wood, like youth."

Soon I got my first glimpse of the ballroom peeking through the trees up ahead. It was a beautiful little building, nestled in the middle of an elevated clearing, very classical in feeling, square, domed, with columns in the front, and wide, shallow steps leading up to the entrance. A miniature Palladian villa. Moss was growing up the sides and it was surrounded by tangled underbrush. It hadn't been kept up.

"This way," Mrs. Griffin said, leading me up the steps.

She thrust open the French doors, and we went inside, where I paused for a moment to take in the scene. Standing atop the wide circular steps flowing down into the room, I saw that the entire building consisted of a single space: a round marble dance floor ringed by a low balustrade in front of a deep, elevated gallery for people to sit and dine, or walk around, observing the dancers. There was a special podium for musicians; French doors opened out onto the garden. The area was quite large, yet so skillfully proportioned it retained a sense of intimacy.

Mrs. Griffin let me wander around by myself while she stayed near the main entrance, watching. I circled the room, examining the walls, running my hand along the marble columns, the steps, and the gallery railing. No expense had been spared in either materials or craftsmanship. I decided the snowy white marble of the dance floor and that of the columns was almost certainly from Carrara. It had the unmistakable luster of that famous quarry.

"Does it speak to you?" she said after a time.

"Oh yes, it's chattering away," I said happily.

"Getting any ideas?"

"Hundreds. The trick is to narrow them down to one."

"Quite right," she agreed. "It's so important to specify one's vision. Don't you find that ideas often shimmer in front of you like a mirage, but when you try to get close to them, to make them concrete, they vanish?"

"Unfortunately yes."

"Making a theme or an idea real in human terms is the secret, isn't it?"

"How do you mean?" I asked.

"Well, for example, we may yearn for love in the abstract until we have a lover or a child. Then our notion of love becomes defined by that person, and we can't think of it without the embodiment in mind."

I didn't attempt to respond. I just listened as she went on:

"So I suppose the moral of all that is one can't be vague— in life, or art, or even decoration. One must find the embodiment of one's passions."

I found myself wondering what might have happened had this remarkable woman applied her talents to something less ephemeral than style.

"Did you ever think of becoming an artist?" I said.

"No, heavens no!" she cried. "I leave art to the strong." She paused for a moment and then said wistfully: "You remind me so much of my daughter."

"Do I? In what way?"

"Well, it's not so much the way you look, although, as I said, there's a certain similarity. It's more, well, a sort of presence you have. A kind of enthusiasm. I can't tell you how much you remind me of her, standing there."

"You built this just for your daughter's coming-out party?"

"Yes. Just for that."

"Only for that one occasion?"

"Yes . . . well, of course, we did think we'd use it again. But you know how things are. We never did," she said sadly.

Mrs. Griffin was staring at me from across the room. Perhaps it was the physical distance between us that made me bolder. She didn't seem so formidable, perched on those sweeping steps, and I thought to myself that now was the perfect opportunity to let her know I was aware of the tragedy. I felt I needed to bring up the subject in order to lay it to rest. So I blurted out my next sentence before I could take too much time to think about it.

"I understand your daughter died," I said.

She stiffened slightly. "You understand correctly."

"I'm so sorry, Mrs. Griffin, I didn't mean to offend . . ."

"Don't apologize." She raised her hand to cut me off. "Let's discuss what we're going to do in here, shall we? I assume you're going to accept the commission."

"Yes. I accept it."

"Good," she said firmly. "Well then, I think trompe l'oeil, don't you?"

"Yes," I concurred. "Trompe l'oeil seems appropriate."

CHAPTER
3

Having accepted the commission, I finished up all my other work and notified my clients I was taking a leave of absence until further notice. Two weeks later, I drove out to The Haven to begin my preliminary sketches of the ballroom. The butler showed me through the garden to the little pavilion, which, to my amazement, looked completely transformed. The scruffy vines around it had been cleared away, the grit and moss scraped from its walls. Scrubbed clean, it gleamed proudly in the bright spring sun.

"My lord, what's happened to it?" I asked the butler as we approached.

"Mrs. Griffin's had it prepared for you," he said.

"How very thoughtful of her."

He led me inside and asked if he could bring me anything. I requested a chair, a small table for sketching, and some black coffee, very strong. When he left, I began to settle in.

The ballroom was cool despite the rising heat of the morning. I stood at the center of the round dance floor turning slowly in place, focusing on each wall until I could imagine the entire area with my eyes shut. I always needed to feel the structure and rhythm of a room before attempting any sort of scheme for it. I tore it down and built it up again in my imagination in order to know it inside out. Though the ballroom was a much grander scale than I was used to, my goal was the same: to fit my artistry over the space like a glove; to enhance without overburdening.

The butler came back promptly with the things I'd asked for. As he worked setting them up, I studied him for the first time. He was a slim, older man of medium height, with slack, nondescript features, and fine white hair combed meticulously over a bald spot at the top of his head. In his black-and-white uniform he looked as neat as a printed page. He set up the table and chair and poured the coffee, moving swiftly and quietly with the precision of one who takes pride in the art of serving others. I thanked him and asked him his name.

"Henry Deane, but I'm called Deane," he said quickly, as if the question somehow embarrassed him.

I thought about Deane after he left. I wondered how long he'd been in Mrs. Griffin's employ, wondered what he knew about the murder. Had he known Cassandra? Had he been here when it happened? I wondered if I'd ever get up the courage to ask him.

I sat down on the chair Deane had brought and began to draw. My preliminary sketches were quick and rough, abbreviated renderings of the room itself. I viewed them only as notes to myself, useful for going over the room's architectural details and discovering where some of my main problems might lie. After these had been completed, I sketched out several ideas for schemes off the top of my head, though none of them seemed exactly right. It wasn't turning out to be a particularly productive morning, but I wasn't discouraged. I knew there would be many frustrating days to come, and many rewarding ones—that was the nature of creation.

I had hoped Mrs. Griffin would make an appearance to discuss some of my ideas, but there was no sign of her all morning. At twelve-thirty, Deane came back and asked me if I cared for some lunch. I held up the sandwich I'd brought with me and shook my head.

"Wouldn't you like something a little more substantial?" he said coaxingly.

I thanked him, but declined. It was my habit to have a quick, light lunch on the job so as not to interrupt my train of thought. I ate alone in the garden and mulled over the morning's work. However, as I sat there on the lawn eating my sandwich and sipping my Coke, I couldn't help but reflect on the weird nature of this assignment: trompe l'oeiling a room built for an antiquated ritual in honor of a girl who'd been dead for years!

My thoughts kept drifting toward Cassandra. I wondered what the enigmatic girl in the photograph in the library had thought of her first step into society. Had she felt the glory of her moment and danced the night away with a dozen admiring suitors? Or had she watched it all from a distance, isolated from the crowd, feeling herself to be an excuse for yet another party? I suddenly felt a chill and shivered, as if a ghost had swept by me. I got up and went back inside.

Returning to my worktable, I tore up all the sketches I'd made, including one or two I'd thought were quite promising. They were all too stilted and formal. None of them captured the haunted quality of the room. I hadn't found the key.

Toward the middle of the afternoon, I decided to call it a day and let the power of a good night's sleep work on my subconscious. I left The Haven at three-thirty and drove back to the city. Instead of settling into the car and relaxing, as I usually do when I drive for a distance, I felt myself becoming more and more tense. At first I thought it had to do with the day's unproductiveness. But gradually I became aware it was something else, something I couldn't quite put my finger on, having to do with Cassandra Griffin.

Before going home, I decided to stop off at the library. An assistant helped me locate the pertinent *New York Times* microfilm on Cassandra Griffin. I went upstairs to one of the cubicles and settled into the story.

Newspaper references to Cassandra Griffin began with a

feature about her coming-out party entitled AN AMERICAN PRIN-
CESS MAKES HER DEBUT. The article was accompanied by grainy
photographs of the ballroom, both under construction and completed. There was also a picture of Cassandra, the same picture
I'd seen in her mother's library.

There were no more articles about her until her murder
eight years later, when she was twenty-six. The brief explosion
of news associated with the crime engendered lurid headlines
in the city section. Her old deb photograph ran with every article
about the crime. One couldn't help imagining that young, privileged girl sprawled out on the bedroom floor of her palatial
house, stabbed through the heart like any other blood-spattered
victim in the tabloids. Yet there was a difference, and perhaps
more of a fascination, because of who she was and what she
represented.

In several follow-up features about the case, the paper
printed elegant pictures taken of Frances and Holt Griffin, as
well as a stern-looking tintype of Holt Griffin's entrepreneurial
ancestor, Elias Holt, the founder of the fortune. The photograph of Frances Griffin, a cool studio portrait of a woman of
style taken by Cecil Beaton, surprised me. I hardly recognized
her. The Frances Griffin I knew looked like a former beauty
who had aged well. The woman in this picture was not even
very pretty. The youthful face seemed devoid of a certain character and mystery which the aged one possessed. They might
have been two different people.

All the articles made reference to the great ballroom that
had been built especially for Cassandra's coming-out party, the
extravagance of which had apparently caused quite a stir in the
late sixties when such rituals were considered wasteful and
passé. All delved into the unfortunate girl's illustrious heritage,
reminding readers that she was the sole heir to the Griffin mil-
lions. They referred to her as "the Griffin heiress" or "the tragic
American Princess." One or two articles noted briefly that Cassandra had married a ski instructor—one Roberto Madi.

Tantalizingly little was written on the subject of Mr. Madi

and nothing on the event of the marriage itself. I searched and searched, but there was no wedding announcement. This meant that the marriage probably hadn't been conducted in any celebratory way, which was rare for girls of Cassandra's background. Nothing in any of the articles on the murder elaborated on Madi's life or gave any indication of what had become of him after the crime. He seemed to begin and end in one or two sentences. However, from the moment that I read he existed, Roberto Madi was there, lurking like a shadow between the lines.

At precisely the time when, presumably, public interest in the case had reached fever pitch, the press fell inexplicably silent. There suddenly wasn't one more word or mention of the crime, and nothing further regarding any of the various leads, suspects, or impending arrests. There were no more human interest stories on the family, no further speculation, no more articles, period.

Then, several months later, there appeared a follow-up item tucked away in the back pages of the city section, headlined "Socialite's Murderer Still Eludes Police." This innocuous story briefly described a trail of inconclusive evidence in the case leading to a dead end.

The last references to the crime I managed to locate were largely indirect. One was the obituary of Holt Griffin, in which the glowing record of his generosity and service to the nation seemed to dwarf the murder of his daughter, making it almost an afterthought in this distinguished life. The piece did say, however, that the still-unsolved crime had taken its toll on the great philanthropist and diplomat, and probably contributed to his death from a heart attack at the age of sixty-six.

Then there was the obituary of the police detective who had been in charge of the frustrated investigation. In this article, Cassandra Griffin was mentioned almost as many times as the deceased himself, and I suspected Detective Miles M. Sarnoff received a more prominent death notice than he might have otherwise on account of his role in the case. He was quoted as saying he could never forget the "vile sight of that young girl lying all bloody on the carpet," and that the sorrow of his life was having failed to solve that particular crime. All told, the coverage was as puzzling as the murder itself. I photocopied the articles from the microfilm and took them home to study.

Out on the street in the twilight, I felt depressed. Here I was, I thought, walking home with a young woman's entire life tucked under my arm, a life of extraordinary privilege, that could be summed up by nothing more than a few sensational articles in a newspaper.

I recalled the human skeleton in a satin wedding gown I'd once seen in the window of a Mexican folk-art store on Third Avenue. I had stared at the mantilla draped over her skull, mesmerized by the grin under that veil of white lace.

Morbid thoughts have plagued me throughout my life. I've often wondered what would have happened had I not been granted a certain facility as a craftsman. Having no family left, no husband, no children, no ties to the world through its traditional trade routes, I might easily have succumbed to the forces of self-destruction. I'd been saved from the abyss only by my firm belief that art is a kind of salvation, a footpath through the wilderness. But what about Cassandra? What had she believed in? Who was she really? Was she the victim of circumstance or of her own dark impulses?

When I arrived home, a delicate white narcissus plant was waiting for me outside my door with a note attached to it. The note read, "Art is the accomplice of love. Work well." It was signed, "Frances Griffin."

I wasn't quite sure what to make of this. "Art is the accomplice of love." What did she mean? I took the plant inside and set it on the kitchen table while I fixed myself and Brush some dinner. I was slightly skeptical of this gesture. Was it simply a kind offering, or the first step in some sort of seduction? I was wary.

As the sun in a solar system of her own creation, Frances Griffin was undoubtedly very adept at drawing people into her orbit. The question was why did she want my good opinion of her? I was just another person in her employ. Something about it was odd. I looked at the plant again and again, wondering what it was meant to cover up. I was good at spotting cover-ups. They were, after all, my trade.

That night in bed, with Brush curled up beside me, I studied the newspaper articles on the murder more carefully. The clippings raised more questions than they answered. However, after going over them a couple of times, I began to form in my mind an interesting, if spotty, picture of Cassandra Griffin's life.

On the face of it, Cassandra had been brought up in the safe and pleasant circumstances of an upper-class WASP: boarding school, coming-out party, college. Some of the articles mentioned her talents as a painter and as an equestrienne, but all cast her in the socialite mold. I noticed she was never called by her married name, but always Cassandra Griffin. Her husband, Roberto Madi, was referred to as a ski instructor, but there was no mention of where he came from or who his family were. One could assume the marriage had not been a particularly felicitous event for Cassandra's parents. Given Frances Griffin's former penchant for parties and festivities, it seemed likely she would have feted her daughter lavishly had the union pleased her.

The murder itself was bound up in a tangle of conflicting accounts and backtracking regarding what exactly occurred, as well as who was present. The first stories said Cassandra and her mother and father had dined together at The Haven the night of the crime, just the three of them. They had all gone to bed early. Sometime around midnight, according to the police, the perpetrator had shimmied up the trellis outside Cassandra's bedroom and entered her partly open window. Cassandra, apparently awakened by the intruder, had gotten out of bed and either confronted him or tried to escape. Whatever the circumstances, she and her assailant then engaged in a brief, fierce struggle which ended with his stabbing her once, directly through the heart. After that, police surmised, the intruder panicked and left—without taking anything—the same way he'd entered, through the window, shimmying back down the trellis and fleeing the premises. This seemed to be a logical explanation, given that nothing was stolen and there was no sign of a forced entry anywhere in the house.

The five people in residence at the time were Mrs. Griffin, Mr. Griffin, Cassandra, and two servants, both of whom had been with the Griffins for years. No one heard anything, no one saw anything. The next morning, Mrs. Griffin went to wake up her daughter and made the grisly discovery. Upon entering the room, she apparently screamed and fainted. Small wonder, I thought. What a sight for a mother to see—her only child lying on the floor, eyes wide, face pale as the moon, clothes soaked in blood. Death, according to the coroner, had been "mercifully instantaneous." This was meant to be a consolation, I suppose.

Stroking Brush, I wondered again how on God's earth Frances Griffin had remained all these years in the same house where her daughter had been butchered? After all, I thought, it wasn't as if she couldn't afford to move. Did she remember her unspeakable discovery every time she passed Cassandra's bedroom, even today? How could she stand it? And that was another thing: which room was it? On my tour of the house, Mrs. Griffin never identified the room that had once belonged to her daughter. Was it the Indian Room, the Chinese Room, the Room of Glass Bells?

I've always believed that violence irrevocably alters the place in which it occurs. A violent act pierces the atmosphere, leaving a hole through which the cold, damp draft of its memory blows forever. I wondered in which one of those rooms I might one day feel a chill.

I reflected on these first accounts for some time. The more I thought about them, the more incongruous they became. I read on. Subsequent stories, though more comprehensive, began to change certain details of the events leading up to the crime. Though these changes were played down as being minor and irrelevant to the case as a whole, I found them fascinating and extremely significant.

For example, a later story said that Cassandra and her parents had *not* dined alone that night. The elusive Mr. Madi had dined with them, but left early. His presence had not been mentioned initially because, according to the police, Mr. and Mrs. Griffin had been so traumatized by the murder, it had simply slipped their minds.

Slipped their minds? Now this was a tough one to swallow. But assuming it was true, assuming it had slipped their minds, there were still a lot of unanswered questions. If Madi had been there for dinner, why did he leave? After all, he and Cassandra were married, so why would he dine with her and her parents and then leave her there alone for the night? Why didn't he stay with her?

I kept coming back to their omitting to tell the police about him in the first place. Why not say he'd dined with them? Were they really so distraught that they'd forgotten he'd been there? Or did they have a hidden reason to try to eradicate his presence on the scene?

There was also the question of the murder weapon. In the first accounts, the weapon had been found and identified as a silver fruit knife belonging to a set from the house. Subsequent stories said the knife could not be positively identified as one from the Griffin set. According to the butler, no knives from the set were missing. There then was a story that the knife, formerly identified as the murder weapon, was perhaps not the murder weapon after all. According to the testimony of one expert who examined the body, the wound was too large to have been inflicted by that particular knife. Therefore, the murder weapon had to have been another knife, one which had not been found. A piece, entitled "Missing Murder Weapon a Mystery in Griffin Case," recounted the story of the discredited knife. Then the knife in question disappeared from the police evidence locker. This was followed by a short, damning article speculating on the possibility of a cover-up in the case. That, in turn, was quickly followed by outraged denials by all concerned, as well as a flurry of articles relating to inefficient police procedures regarding the handling of evidence. Whichever way you sliced it, the murder weapon was missing.

By the time I'd gone through all the articles, it was well past midnight. I was familiar with the relevant facts of the case as well as their apparent contradictions. In my view, the strangest and most damning thing of all was what I called "The Question of the Locked Window."

The butler—a man named Frank Beridge—had told police that the morning after the murder, at around nine o'clock, he'd heard a woman screaming. According to his first account, he followed the screams upstairs to Cassandra's bedroom, where he found Mrs. Griffin passed out on the floor next to Cassandra's mutilated body. Beridge said the first thing he did was unlock the window to let in some fresh air. Then he made an unsuccessful attempt to revive Mrs. Griffin. This meant, of course, that the intruder couldn't possibly have come in through the window. Or, that he came in the window, locked it behind him, then left by another route, not down the trellis, as the police suggested. The idea of a blood-soaked madman traipsing around the corridors of that labyrinthine house with a knife, trying to find his way out, leaving no trace of his steps, was utterly ridiculous.

In any case, no one questioned this startling story because in another article Mrs. Griffin apparently cleared the whole thing up by saying that she'd come into her daughter's room in the morning to close the window (never mind that it was midsummer) and that only after closing the window and locking it did she realize her daughter had been stabbed to death. That was the point at which she'd screamed and fainted. So, if you believed that, the murderer could have come in and left through the window, as the police had postulated in the beginning.

This was a tough one to buy, even for me, the observer far away in time and place. I wondered why the police had bought it, and, in fact, *if* they'd bought it. Why had she told it? Was it true? It seemed a ludicrous account, because it meant that Mrs. Griffin had walked into the bedroom, stepped over her daughter's body lying on the floor in a pool of blood, and closed the window on a summer's day. Then she'd turned around, seen the body, screamed and fainted. All right, it was morning. Peo-

ple are groggy in the morning. But was she in such a fog she
didn't even notice a murdered girl on the floor when she first
came in? Vagueness has its limits.

Others must have felt the same way I did because at the
inquest, Beridge the butler changed his story entirely. He said
he'd been mistaken—he'd never opened the window, never
even went near it. In his official account, he swore to the coroner
that when he came into the room, the window was already open.

I finally finished reading at two o'clock in the morning. I
turned out the light. Brush was curled up peacefully. I had to
get up early, but when I closed my eyes, I couldn't go to sleep.
A flock of thoughts flitted through my brain, like birds hitting
a propeller, exploding one after another, in little bursts of blood.

It seemed so obvious. The murder had been an inside job.
Everyone in the house must have known the true story and for
some reason they'd all covered it up. But why? Why cover it
up? Especially when it seemed clear to me *who* had done it. I,
the amateur detective, had pieced together the evidence from
a few newspaper articles and was convinced that Roberto Madi,
the shadowy ski instructor and unacceptable husband, had in
fact murdered Cassandra Griffin. It made all the sense in the
world. He was there, and he had a motive: money. So why had
he never been charged?

I stared at a streak of moonlight on the wall between the
dresser and the closet door. No use trying to sleep. It was Madi
all right. He was the one. Why had he never been brought to
justice? Why was he never even named as a suspect? Where had
he disappeared to? Why were all the reports about him so
vague? Who was he really?

I knew I was probably letting my imagination get away from
me, but still, I had a special interest in men who victimize women
and in the women who fall into their hands. My mother had
been the target of a strange, careless man—my own father. And
I had just barely escaped her fate . . . Or had I? There was no
tangible evidence of my encounter with masochistic love, no
unwanted child, no visible scars, no addictions to dull the edges
of broken dreams. There was, however, a void in my romantic

life in which I'd floated, alone and disconsolate, for the past twelve years.

Yes, Madi intrigued me. Of course Madi intrigued me. Another shadowy male figure for me to dwell on, to fantasize about. There were no pictures of him in the newspapers, so I lay in the dark, trying to imagine what he must have looked like. The only face I could readily conjure up was that of my old lover, John Noland. He'd been to me what I suspected Roberto Madi had been to Cassandra. I thought of John as the model for all such men.

Early on, my abandoning father had set the pattern of my love life on the loom of my subconscious. Because he'd left us, I defined a man's love by its absence rather than its presence, by the pain it inflicted, rather than the joy it was supposed to bring. I saw my mother rise again and again, phoenixlike, from the ashes of her daily life, both cursing my father and being grateful to him for giving her the great consolation: a child. Me.

I remembered very little about my childhood, and nothing about the man who had sired me. I did remember my mother confiding to me in later years that the night my father quit our house forever, she had cried and cried, rocking me back and forth in her arms, singing to me. After that, she never cried again.

Watching my mother's pain over my father produced scant enthusiasm for attaching myself to a man. In my early twenties, I had half a dozen boyfriends, whose attentions I experienced rather like a sleepwalker. Then, at twenty-four, I met John Noland. John Noland intrigued me because in him I'd finally found someone who was as elusive and tricky as my definition of love.

John Noland was divorced when I met him, several years older than I—a just-about-to-be-celebrated writer whose prose was fluid and elegant. He was known as "a beautiful stylist," as smooth in life as he was in art. Women adored him. How women adored him! They were always lapping up against him like little waves, caressing him with coyness and flattery. I used to watch them at parties, laughing and flirting with him, while he turned them inside out with his dark blue eyes. His riding crop wit combined with an aloof, ironic attitude made them dance and flutter around him all the more. During the course of an evening, I would observe him as he gradually singled one woman out, stalked her, and isolated her from the herd. Though varied in looks and type, the women he fancied all had one thing in common: they were all profoundly lonely. One could see it in their eyes, the way they were begging to be hurt and betrayed. Like a lazy lion, John Noland knew how to pick on wounded game.

When he singled me out, as he did one night at one of those smoky, crowded loft parties we all went to then, I felt flattered, confident, special. I didn't immediately identify myself as one of the wounded herd, though that feeling soon changed in the wake of experience. No, that night I thought I was clever and irresistible, different from the women he was used to. I didn't think of myself as a victim, but as a crusader. I told myself I'd be the one to change him.

Soon after we began our affair, I sensed he was a disappointed man who felt the world was not giving him his due. He was angry when he was dismissed by the critics while other writers soared to fame on books less well crafted than his. His dissatisfaction with life made him restless and incapable of remaining in one place for any significant length of time. Staying put meant too much time to reflect on disappointment. John was, therefore, constantly on the move, traveling here and there to remote places, researching his books, engaging in brief romantic encounters, basically uninvolved with anything or anyone beyond his writing and himself. When at last he finally had a measure of success with his work, I remember his complaining it was "too little too late." He'd gotten what he wanted, but didn't seem to want what he got. For John was always searching for something more, though what that was I don't think even he knew.

Together almost constantly for a year, we gradually began to drift apart. Increasingly I sensed the anger in him arising from despair. He began neglecting me, first in little ways, then in large ones. Without warning, I wouldn't hear from him for a week. Then he'd call me up as if nothing was wrong, with no explanation. I'd cry, berate him, scold him, and he would comfort me by telling me it would never happen again—but it did, more and more frequently.

Yet as he withdrew and I struggled with long bouts of loneliness and fury, I felt myself becoming bound tighter to him. Each new wound he inflicted only made my passion flare. I turned detective, uncovering his lies and infidelities with a maniacal glee which sent me racing to confront him. He was always penitent, always passionate, always able to convince me I was the only one he really loved. I went back to him time and time again, convinced it was he to whom I was returning, rather than to the hurt and the disappointment. Having pried the masochist from her shell, he made her into a sadist as well. We saw one another off and on for three years, torturing each other with our mutual obsessions and inability to love.

The routine of my life—how I worked, ate, slept, relaxed —was governed by my thoughts of John. When I finished a piece of work, I immediately wanted to show it to him. If I saw something interesting, I thought only of taking him to see it. If I bought a new dress, I imagined him admiring me in it. If I cooked a meal, it was for him to eat. If I listened to music, it was for him to hear. Day and night, he was in my life, yet we rarely saw one another. We lived in constant but distant com- munication, speaking on the telephone, meeting once or twice a month for a night or two. Between the moments I spoke to him or saw him, I didn't live, I only marked time.

There was a certain point at which my obsession became so intense, I felt as if it would kill me. I didn't know what was happening until much later when, after going back and forth time and time again to the same brief ecstasies, the same long punishments, the same deep disappointments, I began to un- derstand that what I'd thought of as an escape from the sadness of my childhood was actually a re-creation of it, using bolder, more colorful designs. I longed after John Noland as I'd longed after my father. In acting out the longing, I was able to fool myself into thinking I loved him.

And so I felt a kinship with Cassandra Griffin. I suspected we were both victims of a passion beyond our control, only she had died, and I had survived.

CHAPTER 4

The Haven seemed far more sinister to me when I saw it again, as if its beauty were a clever disguise for evil. As I got out of the car, I glanced at the row of upstairs windows, wondering which room had been Cassandra's. Deane greeted me at the door and said Mrs. Griffin would like a word with me. I followed him down the hall.

Mrs. Griffin was arranging flowers in the pantry, standing behind a large table covered with a white cloth. She was wearing gardening gloves and an apron which looked as if it was made of mattress ticking. She had on a straw hat with a wide brim. Pom-Pom was in attendance, dozing at her feet. She reminded me of one of those English county ladies whose lives revolve around their gardens and dogs. A diminutive maid in a gray-and-white uniform stood nearby, tending to three large pails containing neat bunches of flowers.

"One of my little hobbies," Frances Griffin said as I entered.

I stood for a moment, admiring the arrangement she was working on, an explosion of pale orange tulips packed so tightly together they formed a perfect globe.

"There must be a hundred tulips there," I said.

"Eighty-two. More is more. That's the motto of this house. No minimalism for us, right, Bridey?" The maid didn't look up.

I ran my finger along the feathered edge of one of the tulips.

"Parrot tulips," I said.

"Yes, I have them specially grown for me at my house in the country. You can't get really good flowers from a florist nowadays."

"Where's your house in the country?" I asked, somewhat perplexed by the remark.

"France," she replied. "About sixty miles outside Paris. Near Chartres."

"These flowers are from France?"

"I have them flown in once a week," she said. "It's extravagant, I know. I should sell that house. At least it's good for something. So much less complicated keeping things than getting rid of them, don't you think?"

"Well, I suppose if you can do it, why not?"

A few of my wealthy clients who complained about the sorry state of commercial florists had flowers trucked in from their houses in the country or else from private greenhouses out of state. However, this was the first time I'd heard of having flowers flown specially across the Atlantic on a regular basis. Even I, who encountered all sorts of extravagances in my line of work, found this extraordinary.

"Did you like your narcissus?" Mrs. Griffin asked.

I suddenly remembered the plant she'd sent me. In the wake of the evening's reading, I'd forgotten all about it.

"Oh yes! Sorry! I meant to thank you for it. It's lovely. But you didn't have to do that."

"I thought you should have a little something to cheer you up."

"That's very kind of you but I'm not sad, Mrs. Griffin," I said, trying to make light of a perplexing remark.

"Never mind, we all need cheering up," she replied.

Using a garden clippers with the precision of a surgeon, Mrs. Griffin trimmed the leaves and thorns off a sunset-colored rose and placed it strategically in the middle of all the tulips. She stood back a little, admiring her creation.

"Voilà!" she said crisply, removing her gloves. "I'm finished here. We'll do the rest later, Bridey."

The maid nodded and began picking up the debris.

"Why did you put a rose in the middle of all those tulips?" I inquired.

"I enjoy the unexpected," she said. "Will you join me for lunch later on?"

"I don't usually take a long lunch."

"It will be short and light. I promise."

"Well, thank you," I replied, accepting her invitation against my better judgment.

"I'll meet you in the living room at a quarter to one," she instructed.

She disappeared down the corridor. I went off to the ball-room to begin work. I had qualms about joining her for lunch. Dining alone with her was bound to produce a certain intimacy, and I wanted to remain as independent from her as possible. But a part of me, the part that had stayed up half the night studying the newspaper clippings of her daughter's murder, that part wanted to know how she'd remained all these years in the same house where the crime took place, that part was interested in getting to know her.

The morning passed slowly. I made several sketches I wasn't happy with and smoked too many cigarettes. By noon I was famished and wished to God I could just go out and eat my sandwich on the lawn as I'd originally planned. I was in a bad mood on account of the work not going well, and the last thing I felt like was having to make polite conversation with my employer.

I walked back to the main house at the appointed hour and waited impatiently for Mrs. Griffin in the living room, anxious to get lunch over with as quickly as possible and go back to work. I glanced at the fine Louis XVI ormolu-mounted mantel clock above the fireplace. It was set at exactly twenty to one, as was a charming blue enamel clock by Fabergé on the table beside the sofa. I adjusted my wristwatch, concluding it was fast. I was pleased when Mrs. Griffin appeared at the door at exactly a quarter to one, according to those supurb time pieces. She kept a punctual house. I liked that. And she looked refreshed, having changed into a pale blue linen dress and pearls. Her hair was perfectly in place and, I detected, a slightly lighter shade than it had been in the morning. This was the first time I suspected she was wearing a wig.

I followed her into the dining room, where Deane served us lunch at the small round table in front of the bay window facing out onto the garden. As he passed the platter of fish to Mrs. Griffin, he whispered: "The piece on the left has no butter, Madam."

She nodded.

"I'm on this ghastly diet," she said, serving herself the dry filet of sole. "My cholesterol—whatever *that* is—has suddenly shot up for some unknown reason and the doctor's put me on this ridiculous regime for at least six months. Such a bore, I can't tell you. When I was your age, no one had ever heard of things like cholesterol and plaque and whatnot. You ate what you wanted and you were either fat or thin. The older I get, the more I think there's such a thing as too much information."

"Or not enough," I said.

She let the remark pass.

"My cook hates preparing food for me these days because I've told him he can't use any oil or butter or cream. You don't know what that does to these prima donna chefs. It's like telling an artist he can only paint in black and white. So he loves it when I have company and he can show off. How is it?"

I tasted my fish.

"Delicious," I said enthusiastically.

"Good. I don't want him to lose his touch."

I sipped some mineral water, avoiding the wine, and looked out onto the garden. The trellises were weeping great bunches of wisteria. A lone bird was warbling softly. Everything seemed so perfect and tranquil.

"It's lovely and peaceful here," I said.

"I loathe noise. I have what my doctor calls hyperacusis. Which means I'm oversensitive to sound. I hear things no one else can hear."

What an interesting bit of information, I thought. That being the case, wouldn't she have heard something the night Cassandra was murdered?

"I don't know how you stand living in the city," she went on. "I couldn't stand the noise."

"I'm used to it now. I think of the noise as company."

"You live alone?" she asked.

"Except for Brush."

"Animals are so comforting and you don't have to worry about them like you do about children. But Pom-Pom is a very bad little man and he's ruining all my rugs." She glanced down at the sleeping dog. "Did you have a productive morning?"

"Not really," I sighed. "But I'm just getting started. I did have some ideas I wanted to discuss with you."

"I'd really rather see things than discuss them, if you don't mind."

"I'll plow ahead on my own then. Right now, I'm just trying to get to know the room as well as I can."

"Oh yes," she said sympathetically. "Rooms are like people. It takes time to get to know them. And even then, the interesting ones keep revealing themselves more and more."

Mrs. Griffin finished eating before I did. She leaned back and took a cigarette from a silver box on the table, hesitating before lighting it.

"Will the smoke bother you?" she asked.

"No, not at all."

She struck a match and lit the cigarette, inhaling deeply, then exhaling the smoke through her nose and mouth like a practiced smoker. I'm not sure why the sight of her smoking surprised me, but it did. I hadn't pictured her with that particular habit.

"My doctor's absolutely forbidden me to smoke. But I don't care. There are some things in life I simply won't give up," she announced.

"What's another one?"

She cocked her head to one side as if the question amused her.

"Linen sheets," she replied.

"Linen sheets don't sound like a vice, and they certainly won't kill you."

"No, they kill the maids though," she chuckled. "They're a terrible bore to wash and iron. I have a lady who comes in once a week just to do them, but she's getting so old she can hardly hold the iron. The young ones don't know how to do them correctly. And they're not interested in learning. Nobody wants to work for anybody anymore. The days of real service are gone, along with all the lovely old-world amenities and craftsmanship. Don't you notice that?"

"People say that, but I try to use the old techniques whenever I can. I've studied with people who know them. Certainly in my craft the older techniques are the most reliable."

"Chocolate!" she said suddenly.

"Sorry?"

"Another thing I won't give up."

I laughed. "Oh I can certainly sympathize with that. I'm a chocoholic."

"Let's see . . . What else?" she said thoughtfully.

She seemed as fixated on this notion of things she wouldn't give up as she was on the blue string of smoke rising from her cigarette.

"This house," she said. "I won't give up this house." She said it defiantly, as though someone had asked her to.

"Why should you?"

Of course I knew perfectly well why she should, and I honestly didn't know whether I'd asked the question out of nervousness or in order to be provocative.

"Why should I?" she asked. "Well, for one thing, because my daughter was murdered here."

I shifted uncomfortably in my chair and picked through the fish. When I looked up again, she was staring hard at me.

I felt my mouth shape itself into a nervous little grin. I said nothing.

"You knew that, didn't you? That Cassa was murdered right here, in this house?"

"Yes," I said softly. "I did know that."

Now the question: was I going to tell her how much I knew?

"I suppose you wonder how on earth I continue living here."

I nodded.

"Everyone does," she said.

Her mood changed to one of reflection.

"I wonder it myself sometimes," she said, making careful cross-hatchings with her fork on the tablecloth. "My husband wanted to move after it happened. But I wouldn't. I just couldn't bear to leave. I know this is going to sound odd, but, you see, I feel close to Cassa here. She grew up here. I feel her all around me still. I need to feel her all around me, especially now that I'm getting old. It comforts me."

She put the fork down and sat very still. She looked smaller and frailer than before, dwarfed by a memory which seemed to hang on her like some huge, ill-fitting coat.

"Did they ever find out who did it?" I asked.

She took one last puff of her cigarette and dabbed it out on the little silver ashtray in front of her.

"No."

"How awful for you."

"Yes," she sighed.

"They never found any clues?"

"How much do you actually know about what happened?"

"Just what I read in the newspapers," I replied.

"The newspapers? It happened over fifteen years ago."

I swallowed and took a deep breath.

"Ah—I want to confess something to you, Mrs. Griffin. I didn't know very much about the crime before coming to work for you. But yesterday afternoon I went to the library and photocopied some newspaper clippings. I took them home with me, and I, uh, read them. Actually, I was up half the night."

She smiled a strange half-smile.

"Yes. I know."

"I beg your pardon?" I said.

"Well, I know you went to the library and got newspaper clippings about the murder. I didn't know you were up half the night reading them."

I was stunned.

"How did you know I went to the library?"

Resting her head on the back of the chair, she closed her eyes and talked to the air as if she were exhausted or in pain.

"I don't have to tell you this, but I want to," she began. "When people first come to work for me, I feel it's necessary to have them watched for a time."

This took a few seconds to sink in, but when it did, I was truly astonished. And rather horrified.

"You mean I'm being followed?"

"Yes."

"You had me followed?"

"Yes."

"For how long?"

"Long enough."

"How long, exactly?" I felt my anger rising.

"Let's just say, ever since you were chosen for the job."

I could feel my head swelling up with blood. I was furious. I ran my fingers through my hair.

"Mrs. Griffin—I can't believe this. I'm speechless. I mean, what a terrible thing to do!"

"Oh yes," she said wearily. "I suppose it is from your point of view. But it's just a precaution." She opened her eyes and looked at me. "And, naturally, everything I learn is confidential."

"Is that supposed to be comforting? My life is none of your business."

"No, I know it's not," she said quietly.

"Well then, how dare you? Really, Mrs. Griffin. How dare you?"

"It's just a precaution, that's all."

"Look, Mrs. Griffin, I've worked for an awful lot of very rich, very prominent people and nothing like this has ever happened before."

She narrowed her eyes.

"How do you know?"

She had a point there—I didn't know. I suppose some of them could have had me followed. But the idea still seemed outrageous.

"Well, I'm glad I didn't know it because my reaction to it would have been the same as it's going to be now—which is to say, I quit."

I threw my napkin down on the table and got up. Mrs. Griffin quickly grabbed my arm. Her frail, bony hand felt like a bird claw. There was no strength in it. I could easily have wrenched myself away, but something in me stopped and let her hold me.

"Please! Please don't go!" she cried. "I didn't *have* to tell you. I *wanted* to tell you because I want to be honest with you. I don't want there to be any secrets between us. Please . . . please sit down and listen to me."

She tugged at my arm, looking so pathetic and needy, I just couldn't refuse her.

"All right," I said, gently extracting my arm from her grip.

I sat down again, crossing my arms in front of me, glaring at her, defying her to explain herself. She spoke slowly as if she wanted to choose her words carefully.

"You see, after Cassa died, there was a terrible fear," she began. "A terrible fear that took hold of us, Holt and me. Not just a fear for our own lives, but a fear of life in general. Can you understand that?"

I nodded.

"When a child dies, it breaks the pattern, the most fundamental pattern in life. Cassa was our only child. And I'd had some trouble conceiving her. Consequently, I was overprotective of her. We both were. I wanted everything to be perfect for her. I never wanted her to go through what I'd gone through in my life."

She shuddered.

"But somehow," she said after a time, "somehow she got away from me. I don't understand how exactly. There was a kind of wildness in her, I suppose. People have their own destinies."

She paused again, then went on: "I didn't understand at first because I thought, well, we've given her everything. And when I came to understand it, by that time it was too late. She'd gone off and married Roberto."

"Roberto Madi?" I asked.

"Roberto Madi," she said with distaste.

"You didn't like him?"

"No," she said. "I didn't like him. She married a handsome ski bum. I hated his face."

"Where did she meet him?"

"In Europe. He was her guide. I'm convinced that he knew who she was before he met her and just set out to get her, although he always denied it. Oh no, according to Cassa, they had a great love, a great passion—ha! Filthy man."

"They didn't say much about him in the paper."

"Oh, he had no background, no family, nothing. He could have been wanted by the police for all we knew."

"Do you think he was wanted?"

"Certainly by my daughter," she said, as if the idea was repellent to her. "Nothing we said could dissuade her. Nothing. Holt threatened to disinherit her if she married him, but she didn't care. She had a little money of her own, and most of the trusts ended with her anyway, so she knew one day, whether we approved of her or not, she'd be rich. She wouldn't listen to either of us." Her voice had grown hoarse.

Mrs. Griffin picked up her glass of wine. Her hand was shaking. She nearly spilled some of it before managing to take a sip.

"He married my daughter in secret and was planning to steal all her money," she continued. "He manipulated her. But we found out. I can't tell you the horrors we lived through.

Holt was trying to get him deported. Anyway, finally, she agreed to leave him. The night she was killed, there was an awful scene. Holt and Roberto had a terrible fight . . . Afterward, Cassa told us—she *promised* us she was going to leave him, but she said we had to let her alone and allow her to work things out in her own time. Holt got so angry. I never saw him like that. And Roberto—my God—the two of them . . ."

She buried her head in her hands and began to cry. I reached out and patted her shoulder.

"Oh God, oh God, I should have protected her more," she sobbed. "It's all my fault."

"I'm so sorry, Mrs. Griffin. Is there anything I can do?"

She shook her head, wiping her eyes with her napkin.

"So you see," she said, looking up at me, "it's very difficult for me to trust anyone."

"All right," I said, feeling more sympathetic toward her, "I understand now."

Sensing her vulnerability at that moment, I decided to ask the question I'd been longing to ask ever since reading the newspaper accounts.

"Didn't you ever suspect him?" I said.

"Who?"

"Roberto Madi? Didn't you ever suspect him of the murder?" I pressed.

"Oh, please don't ask me that."

"You said she was going to leave him and he'd tried to steal her money. Wasn't he the logical suspect?"

"I can't answer that. Please," she groaned.

"Why not?"

"I can't. I just can't. Please don't ask me."

She began crying again.

"I wish," she said, her voice faltering, "I wish to God I'd known that night was the last time I was ever going to see Cassa alive . . . If I'd known—" she stopped.

"Go on," I urged her.

"If I'd known . . . I would have said—" She halted again.

"What? What would you have said?"

The old woman took hold of my hand and studied it, measuring it against her own.

"Tiny, delicate hands," she mused.

She looked at me with an expression of surprise, as if she weren't seeing me at all, but someone else.

"I'm sorry, my darling," she said plaintively, staring into my eyes. "Please forgive me, Cassa . . . I'm sorry . . . I'm so sorry."

"Mrs. Griffin, I'm not Cassa."

I can't say whether or not she heard me for she just sat there for a long time holding my hand, swallowing thick sobs. I didn't know what to do so I just watched her. Her grief was so intense, so full of passion, I felt embarrassed, as if I were witnessing some sort of sexual act. I hadn't the vaguest idea what to say to her. What does one say to a person who's grieving over such an irreparable loss? Had I been an old friend or someone with more of a shared history, I might have felt comfortable reaching out and hugging her in her moment of distress. But as it was, I felt powerless to help her, fearing that any gesture on my part might seem hollow or be misinterpreted as too familiar. I longed to turn away, to get up and leave that stifling room.

Mrs. Griffin let go of my hand. She cleared her throat as if she were about to say something. But instead, she simply rose from her chair and walked slowly toward the door without uttering a word. I watched her leave, then sat motionless in my chair for a long time, staring out the window with her last words ringing in my ears.

"Please forgive me, Cassa . . . I'm sorry . . . I'm so sorry."

What did she mean? Sorry for what? What did she want Cassandra to forgive her for?

Finally, Deane came in and announced that Mrs. Griffin was tired and that I was free to go back to work or take the rest of the afternoon off, as I wished. To which room, I wondered, had she retreated for solace—her bedroom or some other? The room in which Cassandra had lived as a child, the room in which she had died?

Later that day, when I left the house, I wondered if Mrs. Griffin was watching me. I knew one thing: I was going to be watching her.

Instead of going back to work, I took the afternoon off. Leaving The Haven I began to drive, just drive, with no particular destination in mind. I kept seeing Cassandra and Roberto Madi as myself and John Noland. Suddenly I pictured John Noland stabbing me through the heart. I pulled over to the side of the road to catch my breath.

I started up the car again and drove around aimlessly until I found myself in my old neighborhood in the Village, near Washington Square. Except for the more apparent seediness of the sidewalks, the area hadn't changed much since I'd lived there fifteen years earlier. The turn-of-the-century architecture and the narrow, winding streets always reminded me of a slower, more graceful era. It was here that I'd met John Noland, here that we'd conducted our affair around the cafes, jazz clubs, theaters, and restaurants that shaped the neighborhood. We lived near enough one another for felicitous encounters, for last-minute trysts, and for me to spy on him. Now, once again, I found myself driving by his house, looking up at his window to see if he was home.

He lived on the second floor of a brownstone off Bleecker Street, or at least he'd lived there once. After we'd stopped seeing one another, I would go out of my way to walk past his apartment. Sometimes I even lingered around, waiting to catch a glimpse of him, dreading the thought of seeing him with another woman, yet morbidly titillated by the idea. Once, I actually staked him out. I stood on the street until dawn, staring up at his windows, catching intermittent glimpses of him smoking, drinking, pacing around his apartment as he worked through the night. During that vigil I realized how much closer I felt to John when I wasn't with him, when I was observing him from a distance, or just thinking about him. I finally grasped how unsatisfying our relationship had been.

I didn't know if he still lived there. It had been so long since I'd seen him or been in contact with him. Had he moved? Had he died? No, he couldn't be dead, I thought. I'd have heard, or else I'd have seen his obituary in the *Times*. I'd taken to reading the *Times'* obituary pages in the last couple of years. They had replaced marriage announcements as a source of personal news for me. Surely John Noland, the now-esteemed writer, would have been as respectfully reviewed in death as he had been in life, perhaps more so.

I parked my car and looked up at the familiar row of windows on the second floor. The old routine. The third window to the left, I knew, was his office—or used to be. The one next to it his bedroom—or used to be. The shade had always been drawn in that room. It was drawn now.

I got out of my car and went into the entranceway of the brownstone to check and see if he still lived there. No harm in that, I thought. It was still the same old hall, dim, butter-colored, with blackened cracks in the white tile floor, still the scent of cats, and, by God, still his name in a slot in the same mailbox, scrawled on a yellowing file card: John Noland.

The mailbox was stuffed. He must be away, I thought. Well, that was par for the course. He would go away frequently to research those elegant books of his. It was fascinating to me how a man harboring so much personal angst and passion could write in such a detached manner. What was that last book of his? I stood in the hallway trying to recall the title. I remembered reading a review a year or so ago, which said that it was "nobly historic." Then it came to me: it was about the colonization of

Peru as seen through the eyes of a missionary and an Inca who become friends and then die together in some violent, worthy way. What was it called again? I thought for another moment. Oh yes: *Men of Stone*. Perfect.

I walked out onto the street again thinking of the time John and I spent together, making love, fighting, making up. I recalled the day I'd gone into his office and rifled through a pile of correspondence, my heart thundering as I found and read a letter from another lovesick woman. I confronted him with it.

"Who *is* this woman who says she loves you and that you love her?!" I had screamed at him.

"It's none of your business," he said, easing the letter from my hand.

"Why do you do this to me?"

"You do it to yourself," he replied.

And it was true. I did. Again and again.

We talked about getting married. I even bought a white lace dress in case we decided to go and do it on the spur of the moment. I wanted to be prepared. I'd always wanted a white wedding. Now, I reflected as I stood on the sidewalk, if I have a wedding, it will be white all right: white dress, white flowers, white hair.

Standing on the street, unable to tear myself away from the building, I remembered the day John phoned and I told him, on impulse, that I didn't want to see him anymore. And this time I really meant it. I think I surprised myself as much as I did him. My tone of voice was uncharacteristically cool. He asked me what he'd done. Was there someone else? No, I said, he'd done nothing in particular and there was no one else. I just didn't want to see him again—which wasn't true. I did want to see him again, but I was suddenly sick of the pain, maybe even a little bored with it. Hearing him plead with me, I was tempted to give in, but instead I said, "Good-bye," and hung up. He never called me back.

I found the strength to move out of the neighborhood, uptown. I stopped wondering if I'd made the right decision, stopped making surreptitious pilgrimages to his house, stopped sitting by the phone waiting for him to call. I stopped searching the mail every morning for his cryptic notes and postcards. When they came—and several did—I read them and threw them away instead of keeping them. John Noland's early correspondence and my father's birthday cards to me from distant places had lain in two piles, side by side in a hidden drawer in my desk for years, until one day I got tired of knowing the piles were there and burned them both. I went about my life in a different way, forming a new collection of feelings, settling into my state of resigned contentment.

Whenever I saw John Noland's books reviewed, I smiled. Occasionally, browsing through a bookstore, I'd pick up a copy of his latest novel. I'd look at the picture on the back of the jacket and think, there he is, still craggy-handsome, still taut and lean, still the ladies' man, but getting older. I always glanced at the dedication in his books. One read: "For S. R.—With Love." Poor "S. R.," I thought as I replaced the book on the shelf. Poor love.

When I got home that evening, I thumbed through all the newspaper clippings about Cassandra again, reading snippets of them aloud to myself and Brush. I fell asleep with the light on and had a dream I didn't remember clearly. I awoke the next morning considerably more tired than when I went to bed.

I didn't see Mrs. Griffin for more than two weeks after our strange lunch together. I went to work every day, but there was no sign of her and no word from her. That was fine with me. Our encounter had left me feeling vaguely embarrassed, and her words, "Please forgive me, Cassa . . . ," kept echoing in my mind. The incident had jolted the rhythm of our relationship, and we both needed to recover. She'd revealed too deep a part of herself too soon. We really didn't know one another well enough for a dramatic scene of tears and mistaken identity. I felt the necessary balance could only be restored by time and distance.

During this period, I worked hard to little avail. I sat for hours in the ballroom smoking, sketching, conjuring up ideas, only to dismiss them the next day as too trivial or too bland. I found myself wondering just exactly how Mrs. Griffin was spending her days. As far as I could tell, she never went outside and she never received visitors. No one but tradesmen called at the house. She never came down to work or stroll in her garden. She never looked in on me. She remained all by herself, attended only by servants. So, I asked myself, what on earth did she do all day? Did she read or watch television? Did she spend time in her costume rooms trying on her memories? Or did she have some secret project to fill her hours?

Though I never saw her, I felt the old woman's presence as I worked, and I developed the uneasy impression of being watched by her. Little things happened. The birds would suddenly stop chirping, and I sensed there was someone walking around outside. But when I went to look, there was never anyone there. Sometimes I strolled around the building at lunch and noticed faint footprints in the soil, small, made by a woman's shoe. Sometimes I could have sworn I heard someone crying softly outside.

At first I dismissed these incidents and thoughts. Gradually, however, the feeling of being watched became so pronounced I wondered if she wasn't somehow spying on me from a secret hole in the wall. I found myself turning around abruptly in the middle of a sketch to search the walls for an eye.

One day, I made a point of coming to the ballroom very early in the morning when the rising sun was still low in the sky. I stood in the center of the room turning around slowly, and, by God, there it was: a tiny pinprick of sunlight, barely visible behind a column, stabbing the east wall at eye level. I walked over to it in order to examine it more closely. It was a miniscule hole just big enough to peer through. I stuffed it with paper and made a note to have it plastered properly. This particular game was over, and I had won. At least for now.

In time, I got to know the ballroom as one gets to know a close friend, complete with moods and flaws. Built for an old-fashioned ritual, it had an air of sadness about it, perhaps because it would never again be used for the purpose for which it was intended. I knew Mrs. Griffin would not give another ball there. She was too reclusive, too old. This brought to mind the question of just why she wanted the room done up at all. Perhaps, I thought, it was to fix some sort of memory she had, or wanted to have, of lighter, more innocent times. Increasingly, I felt a desire to make the room—how to put it?—happy. Slowly, with this idea in mind, a plan for its design began to take shape.

Since every great ballroom must always look as if it's ready for a ball, I decided simply to make it ready. I planned to give the stark, classical space lots of company, fantasy, and music—to create a dance, a coming-out party, in the middle of which I'd place the debutante herself—Cassandra Griffin—poised to step onto the dance floor, a true princess in her long white dress and tiara of youth.

As this inspiration settled into place, I thought to myself, Cassa, you and I will live together for a few months while I immortalize your crowning moment. I'll come to know you and perhaps even myself a little better as a result. I'll live with you and re-create your finest moment, and maybe even solve the mystery of your death.

Having decided to proceed with this scheme, I began sketching directly onto the ballroom walls. My charcoal pencil flew across the plaster as a hundred ideas occurred to me at once. I felt the burst of energy every artist longs for when ideas start gushing from that magic spring deep in the subconscious. I worked furiously until I'd realized my inspiration with a series of detailed sketches.

At the end of a week, the ballroom had come alive with people and musicians, animals and flowers. Each panel told a little story, and each story had in it a touch of whimsy. I was particularly fond of the vignette in which a small dog, hiding in the folds of a woman's long dress, has lifted its leg on her escort. The woman, smoking a cigarette in a long holder, and the young man, in white tie sipping champagne, are oblivious to the dog's mischief. I sprinkled other, similarly irreverent scenes over the generally decorous cotillion crowd: a waiter staring down a grand dame's décolletage as he offers her a plate of hors d'oeuvres; an old roué pinching a young girl's bottom; a woman pulling up her skirts too high to the delight of her escort. At the center of the gala was a blank-faced portrait of the debutante herself, Cassandra Griffin.

My supporting characters in place, I now needed Mrs. Griffin to approve the plan. I knew she wasn't spying on me anymore—I figured I'd taken care of that. I wanted her to come to the ballroom to see what I was proposing, though I suspected she came to look over my work every night after I'd gone. After making my request to Deane, who said he would consult with Mrs. Griffin and get back to me, I wandered around the grounds waiting for her answer, feeling both elated and nervous at the prospect of seeing her again.

I knew I'd done good work and hoped she would approve, but I was still wary of her. I couldn't quite figure out this odd little game she was playing with me, or if, indeed, it was a game at all and not just some figment of my imagination. I wondered how she would behave, given the unexpectedly intimate nature of our previous encounter. I knew it was best to let her set the tone for this meeting.

Later that day I was summoned to Mrs. Griffin's bedroom. She sat propped up in her silk canopied bed, resting against a mountain of pillows, looking so old and shrunken that for a moment I didn't recognize her. Her head appeared much smaller. Wispy gray strands of hair covered her skull.

"Get me my hair," she said imperiously to a maid, who promptly disappeared into the dressing room.

"I've had a spell," she said.

She held up a hand mirror and examined her face in the glass.

"Hideous," she said with a self-deprecating little laugh. "Simply hideous."

Putting the mirror down, she looked at me with those large pale blue eyes of hers.

"I used to take great pains with my appearance, you know.

I was famous for it. Never a hair out of place, even to go around the corner. Good grooming is a full-time occupation, and I was very good at my job. No one's ever seen me like this, except my maid, of course."

I wondered why she was allowing me to see her in this sorry state, and then, as if reading my mind, she said: "But I wanted you to. I wanted you to see me without any artifice."

"Why?" I asked.

She thought for a moment. "I think perhaps it's because I want your good opinion, and it's easier to get people's good opinions when they feel slightly sorry for you."

I let go a perplexed little laugh.

"Why on earth should you want my good opinion? I don't understand."

"No. I know you don't. And you won't for a while. I'm not sure I quite understand it myself. But I think it's fair to say that one day I'll need all your compassion. Compassion is the most necessary ingredient in all relationships. Everything depends on it. Everything rises and falls with the amount you use. You'll need quite a bit for me."

She picked up the mirror again and studied herself.

"I used to love looking in the mirror," she said. "It reassured me." Tracing one or two deep wrinkles on her face with the tip of her finger, she sighed, "I never imagined myself getting old . . . How old are you now?"

"Thirty-nine," I replied without hesitation.

"Ah! At thirty-nine I was immortal. . . . Do you imagine yourself getting old?"

I shrugged. "Yes and no. I try not to think about it. Sometimes I feel quite old already."

"That's because you're alone," she said. "Being alone ages you."

"You think so?" The thought had never occurred to me.

"Oh yes," she said firmly. "One needs contact with others to stay young."

The maid brought in two wigs on stands. Mrs. Griffin chose

one, and placed it on her head, expertly tucking the errant wisps of her own hair beneath it.

"Did you know I wore a wig?"

"I thought you might," I said.

"I hate them. They're hot. But, as you can see, my own hair is impossible now. It used to be luxurious—though not, if I do say so myself—my best feature as it often is with plain women. If I weren't so vain, I'd just wear a scarf. But I am vain. I used to lie about my age all the time. I was nearly thirty-three when Cassa was born but I told everyone I was twenty-eight. Now there's no point in lying about anything. There," she said, holding the mirror away from her to get a better view. "That's a bit better . . . Well, maybe not."

The wig did make her look better. But I couldn't forget the bizarre image I had of her without it—a shrunken head sprouting thin gray strings.

"Oh, it's so boring to know I'll never look well again," she said irritably. "I have terminal cancer."

I didn't know how to respond. She rattled on.

"The doctors don't give me more than a year or two. It's odd, you know, because I don't feel as if I'm going to die, and yet I know I am. And soon. But I feel as if it's all happening to someone else and I'm sort of watching it. Do you know what I mean?"

"I think so."

"I must say I do dread the night," she went on. "One feels so alone at night for some reason. I don't know why that should be true since I'm alone all day. But there's something about the darkness and the stillness. I lie in bed and think about all those evil cells eating up my insides. I can almost hear them—chomping away. I'm not so wedded to this life that I can't give it up. But I loathe the idea of disintegration. I don't want to disintegrate."

"My mother died of cancer."

This interested her.

"You took care of her?"

"Yes."

"Yes, I'm sure you did. Was it difficult?" she asked.

"Very."

"What was the most difficult thing about it?"

I thought for a moment.

"The most difficult thing . . . is now."

Mrs. Griffin stroked my right hand.

"There's a good girl. Well, enough of all this crepe-hanging," she said abruptly. "Help me out of this grave, will you? I want to go to the ballroom and see what you've been up to."

6

Mrs. Griffin took my arm and leaned on me as we walked downstairs, hardly speaking. The effort of the journey seemed as much as she could bear. When she faltered I bolstered up her by putting both my arms around her, a gesture for which she thanked me almost too effusively. Her pathetic gratitude and frail demeanor reinforced the protectiveness I was developing toward her. I felt the power of my own health and youth more keenly as we went on. Walking with her and having to support her from time to time seemed to fuse us together in some primal way. I thought of my mother, remembering what it had been like to be with her in the last few months of her life. She, too, had clung to me during those desperate days as though I could save her. I wondered, as we made our way across the garden, if Frances Griffin was thinking what it would have been like to walk with Cassandra through this, her final season.

By the time we reached the ballroom, a new closeness had enveloped us. I felt more relaxed in her company. Nevertheless, I held my breath as we entered the room. As eager as I was to see the legendary Frances Griffin's reaction to my work, I was equally terrified she wouldn't like it.

I led her inside. Standing at the top of the stairs, she looked around for a moment and let out a little cry. Breaking away from me with some effort, she walked slowly down the stairs into the middle of the room, where she stood still, examining each of the panels in turn. She spurned my offers of help and, using what I imagined was all the effort she had left in her, pulled my sketching chair into the center of the room, placing it directly in front of the main panel. She sat down and gazed at this, the centerpiece of my creation, with a grim intensity.

It was the largest panel by far, with the most figures in it, the most activity, and the one on which I'd worked the hardest. Like the others, it had been executed in the primitive lines of a charcoal pencil. At its center was the figure of a faceless young woman making her entrance into the ballroom, wearing a sweeping white dress, holding a delicate spray of flowers in a lace cone, bound with streaming ribbons. A handsome escort, in white tie and tails, was standing behind her, slightly off to one side, so that she alone dominated the room. The blank oval where I would ultimately paint her face looked surreal amidst the completed countenances of the other people on the walls.

"This girl," Mrs. Griffin began, continuing to stare at the faceless figure, "who is she?"

"Your daughter," I replied softly.

"My daughter . . ."

"Yes, if you don't object. I thought since she was the reason for the room's existence, I should put her at the center. You built the room for her coming-out party, didn't you?"

Mrs. Griffin didn't answer. Her silence made me nervous. I couldn't tell whether the idea appealed to her or offended her.

"You see," I went on, "I thought it might be rather interesting to freeze that wonderful moment in time forever—as a kind of tribute to you and your daughter, as well as to the purpose of the room."

The old woman said nothing.

"Of course," I continued anxiously, "it's far from finished. I can change it if you like. I can change anything or everything. It's charcoal, easy to erase. Please consider these only as sketches for your approval. I can wipe them all away and start over again."

I heard myself rattling on apologetically and stopped. Mrs. Griffin still didn't say anything. I stood for what seemed like an interminable amount of time, wondering what in God's name was going through her mind. Then I saw a single tear drop from the corner of her eye.

"How did you know about the ribbons and the lace cone?" she said, finally, her voice hollow.

"In the bouquet? I didn't. It was just something I imagined."

"And the dress? How did you know what it looked like? There's never been a full-length photograph of it."

"I didn't. I just imagined it."

She turned and stared at me, stony-faced.

"That's her dress, her bouquet. The attitude, the shyness, everything is her. Except the face. You haven't drawn the face."

"I hope I haven't offended you, Mrs. Griffin."

"Offended me . . ."

I held my breath. I couldn't make out at all what she was thinking. Then she raised her hands up in front of her face, angling her fingers so they formed a frame through which she could examine certain portions of the mural in isolation. She glanced around at the other panels, but her attention kept coming back to the center one and the figure of her daughter. Suddenly, she stood up with an unexpected burst of energy and announced: "It's absolutely right! It's going to be marvelous."

I stood there in disbelief watching her walk around to each panel, picking out details she liked. She was a new person—younger, invigorated.

"I love what you've done here," she said, pointing to a section I was particularly pleased with. "And there—you've been very whimsical there . . . so inventive . . . This part will be wonderful when it's filled in." And so on.

Her comments were not only flattering but incisive. She seemed to understand what I was trying to get at, what attitudes

I was trying to convey. She went on and on with her praise, drawing attention to all the best portions of my work, dwelling on a fold of drapery, a flower, an expression, as though each was a special treasure. Her initial silence and the resulting suspense made my triumph all the sweeter. I was thrilled that her legendary eye was capable of seeing through these sketches to the end result. She made me feel as if I had succeeded almost as well as my hero, Veronese.

We then discussed color for a while, both agreeing that the overall effect should be somewhat muted so that the creamy whiteness of Cassandra's dress could stand out, luminous.

"You must take your time," she said. "Take all the time in the world. It must be perfection."

"I'm so glad you approve, Mrs. Griffin. At first I thought you didn't like it."

"I was simply stunned, that's all. It's just what I wanted. And one so rarely gets just what one wants the first time. Of course I didn't know it was what I wanted, but now that I see it, it's the perfect thing. I can't do things myself, or even imagine them properly. But I have an eye for people who can. That's the secret of life—knowing whom to choose."

She began to speak more slowly and with greater effort. I could feel her energy beginning to flag.

"Forgive me," she said at last. "I'm very tired."

I offered to walk her back to the house, but she declined, saying she needed to be by herself for a time. I watched her as she left the room, walking slowly and carefully up the staircase, gripping the balustrade, as if she were terrified of falling. As she reached the top, she turned to look at the large center panel once more.

"Very striking," she said. "Even from a distance."

She disappeared into the garden.

I stood alone in the ballroom for a long time after she left, reflecting. I still had my work cut out for me but I was elated that Frances Griffin, the great Frances Griffin, had liked my efforts and praised them so highly. Her enthusiasm infused me with energy. I couldn't wait to get started on the final stage, but I allowed myself time to savor this moment.

I stared at the faceless Cassandra and said aloud, "Your face is the very last thing I'll paint. I promise I'll paint it when the evening I create for you is ready for your approval."

I set to work immediately, sorting out colors and brushes, and laying out a general work plan. In the midst of my elation, however, something began to trouble me. Mrs. Griffin's adulation had been too freely given. In retrospect, there was something false about it, something calculated.

The Frances Griffin I'd always heard about—the legendary Frances Griffin who had shaped the taste of a generation of rich women with her high standards of style and craftsmanship—was known as a stickler for perfection. Much as I liked the work I'd done, I knew it was far from perfect. Even I could see some of the mistakes I'd made and intended to correct. So why had Mrs. Griffin been so effusive in her praise? From all I'd heard about her, I doubted whether Veronese himself could have presented her with a work she wouldn't have managed to criticize in some small way. Yet she'd found no fault with anything I'd done in these murals. And I certainly wasn't Veronese. If only she'd made the slightest criticism, the smallest suggestion, I might have felt less uneasy.

Once again I found myself wondering if Mrs. Griffin was playing an elaborate game with me, or whether my overactive imagination was looking for hidden motives that didn't exist. I decided to cast my doubts aside, chalk them up to artistic insecurity, and get on with it. Maybe I was better than I thought. Or maybe the great lady had become less demanding with age. Whatever—I became determined not to let my own doubts about my work undermine the victory of having pleased her.

That afternoon, just as I was leaving for the day, Deane presented me with a fancy dress box tied up with a ribbon.

"Mrs. Griffin asked me to give this to you," he said. "She would prefer that you not open it until you get home."

I thanked him as he helped me into my car with the box.

I decided not to open it until I got home, not because Mrs. Griffin had requested it, but because I was getting used to being a participant in an ongoing drama I didn't quite understand. I did wonder what she had given me, however. I kept the box beside me on the passenger seat, eyeing it now and then as I sped down the parkway.

Brush was lurking by the front door when I walked in. He greeted me warmly, as usual, rubbing up against my leg, purring like a little engine. His long days of solitude always put him in the mood for some affection in the evening when I came home. I was so eager to get to my present, however, I ignored him for the moment.

"You'll just have to wait, my little friend," I said, laying the box on the sofa in the living room.

Undaunted, he hopped up on the sofa alongside the box, watching me as I opened it. The box was made of thick cardboard and covered all over in lavender cloth. The thick dark purple ribbon around it was pure silk velvet. When I tugged gently at the luscious bow, it wilted away. I couldn't help thinking how typical it was of Frances Griffin, a woman whose entire life was a series of presentations, to make even the wrapping of a gift so stylish.

I lifted the top off the box to reveal a flat sea of pale blue tissue paper. Diving into it, my hands itching with curiosity, I discovered a cream satin evening dress, delicately embroidered with seed pearls and alençon lace. Wrapped in a separate parcel was a bouquet of dried flowers sheafed in a lace cone streaming with long white ribbons. There wasn't a note, nor did there have to be. I knew exactly what it was.

"My God, Brush," I heard myself exclaim aloud, "it's the dress! *The* dress! Cassandra's coming-out dress!"

Brush watched as I extracted the rich garment from its box. I held it out in front of me and examined it. Indeed, it was almost exactly like the one I'd sketched for the Cassandra of my panel: sleeveless with a simple scoop neck, a fitted bodice, a full skirt with a train, its thick satin still lustrous.

Judging from the looks of it, Cassandra had been about my size. Just out of interest, I went into my bedroom and held the dress up to myself in front of the full-length mirror inside my closet door.

"Looks like it'd be a perfect fit," I said out loud to Brush, who had followed me. "What do you think she means by giving this to me? Do you think she wants me to keep it or give it back? What do you suppose she's up to?"

I examined myself at all angles, pressing the dress close to my body.

"It's amazing how right I got it in the drawing, isn't it? Down to the bouquet with the white ribbons. How did I know that, Brush? Do you believe in ghosts? In telepathy?"

Brush blinked his large gray eyes.

"No . . . neither do I. Just coincidence, that's all."

Though I thought of actually trying the dress on, I didn't. It seemed too morbid an act. Instead, I folded it up and re-placed it carefully inside its cove of blue tissue paper. I decided it would be politic to call Mrs. Griffin that evening to thank her, as I wouldn't see her for the rest of the weekend, but when I phoned, Deane told me she was resting and couldn't be dis-turbed. Was there any message? No, I said, it could wait until Monday.

While preparing supper, I played back the messages on my answering machine. There were several from Harry Pitt, who was anxious to know how everything was going at The Haven. I felt guilty about not having called him. In one, he suggested we get together soon and asked me if I cared to accompany him to the Goya exhibition at the Metropolitan Museum on Satur-day. There were messages from two friends, one male, one female, wondering where I'd been lately—was I away? What had happened to me? There was a message from a potential client, a decorator, asking me to return his call as quickly as possible regarding some large job on a plantation in South Car-olina. And several hang-ups. The hang-ups were unusual and I wondered who could be trying to get in touch with me who

wouldn't leave a message. Could it be Mrs. Griffin? She was an
unlikely choice, but I couldn't think who else it might be, unless
it was a solicitation of some sort. I decided to let them all go
until after I'd had a bite to eat.

Brush and I enjoyed our respective suppers. I read one of
my favorite books, Giorgio Vasari's *Lives of the Artists*, as I ate
my pasta with fresh tomatoes and basil. I treated myself to a
half bottle of Chateau Haut Brion, '86, since it was my custom
to indulge myself on Friday evenings after the week's work.
Brush licked his liver scraps clean and hopped up on the far
end of the table to take a snooze while I read parts of the text
to him, the lives of artists being of special interest to us both.

" 'In my opinion painters owe to Giotto, the Florentine
painter, exactly the same debt they owe to nature, which
constantly serves them as a model and whose finest and most
beautiful aspects they are always striving to imitate and
reproduce. . . .' " I read aloud.

I enjoyed linking myself with painters and craftsmen of the
past. Today, alas, it is the scientists, not the artists, who are
painting the great new pictures with their theories and equa-
tions. Their strange, computerized symphonies are the inno-
vative music of these times. So I look to the past for my
inspiration.

After dinner, I returned my calls. The poor decorator
sounded agitated when I told him I couldn't fly down with him
to South Carolina to look at the plantation he was restoring. I
apologized, saying I was busy, without giving any details. I rec-
ommended a friend of mine who was a very competent trompe
l'oeil painter and whose favorite period in history was the Civil
War. He seemed grateful.

I then spoke briefly with my two friends in order to catch
up with them and told them that until this job was finished I
was pretty much incommunicado. They were both quite taken
aback and impressed when I mentioned for whom I was working. I'd almost forgotten what magic the name Frances Griffin
still conjured up.

I called Harry back and made a date to meet him at the Met the next day at eleven. He was anxious to talk, but I said I was tired and had a lot to tell him. I told him he'd have to wait and let me take him to lunch after the exhibit. He agreed.

I got undressed and ready for bed. Just before retiring, I took out Cassandra's dress once more, immersing my hands in the heavy cream satin as if it were a rich batter. This time, I couldn't control the urge to try it on. I slid the dress over my head and stood in front of the mirror looking at myself for a very long time before even attempting to hook it up. I was never a very pretty girl, I thought. However, I noted with pleasure that I'd grown rather more handsome over the years, as if I'd once been pretty and my looks were just now beginning to fade.

I smoothed the bodice of the dress down over my torso, trying unsuccessfully to fasten the endless hidden hooks and snaps at the side, which are the hallmark of the custom-made gown. I imagined Cassandra Griffin, small-breasted, lithe, aristocratic, being put into this dress by a maid on the night of her debut. It was, after all, a dress one had to be "put into" by another person, a dress that assumes the presence of servants for its fitting and maintenance.

I did the best I could getting it hooked up properly. Although it fit perfectly—even the length was right—it was still the dress of youth on the body of middle age. Its regal stiffness and smiling neckline only served to highlight the slackness of my features. In the end, the dress did little to transform me.

I wondered if Cassandra had stood staring at herself in the mirror the night of her debut, taking all the promise in front of her for granted, like a view she'd grown up with? Or if she had looked out on black waves of uncertainty, never truly feeling the privilege of her position, or perhaps not wanting it?

I took off the dress, put it away once and for all, and went to bed. I was fast asleep when I heard a persistent alarm sounding through my dreams. In my stupor, it took me a while to realize what it was. I grappled for the receiver in the dark, nearly knocking the phone off my night table.

"Hello?"

"You're there," said a familiar but unplaceable male voice on the other end of the line.

"Who's this?"

"Who do you think?"

Speak of the devil, I thought, now recognizing those low, husky tones.

"John? John Noland!"

"How've you been?"

"What time is it?" I groaned.

"Late."

"In more ways than one. What the hell are you doing calling me at this hour? Or at all for that matter?"

"You're never home. I tried you several times today."

"Why didn't you leave a message?"

"You know me. I hate messages," he said.

I waited for him to continue with the conversation.

"So . . . how've you been?"

"Fine, thanks," I replied curtly.

"Good."

Another interminable pause. This time I broke the silence.

"What do you want, John?"

"I don't know. I was thinking about you."

"What were you thinking?"

I felt myself being pulled back into that net of his.

"Was that you a couple of weeks ago?" he asked.

"What?"

"Coming out of my building?"

So he'd seen me.

"Yes," I said.

"Thought so."

"You saw me?"

"Uh-huh."

"Why didn't you say hello?"

"I'm saying hello now. Hello."

"Hello," I replied.

"What were you doing there?"

"I was in the neighborhood and curiosity got the better of me," I said, trying to sound as nonchalant as possible. "I wondered if you still lived there."

"Why didn't you ring up?"

"How do you know I didn't?"

"Because I was home," he said.

"You were in your apartment?"

"I saw you from the window."

"Oh. Why didn't you yell down?" I said.

"Why didn't you ring up?"

We were back where we started from.

"Okay, John, why are you calling me?"

"I don't know. I guess I miss you."

He said this as casually as if we hadn't seen one another for a couple of days.

"Uh, John, it's been twelve years since we've spoken to one another."

"Do you miss me?" he continued, ignoring my statement.

I was damned if I was going to give him the satisfaction of saying I missed him, or any satisfaction at all, for that matter.

"So . . . what have you been up to all these years?" I said.

"Writing, traveling. Same stuff."

"I heard you got married."

"Uh-huh," he replied.

"To whom?"

"Someone you don't know."

"Who is she?" I inquired.

"We're separated."

"Who was she?"

"Just a woman. A painter, as a matter of fact."

"Really?" This interested me.

"I have a weakness for painters, as you know."

"What kind of a painter was she?"

"A bad one."

"That's not what I mean," I said, somewhat exasperated by his evasions. "What sort of painting did she do?"

"Abstract."

"Abstract, eh?"

Another brief pause.

"So, when am I going to see you?"

"You're not," I said firmly.

"Why?"

"John, I repeat—what do you want?"

"To see you. Catch up. Give you a copy of my new book."

"Why? Did you dedicate it to me?"

"No."

"Who did you dedicate it to?"

" 'Vanishing species,' " he said.

"To me, in other words."

He laughed. "Still have your humor, I see."

"I'd be dead if I didn't," I said.

"So . . . come out and have some dinner with me next week."

"I don't think that's a good idea, John. I really don't."

"Have dinner with me," he urged.

I was sorely tempted. His voice was still alluring. I suppose I have nothing to lose, I thought. It's just a dinner, after all. I felt myself wanting to do it, wanting to see him again, even though I'd felt nothing for him on that strange sojourn to his house. I couldn't believe he'd actually been watching me. It was intriguing.

As he continued to cajole me, I began to reason faultily, as people do in self-destructive situations. I told myself that *not* having dinner with him was a sign of greater weakness than having it.

"When?" I said softly.

"Tuesday. I'll pick you up."

I hesitated for one last self-preserving moment.

"All right," I sighed, giving in.

"See you."

He hung up.

Well now, I thought, it's going to be interesting to see if I've changed. Accepting the dinner invitation to begin with was proof that I hadn't changed all that much. Well, the die was cast. I found myself unexpectedly elated. For the first time in a long while, I had something to look forward to which didn't involve work. I lay awake in the dark. Tuesday suddenly seemed very far away.

Tell me more, tell me more!"
squawked Harry Pitt from his wheelchair, bobbing his large bald
head up and down excitedly.

I was wheeling Harry around the Goya exhibition at the
Metropolitan Museum, regaling him with tales of Frances Griffin and her house—the theme rooms, the extraordinary paintings and furniture, the regal but septic isolation of the old
dowager herself. Harry didn't really need a wheelchair but he
always requested one, finding it an effective tool for cutting in
lines, which, that day, were enormous. Even though I was growing impatient playing Scheherazade to his King Schariar, I
wanted to wait our turn. But Harry, anxious to see the pictures,
went into his act.

"Let us through! Let us through!" he cried.

Shuddering with vague annoyance at being interrupted
during their contemplation, several viewers turned around and
looked at Harry, who was staring up at them, doe-eyed, from
the confines of his wheelchair.

"Please let a sick old gentleman pass," he said sweetly. "I'm
an invalid. Would you be so kind as to let us through?"

Their expressions immediately changed from irritated to
embarrassed as they stepped aside to accommodate us.

"Theater of Guilt," Harry whispered to me cynically as I wheeled him up to the front of the line.

Though I was mortified at Harry's performance, I had to admit it was effective.

"You're impossible!" I hissed into his ear.

He paid no attention, feeling, I'm sure, that such rights of precedence were the due of persons as knowledgeable as himself. To Harry, most people were Philistines beneath his consideration.

"Knowledge of taste is as rare as knowledge of Latin these days," he lamented. "I often feel as if I were one of those monks in the Middle Ages who guarded the ancient texts from the heathen and kept learning alive despite all efforts to destroy it. We have a grave responsibility to preserve what is left of a past that this hideous century is bent on eradicating . . . Have you noticed that most people nowadays don't have the patience to look at any picture that isn't moving?"

"That's not quite true, Harry. Look at all the people here at this exhibition."

"Yes, but they haven't a clue what they're looking at," he said dismissively. "They're just here because some art critic told them to go."

"I disagree," I said, noting the rapt faces on several of the viewers.

"Of course you disagree, my dear. You're still young."

I wheeled him over to Goya's great painting of the lovely Countess of Chinchón.

"Ah, look at her," Harry sighed. "Isn't she magnificent?"

We both stood transfixed in front of the haunting portrait of the young countess, swathed in white, sitting in a void, an ethereal creature whose soft features and dreamy expression were filled with the sadness of a half-lived life.

"The poor countess," Harry went on. "All that promise and beauty come a cropper. You know her story, of course?"

I shook my head.

"Well," he went on, relishing his knowledge, "she was very grand and she married an awful sadist. Some ghastly upstart general who beat her and squandered her money, then ran off with another woman. Typical. She never recovered. Died young.

"Look how sympathetic Goya is to her in this picture. He isolates her so she appears distant, yet he makes her vulnerable and appealing to the viewer. One just wants to reach out and put one's arms around her, don't you think? Yet one fears for her fragility. She looks as if she's about to evaporate, doesn't she? It's as if the artist were saying that beauty and sadness are somehow linked in this fleeting life." He paused for a moment, obviously moved. "He didn't miss much, old Goya."

"She reminds me of Cassandra Griffin," I said, looking at the countess's haunted face.

"Really?" He seemed intrigued.

We moved on, chatting away as we made cursory stops at some of the other paintings.

"Tell me more about Frances Griffin," Harry said.

"Well, the general feeling I have is that she doesn't live life, she stages it."

"Oh, but that's true of so many of those ladies. The tacky ones do it through publicity, of course. I used to walk a lot of them, when I still could walk," he said with a sneer. "And I noticed that they really weren't happy with an evening unless they read about it the next day in the columns and saw pictures of themselves plastered all over the newspapers, sort of like reviews."

"Don't tell me Frances Griffin ever courted publicity. I can't believe it. She's a complete and total recluse."

"No, she never did," Harry said. "She was far too elegant, far too grand. I remember when she walked into my shop that day I hadn't a clue who she was. But I could tell from the way she was dressed and the way she conducted herself that she was *someone*. She didn't have to announce it."

"Yes, she's very regal for a person who came from nothing, as you say she did."

"Don't forget," Harry warned, "people who invent themselves that successfully can be the most regal of all. They're usually very good at revising the script to fit the character.

Frances Griffin has an infallible sense of story line. She always managed to maintain her mystery, which is, of course, vital for any woman, but de rigueur for the true *grand dame*."

"Don't you think everyone invents themselves somehow?" I asked him.

"To a degree. Especially in this country," he replied. "Certainly people who make great lives for themselves out of sheer will or talent are self-invented. But there are a few who are given a clear distinction at birth that's recognized by society—like, for example, great wealth or a great name or even great beauty. And those people don't invent themselves so much as they spend their lives either living up to what was expected of them, or failing to do so."

"I wonder what was expected of Cassandra Griffin," I said.

"Depends on whom you ask. I'm sure most people would expect a great deal from someone with those kinds of opportunities. But what they don't know is that too much can be as damaging as too little," Harry observed. "Great wealth, great poverty—flip sides of the same coin. The poor thing probably never had a chance, not with that background."

"No. She would have had to overcome all her advantages!" Harry and I both laughed.

"God, we're a pair of cynics, aren't we?" I said.

"Well, let's say we're cautious . . . and experienced. Don't forget, Frances Griffin just appeared on the scene one day. I don't think anyone knew what to expect from her."

"What's your point, Harry?"

"My point is that by the time anybody checked on her, it was too late. She'd swept the path clean. And anyone who wanted to be in her good graces had to swallow whatever story she gave them. So that became the official story. People have short memories around money and power. Tell me, Faith," he said, changing his tone somewhat, "do you like her?"

It was odd but I hadn't really thought about it before. I considered for a moment.

"You know, I do, sort of."

"What do you mean, 'sort of'?"

"Well, it's complicated," I began. "I get the feeling she's playing all sorts of games with me and I can't figure out why."

"Games? What sorts of games?" he inquired.

"Oh, Just little things. She had me followed for example. And I think she was watching me for the first week I was in the ballroom. Then we had a very strange lunch where she mistook me for her daughter."

"Explain, please."

"Well, you really had to have been there, but she sort of apologized to me as if I were Cassandra. And that leads me to what I really want to talk to you about, Harry."

I leaned down to speak to him confidentially.

"I think I know who killed her daughter," I whispered. "And it was no intruder."

"Who was it?"

"Roberto Madi. Her husband."

I expected the revelation of this theory to have as startling an impact on Harry as its formulation had on me.

"Oh yes, the son-in-law," he said dryly. "I seem to remember something about that now. Yes, yes, he was the one."

I was taken aback.

"What do you mean he was the one?" I said.

"Well, of course, everyone assumed he did it."

Harry's dismissive pronouncement was incredibly annoying so I gave his wheelchair an extra little push to let him know I was still in charge. He reacted to the jolt.

"Now, now, temper—."

"What do you mean everyone assumed he did it?"

"I don't know. They just did. That was the rumor anyway."

"Why didn't they do anything?"

"What could they do?"

"I don't know. Prosecute him," I said angrily. "Isn't that what one usually does with murderers?"

"Faith, dear, what a silly question. Your naiveté is so unexpected sometimes."

"Didn't they have any proof?"

"There might have been proof, who knows?" Harry shrugged.

"Do you think there was a cover-up?"

"This is Society, dear. Well, *soi-disant* Society. Society is nothing *but* a cover-up," he snorted.

"You know what I mean, Harry. I would have thought they'd have loved to pin it on the son-in-law. Mrs. Griffin hates him. He was an interloper."

Harry reacted to the mild exasperation in my voice by speaking with exaggerated calm.

"Whatever their reasons, they didn't want him prosecuted," he said.

"You keep saying they didn't *want* him prosecuted, as if they had a choice!" I cried.

I heard my voice above the din. People were looking at me.

"Calm down," Harry admonished me. "Listen, dear," he went on, "when you're as grand and rich as the Griffins, you have nothing but choices. That's what your life is: one big choice. Don't forget, Holt Griffin belonged to the old rich. They still have tentacles in high places, which means to some degree, they're immune to the ordinary rules of life—and death."

"Harry, listen to me, will you? Have you ever read those newspaper accounts of the murder?"

"I certainly did at the time," he said. "It was all anyone could talk about."

"But not recently."

"I don't keep them by my bed like a Bible, if that's what you mean."

"Well, when you do read them, it's so glaringly obvious that he did it. I just don't understand why they couldn't prove it."

"Because they didn't *want* to," he said.

"God, how depressing. You know who murdered your daughter and you don't want to prove it."

"Well, contemplate the scandal if they *had* proved it. It was a huge scandal the way it was, but at least it died down after a while. Just imagine what would have happened if they'd been able to prove that the son-in-law had done it. The mind boggles. The arrest, the trial—it would have gone on for years and years! Can you see Frances Griffin enduring that kind of publicity? And as for old Holt Griffin, he wouldn't have survived. He would have just plain keeled over and died."

"He did anyway."

"Yes, but years later. Listen, Faith, not everyone has your tolerance for the grotesque. Holt Griffin was the most proper, careful, upright man. He just would never have allowed it to happen."

While Harry fanned himself with the catalogue, I reflected on what he'd said.

"Tell me more about Holt Griffin."

"I will if you get me out of here. I'm famished and claustrophobic," Harry said irritably.

"We'll go to lunch."

"It's about time," he sniffed.

I took Harry to lunch in a small outdoor cafe near the museum. It was a pleasant day and we sat outside, watching the passersby. The service was slow, which annoyed Harry at first, but he mellowed after the waiter brought him a carafe of wine. We ordered and settled in.

"All right," I said. "Holt Griffin."

Harry rested his elbows on the table, his hands folded in a prayer position which he frequently broke in order to sip from his glass of white wine.

"Courtly—that's the adjective that comes to mind. A courtly man. I saw him several times, but only met him once. He was quite shy, very unassuming. Elegant-looking, tall, fine-featured, aristocratic. Beautifully dressed in that English tailored way. Understated but perfect. You know the type. And slightly effeminate." He hesitated.

"Go on," I said.

"I was just thinking about that for a moment. I don't think he was actively gay, although, as I think I told you, the rumor was that Frances weaned him away from that proclivity and that's why he depended on her so much. . . . Anyway, the most

striking thing about him was this sense of distance he projected.
I felt it when I met him. I only met him once, as I said, and
very briefly, but I had the feeling I wasn't really speaking with
the man in front of me. There was an incredible air of detachment about him. And yet he was perfectly friendly, nice, man-
nerly. But he never let you get close. Know what I mean?"

I nodded. Harry finished his first glass of wine and poured
himself another from the carafe. He offered me some, but I
declined.

"You know I never drink during the day. It makes me too
sleepy."

Harry nodded and continued on:

"He was fanatically private. You think Frances Griffin is
private? Holt made Frances look like a rock star. He was path-
ologically private. He was of the old school that believed a person's name should only appear three times in the newspaper:
when they're born, when they marry, and when they die."

"I thought he was in the foreign service. He must have
been written up in the papers constantly."

"Not true. You're supposed to stay out of the papers when
you're in the foreign service. But, even if he did get in them,
that would have been in the service of his country. I'm speaking
of his private life. Unlike everyone today, Holt Griffin actually
loathed publicity."

"So you think he might have covered up for his daughter's
murderer just to avoid publicity?" I said with revulsion.

"I don't know it for a fact. But let's just say it's not
impossible."

"Well, here's my theory," I began, "I think they covered
everything up, but I'm not so sure it was simply to avoid the
publicity. I think there was something else going on."

"What, for instance?"

"For instance, I don't know. But whatever it was, I *do* know
that Mrs. Griffin feels very, very guilty about it, and that she's
trying to turn me into a kind of surrogate daughter so that
maybe she can confess it or make it up to Cassandra in some
weird way."

"What makes you say that, Faith?"

"It's just an instinct."

"And what if she were trying to make you a surrogate daughter? Would that be so terrible?" Harry said.

"It's a bit bizarre, don't you think?"

"Not really. She's a rich old woman, alone in life. She's had a terrible tragedy. You're young, around her daughter's age, or the age her daughter would have been. When you think about it, it's only natural she might want to attach herself to you in some fashion."

"It's creepy," I replied.

"Creepy—what a word!"

"She's got cancer. I think she's dying," I said.

Harry furrowed his brow and leaned in, hunching his shoulders.

"No," he protested. "Can't be."

"Why not? She told me herself. God, I'd love to solve this murder."

"Why?" he asked.

"Oh, I don't know," I said. "I feel like this girl's sort of a kindred spirit in a way. I can't quite explain it to you. And I'm curious. Just plain old curious. There are too many inconsistencies. I'm sure somebody knows the truth."

Feeling a little uneasy, I broke my rule and poured myself a glass of wine. I drank it down and poured another. Harry looked at me with an amused expression on his face.

"I thought we didn't drink during the day," he said.

"We do today," I snapped. "She gave me Cassandra's debutante dress, and I tried it on."

"Did it fit?"

"Almost perfectly. It was eerie. You know, we kind of look alike, Cassandra and I. Did you ever see a picture of her?"

"Hmm," he nodded.

"I wonder what she was like. I have a feeling we might have had quite a lot in common."

"In what way?"

"Oh, with men, of course. I'm sure Roberto Madi was a variant on the John Noland theme. In fact, I picture Madi as John Noland . . . Speaking of which, guess who called me out of the blue and who I'm having dinner with next week?"

"Oh, don't tell me—" Harry said warily.

"Yes."

"Out of the blue?" He looked skeptical.

"Well, I did go for a little visit into the old neighborhood and he happened to see me from his window."

Harry rolled his eyes heavenward. He knew my history with John backward and forward. In fact, when we'd first met years ago, John was practically the only thing I ever talked about.

"*Nostalgie de la merde*, eh?" he said.

"I know, I know. But I'm curious, I really am. Especially now that I've become intrigued with this Cassandra Griffin thing. It's brought back all sorts of memories."

"Correct me if I'm wrong, but I thought you'd had your fill of masochism."

"Oh Harry, it's just dinner, for heaven's sake."

"Nothing is 'just dinner'—even dinner," he said. "Why don't you simply go out, buy yourself a hair shirt, and eliminate the middleman?"

"Am I that bad?"

"No, *he's* that bad. Think back, Faith, dear. Have you forgotten all that mean man put you through? All you put *yourself* through? You used to call me up at all hours of the night in floods of tears. I even had to come and stay with you once or twice you were so hysterical, if I remember correctly."

I sighed, suddenly sinking down into the mud of unpleasant memories.

"It's true," I reflected. "He was a cold and difficult man. And, you know, I was so crazy about him that if he'd been an ax murderer, I'd probably be dead—just like Cassandra."

"You keep coming back to her," Harry said in a singsong voice.

"I know, I know. I'm haunted by her."

"I think it would be very interesting for you to actually try and solve her murder. You obviously do feel a real kinship with her."

"I feel a kinship with anyone who has been put through the wringer by a man. Sometimes I wonder how I survived all the shit I did."

"Then, for God's sake, why are you having dinner with John Noland? Dredging up the pain? What's the point? You're better off applying your talents to something more constructive."

"I know," I said, feeling despondent.

"Play the game with Mr. Noland in your head, where you've always played it. Leave the actual field to someone else."

My salad arrived, along with Harry's cold roast chicken. Harry approached the meal with his usual gusto. I, on the other hand, had very little appetite. I picked at the soggy lettuce leaves and made a design with the diced ham.

"Christ, Harry, I don't know, I just don't know . . ." I shook my head. "I'm thirty-nine years old and I just don't know about anything anymore. I used to be so sure of things. Do you think that's what life is? A gradual unraveling of all belief?"

"There are periods of unraveling and periods of knitting everything up again," he said, taking a big bite of food.

"What period are you in?"

"Oh, I suppose I'm knitting myself up a few beliefs for the impending journey, sort of like a warm sweater to take on an endless voyage." He rinsed his mouthful down with some wine.

"Do you think about death a lot, Harry?"

Blotting his mouth with a napkin, he replied quite matter-of-factly.

"A lot more than I used to. Why? Do you?"

"I suppose . . ." I said absently.

"Well, when you get to be my age all the unimportant things

suddenly seem vital, and vice versa. I now find myself looking forward to a good meal with the same zeal I used to reserve for business and love. I can remember when acquiring a wonderful piece of furniture or a new lover was the high point of my life. Now, a good roast chicken is."

He raised his fork in the air waving a piece of chicken on the end of it like a flag.

"I've come to realize one spends most of one's life eating, sleeping, and missing the point!" he announced, popping the forkful into his mouth.

"Do you think people get the point at the end?"

"They either do or they don't. Most don't, I suspect. Very few people want to think about things, don't you find? It's easier to just get on with it."

"Are you getting on with it, Harry? Or are you thinking about things?"

"Thinking . . . I think. But what I really hate is to see you wasting your time on this John Noland character, Faith, I really do."

"Oh, well, you know—anything for a little excitement," I sighed.

"There's one in every life, I suppose."

"One what?" I asked.

"Near miss."

"What do you mean?"

"Oh, you know," Harry said, taking a deep reflective breath, "the person you look back on and think, if only things had worked out with them, life might have turned out all right. The one that got away, so to speak. The object of one's fantasy life. Prince Charming *manqué*."

"John Noland wasn't the one that got away. He was more like the one I got away *from*," I said.

"Then who's the one that got away?"

"There isn't anyone. How about you?"

"Rodney," Harry said quickly.

I knew Harry was referring to an ex-lover he introduced

me to years ago who was a police detective. Most of Harry's
"companions," as he called them, were culled from the good,
solid, butch ranks of the working class—policemen, firefighters,
construction workers. He seemed to prefer their virile and, for
the most part, nonverbal company.

"Oh, I remember—the famous Rodney. Rodney, the married detective from Queens with the little genius son."

"God, I loathed that child," Harry said.

"What ever happened to good old Rodney?"

"I have no idea," he replied wistfully. "He was lovely
though. I was rather upset when he went back to that dreary
wife of his. By the way, he's from Brooklyn, not Queens."

In that moment, I realized how sad, in many ways, Harry's
life had been on the romantic front: a series of brief encounters,
of secret liaisons, of background wives and families, of infidelity
and abandonment. To me, Harry was like an old woman who
should have been spending her later years with a devoted husband, reflecting on a lifetime of shared experiences. He was
even beginning to look rather old-womanish lately. Increasingly,
he reminded me of some of Rembrandt's portraits of old people
where age transcends gender and it's difficult to tell whether
the sitter is a man or a woman. Age had withered nearly all of
Harry's masculine characteristics. The soft, feminine side of him
was bleeding through his face like a pentimento.

"Why don't you call him up?" I suggested.

"And say what? Hello, it's me. I've been alone here yearning
for you for eight years. How are you?"

"You could just call up to see how he's doing. John called
me after twelve years."

"Well, maybe John's more secure than I am," Harry said.
"And anyway, it doesn't work the same way when the person is
married and he left you. You have to be more subtle."

"So be subtle," I urged him. "Think of an excuse."

"Oddly enough, you've given me an excuse."

"What's that?" I said cautiously.

"May I propose something to you?"

"Of course."

"Let me help you play detective."

"What do you mean?" I said.

"You say you have a genuine interest in who killed Cassandra Griffin. You suspect it's Roberto Madi. Let's find Roberto Madi and talk to him."

"You're not serious."

"Listen, Faith, you're not the only one who's bored. I could use a little excitement in my life too."

"How's this going to bring you excitement, Harry?"

"Well, for one thing, it will give me an excuse to call up my old flame, Rodney."

I looked at Harry in utter disbelief.

"I'll call him up on the pretext of wanting him to track down Roberto Madi," he went on. "What about that for an idea?!"

"God, Harry, you *are* serious."

"Damn right I am."

Farfetched as it was, I had to admit the notion intrigued me.

"Do you really think he could find him?"

"Unless he's dead."

"Who? Rodney or Madi?" I said half-teasing.

"Listen, if anyone can find Roberto Madi, Rodney Matusak can," Harry stated with assurance. "That's exactly the sort of work he used to do."

"And what if he did find him?"

"We'd go and talk to him."

"You don't seriously think he'd tell us anything, do you?" I said.

"Who knows? It's worth a shot, isn't it?"

"I think it's worth a shot if it's a way for you to get in touch with Rodney again without seeming too obvious. Although I can't imagine this doesn't look obvious—it's so nuts!"

Harry reached out and took my hand.

"You'll understand one day, my dear," he said, smiling.

They say as one gets older, one's insides turn out, and one becomes, so to speak, the personification of the inner being.

Harry's insides, lately revealing themselves at an alarming speed, were, I observed, far softer and more gentle than that studied and cynical exterior of his ever let on. Like myself, he was all alone, without any family that I knew of, and with only a few close friends. The difference in our ages and our health made his situation seem more poignant than my own. Sometimes I got the feeling I was the only person in the world he could rely on. I always tried to make him feel indispensable to me, so that his need for me would not seem to outweigh mine for him.

"Okay, call him up!" I cried. "And if he actually finds Madi—you can knock me over with a feather."

Harry was elated.

"He's going to be awfully surprised to hear from me after all these years. I can't wait! We were so different, of course. Miles apart on anything intellectual or social. But I felt strangely at peace when I was with him. As though I'd found my other half."

"I know what you mean."

"Dangerous game," Harry said.

"What?"

"Oh—passion."

"Yes, indeed, passion's the real killer in life."

"Or the lack of it," Harry lamented.

We finished our meal trying to speak about other things, but the conversation became tainted with a certain gloom. After lunch, just as we were walking out of the restaurant, Harry suddenly became short of breath and leaned against a wall, holding his neck with both hands. His round face grew very red and his eyes seemed to inflate in their sockets like tiny balloons. Prying his hands away from his neck, I quickly loosened his tie and undid the top buttons of his shirt while a deft waiter slid a chair under him. He sank down onto it gasping for air.

After a few moments, his breathing grew normal again. The color drained from his face, while tiny beads of perspiration sprouted up on his forehead. His eyes were still bulging slightly. He looked horrendous.

"We're getting you to a doctor immediately." I told the waiter to please call an ambulance.

"No, no!" Harry protested. "I'm fine."

"You look ghastly and you're coming with me to a doctor this instant."

"If I could just have a glass of water," he pleaded.

Harry slowly sipped the water brought to him by the obliging waiter. Afterward he seemed refreshed.

"Just take me home."

"No. You're going to the emergency room." I was adamant.

"This happens every once in a while. It's nothing."

"Harry, please—"

"Faith, dear, it's my life."

He looked so fragile and so frightened I didn't dare argue with him.

"You're sure?"

"Sure," he said firmly, forcing a wan smile. "Take me home, will you?"

"You won't have yourself checked at least?"

"No doctors."

"Even though it might be something serious?"

"I hope it is."

"Harry, please don't say that, please—" I begged him.

"I do. I hope it is. Now just drop me home, like a good girl."

"If you won't think of yourself, would you think of me? I'm not ready to lose you, you know," I said tenderly.

"My dear—" He sounded as if he were about to say something quite serious, but then stopped himself. "Just take me home, will you?"

We looked briefly into one another's eyes, and in that moment, I understood for the first time what it meant to be old and sick and weary of life. Harry smiled forlornly. I hailed a taxi. We said very little to one another on the way back to his apartment. The cab lurched up to the familiar green awning.

"Thank you, Faith," he said, as he lumbered out. "You

know, this Madi business really gives me something to look forward to. Thank you."

I offered to see him upstairs, but he declined. After dropping him off, I continued on for a bit, then decided to get out of the taxi and walk the rest of the way home. I needed some air.

CHAPTER
8

Harry's unexpected seizure had frightened me more than I first realized. I walked faster and faster, trying to ignore a growing wave of panic, finding it increasingly difficult to breathe. Finally, unable to catch my breath at all, I had to stop and lean against a building in an effort to calm myself down. I could feel my heart pounding more and more fiercely. Little rivulets of sweat began forming in the palms of my hands. I felt hot and dizzy, as if I were going to faint. Hugging the building, my body pressed tight against the cold concrete, eyes squeezed shut, gasping for air, I prayed for this anxiety attack to go away. Gradually, mercifully, it abated, and I was able to continue. Shaky at first, finding my steps one at a time, I soon broke into a trot and then began to run. I couldn't wait to get back home to my little apartment, my comfortable, well-ordered refuge.

Panting and disheveled, I rounded the corner of my block and stopped dead when I spied a tall, thin, familiar figure lurking around the entrance to my brownstone. At precisely that moment, the street lamp in front of the building lit up. The figure turned his face toward the light. I recognized him: it was John Noland.

What in hell was he doing here now, tonight of all nights? Our date wasn't until Tuesday. Of course I knew what he was doing here. It was so like him to show up unannounced, particularly after we'd made a specific plan to see one another, so like him to catch me off-guard, to rattle me so that once again he'd start with the upper hand.

Well, I said to myself, I won't let him see me. It's as simple as that. I just won't go inside for a while. I turned around and walked swiftly back to the corner, hoping he wouldn't catch a glimpse of me. I had no intention of confronting him in my present state, looking the way I did and feeling as fragile as a foal. That was not my plan. I knew exactly the way I wanted to look when he first laid eyes on me again after all this time, and it wasn't like this. He wasn't going to do me out of my careful grooming, my composure, my air of detachment, of mild amusement. He wasn't going to catch me unkempt, out of breath, frightened of life, and death.

I'd had visions of what our first meeting would be like. They went like this: Calling for me on Tuesday, John would ring the buzzer in the front hall, and I'd keep him waiting just a short while to show him I wasn't overanxious. Then I'd buzz him in. I'd listen to him walk upstairs, the familiar loping walk. I'd be at the front door, wearing a new dress, one I'd bought specifically for the occasion. A discreetly revealing dress to show him I hadn't lost my figure. I'd have on makeup, slightly more than usual, though not a lot, just enough to cover up time a little. My attitude would be light, cheerful, and, above all, disinterested.

We'd engage in a bit of small talk leavened with a few nostalgic innuendos, and then I'd suggest coolly, "Shall we go to dinner? I have to make it an early night." On the pretext of getting a sweater just in case it was chilly in the restaurant, I'd leave John to look around the living room, to soak up the warm atmosphere I'd created for myself. He'd always said he admired my taste and the knack I had for making things cozy. I'd let him see that some things hadn't changed.

We'd go to dinner. He'd take me to one of our old haunts downtown.

"Oh, yes," I'd say, over cocktails, "life's treated me very

well. All things considered, I'm quite happy." And I'd be thinking to myself all the while, "I survived you, didn't I . . . ?"

We'd drink a little too much wine, reminisce a little too
intimately. He'd reach over, take my hand, gaze into my eyes
and tell me nothing had changed. I'd stroke his cheek for a
fleeting moment, pull my hand away, and say that unfortunately
I had to get up at the crack of dawn the next morning, "Could
we please go?" Dropping me off at my apartment he'd say, "How
about a nightcap?" I'd kiss him on the cheek and reply in the
sweetest voice imaginable, "Another time." He'd clasp my arm,
not wanting to let me go. I'd pull away, run up the stairs of my
brownstone, turning to look at him one last time. I'd smile
wistfully and go inside.

That was how I pictured our next meeting, and I wasn't
going to be cheated out of it, or at least a version of it, that
easily. I wanted John to see me at my best, my coolest, and most
prepared, not catch me off-guard, looking like hell, feeling anxious and derailed. Not after all these years. I wanted my
moment—the moment in which I proved to him and to myself
that I'd triumphed over his memory, and all the memories he
represented, that I'd survived and survived well. That moment
was going to be mine to savor, on my terms, not at his conven-
ience. And it was going to be on Tuesday night as planned, not
now.

However, it was not so easy to tear myself away. In spite
of all my plans for Tuesday, I was riveted by the sight of him.
I kept watching him from a distance, hoping he would turn his
face toward the light again. It was too dark to tell how he really
looked. He was blurred, indistinct, floating like a shadow. He
continued his vigil, showing no signs of leaving. Finally, I retreated, walking slowly around the block, hoping he would go
away.

The streets were almost empty. Gone were the Saturday
afternoon strollers, the tradesmen locking up their stores, the
last-minute shoppers carrying home bags of groceries and the
odd bunch of flowers. In their place, the night people were
beginning to creep out here and there—people who seemed to

be waiting for something, anything—an event, a fight, an accident—to shape the pattern of their lives for the next few hours. I watched a cat chase a large brown cockroach on the sidewalk. I felt a subway rumbling beneath the concrete. A wailing siren shredded the air. A man in rags, carrying two tattered shopping bags, darted out in front of me, yelped, and ran away. I jumped back, lost my balance, and steadied myself against a parking meter, where I waited for a time, trying not to inhale the exhaust fumes from the cars whizzing by. All around me was that combination of energy, danger, and hopelessness which is the atmospheric brew of big cities.

When I came around the block again, John Noland had gone. Thank God, I whispered, breathing a sigh of relief. I mounted the steps of my brownstone, lead-legged, my head aching. I opened the door to the entrance hall, longing to lie down. I didn't even bother to get my mail, which I could see through the slot, crammed inside its brass box on the wall. Bills, circulars, catalogues, most likely. They could wait. Everything could wait until I'd had a hot bath and a good night's sleep. I put my key in the second door.

Suddenly I felt a tap on my shoulder. I whirled around. "Hello," said the low, insinuating voice I instantly recognized. There was the familiar face in front of me.

"John! You scared me to death!"

He smiled that winning smile of his. I felt weak and unsure of myself as he dangled in the dimness, an old memory beckoning me back in time.

I squinted, trying to bring him out of the gloom into sharper focus. I saw he hadn't really changed that much over the years, except that his features seemed starker now. His skin was less supple with age. There had always been a monastic austerity about John. He was tall, thin, angular, and slightly stylized, like the carved apostles on Gothic cathedrals. I used to tell him he would have made a good model for the Crucifixion. Even now, he looked monklike, despite his blue jeans and red flannel shirt, open to the middle of his chest. He still possessed those grimly handsome, sunbaked, ascetic looks which had attracted me to him all those years ago. And there was still that impish glint in his expression which, I knew from experience, could suddenly harden into cruelty for no apparent reason.

"Hello, Faith." His lips were a smudge in the murky light.

I knew he was studying me. That was quite like him. He was adept at gauging my reactions to him by staring at me until I became so self-conscious I revealed myself in some awkward way. Then he'd pounce like a jaguar, clawing my confidence to pieces. I thought to myself: you bastard, you instinctively knew you'd catch me at my worst. He must have known damn well this wasn't the way I wanted to present myself to him, not after all this time. But there I was, standing in front of him, exhausted and disheveled, looking just as pathetic as I possibly could. In fact, I hadn't felt or looked quite so terrible in years.

I raised my hand in a vain effort to smooth back my hair. John intercepted it, held it for an instant, then kissed the palm. I felt the flick of his tongue on my flesh.

"You look beautiful," he said, as if he'd read my thoughts.

"Rubbish." I pulled my hand away from him. "I look like a rat on a wheel, and you know it."

He laughed. I began trudging up the stairs.

"What happened to Tuesday?" I said wearily.

"I wanted to surprise you," he answered, walking so close behind me I could feel the heat of his body.

"Why?"

"Turn around and let me look at you."

He put his hands on my waist, stopping me mid-step. It had been so long since I'd felt a man's hands on my body, I froze. His hands pressed firmly on my sides. I relished the moment longer than I should have, giving myself away. When I tried jerking free at last, he held me fast, speaking to me in a patronizing tone.

"Stop . . . Relax . . . You're like a scared rabbit."

I wriggled around to face him. I was one step above him,

but because he was so much taller than I, we were now the same height. We looked into one another's eyes. He continued holding my waist.

"Go away, John. I'm exhausted. Come back on Tuesday, will you? Like we planned."

"How've you been?" he said.

"Fine. I'm just tired."

"You're trembling."

"Yes, well . . ." I heard my voice crack.

"Aren't you glad to see me?"

I hesitated. "I don't know."

"No?" He seemed amused.

"I don't know, I—"

He kissed me gently on the lips.

"What don't you know? Hmm? What don't you know?"

I was stunned. I hadn't kissed anyone in God knows how long.

"Jesus, John!" I cried, jerking away.

He looked startled, then wounded.

"What?" he asked ingenuously. *"What?"*

"You think you can just—" I gave up, too exhausted for anger. "You haven't changed one bit, have you?"

"Make me a drink?" he said impishly.

"No."

"A cup of tea?"

"No."

"Love?" he whispered, suddenly leaning in.

"John, you are the limit. You really are."

"Just a drink then. Be a sport."

"No. Look, I'm not ready for you. Come back on Tuesday. We'll have a nice dinner somewhere, talk, catch up."

"I'm all caught up . . . Aren't you?"

"What's wrong with doing things as we planned for once?"

"Doing what things?" he said suggestively, his whole manner coated with a come-on I pretended to ignore.

"Why is it that having a date with you, even an encounter,

always turns into a game where you get to make up all the rules?"

"Is that what you think?" He looked genuinely dismayed. "Well then, I'm sorry. The truth is I couldn't wait to see you, that's all. I got so excited hearing your voice again. I was just carried away, I suppose. I thought it would be rather romantic. Anyway, I apologize. I'll go."

He released me. Suddenly, I felt panicked. There it was—the old pattern repeating itself: I reject him, then I feel abandoned. I felt torn between wanting him to leave and longing for him to stay.

"It's just that I wasn't expecting you now."

"Don't worry." He stroked my cheek.

I inadvertently raised my hand to his, following its path along my skin.

"I've missed you, Faith. Have you missed me?" I nodded. "Come on then," he said, putting his arm around me. "Let's go upstairs."

John insinuated himself back into my life as though he'd never really left it. We chatted easily and flirtatiously over a bottle of wine. He complimented me on my apartment, stroked Brush, whom he'd never met, asked to see the photographs of my most recent work, remembering the leather-bound album in which I kept a record of the jobs I did. He seemed interested in me, in what I'd been up to. I got out the album and showed it to him. Thumbing through it, he said my technique looked as if it had improved—not that it needed to, he added mischievously. We both laughed at the double entendre. There was nothing at all forced or awkward between us, no residual anger or recriminations. Still, I was wary. I asked him what he'd been doing and he was appealingly modest, saying he was up to pretty much the same things as always: traveling, writing, lecturing. He said people were taking more of an interest in him these days. He said he was winning more awards, being asked to give interviews, and speaking for hefty fees. "Standards must be higher at last," he joked.

Underneath John's easy banter, however, I sensed danger. It was as if an old, rusty door were slowly creaking open, and though fearing what I would find behind it, I kept wanting desperately to look.

Quite casually, John started running his index finger up and down my arm as we spoke. He began to massage my neck. Closing my eyes, against my better judgment, I let his powerful hands sway me back and forth in a compelling rhythm. How easy it would be for him to kill me, I thought. And then I caught myself. Why was I thinking of murder? An image of Cassandra flashed through my mind. I snapped open my eyes and quickly pulled away.

"Why so skittish?" John said. "You used to love being massaged."

"I-I'm afraid," I stammered.

"Afraid?" The thought seemed to amuse him. "Of what? Me?"

"Maybe. Or myself."

"Come here," he purred. "There's nothing to be afraid of. I'm not going to hurt you."

"No? You did hurt me once."

"You hurt me too," he replied somberly.

"Yes, but you used to get so furious, so violent. Sometimes I thought—" I stopped myself.

"What?"

"No, no, nothing."

"*What?* Tell me."

"All right." I drew a deep breath. "Sometimes I thought that you wanted to kill me."

"Really?" he said, arching an eyebrow.

"Did you ever?"

"What? Want to kill you?"

"Yes."

We looked hard into each other's eyes for a long moment.

"Not literally," he said, smiling.

"But you used to get so angry. You hit me, remember? Do you think you ever could kill anyone, John?"

"You mean, aside from myself?" he said.

His answer amazed me.

"John, do you really think you could kill yourself?"

He shrugged. "I've thought about it. Hasn't everyone?"

"I haven't—not seriously."

"Well, you're lucky."

We sat in silence for another moment. I hadn't realized, all those years ago, what a melancholy man he really was.

"Yes, probably," he said, after a time. "I probably could kill someone if I had to. If it was them or me."

"I mean a woman," I said, "a woman you were involved with."

He looked at me quizzically. "Why are you asking all these questions, Faith? Do you have murder on your mind?" he said lightly.

I got up to pour myself another drink.

"Oh, I don't know. The subject seems to interest me lately."

"Quite a subject, murder." He didn't seem to take me seriously.

"Murder," I said, refilling his glass, "and passion."

He grabbed my wrist. Some wine spilled out of the bottle. Brush leapt off the couch and slunk away to a corner. John pulled me down to him and kissed me deeply on the mouth. I tried to free myself, but he kept a firm grasp on me, refusing to let go.

"John, no—please!" I protested.

He took the wine bottle from my hand and rested it on a table nearby. Standing up, he enveloped me in his arms. I was frightened, and yet the fear was exciting. I felt how much he wanted me, and that made me want him. For a while, I kept on resisting, but his passion and persistence wore me down. Finally, he lifted me up and carried me down the hall. I clung to him, kissing him, licking his ear, burying my head in his neck, whimpering that we shouldn't be doing this. He paid no attention, slamming the bedroom door behind us with his foot. I heard a small cry from Brush, wanting to get in. Then he threw me on the bed and lunged on top of me. I was his now, and we both knew it. We struggled to undress, not wanting to forego a second of contact with one another. He tried to undo my bra unsuccessfully.

"You never could figure out how that thing worked," I laughed, starting to undo it myself.

John was too impatient. He yanked the bra down around my waist and began massaging my breasts. I pushed my pelvis up against him and started undulating slowly until passion overwhelmed the two of us.

We fucked, and fucked hard. John slid his hands under my buttocks and gripped them tight, lifting me up, fusing our hips together. He pushed deep into me. I wrapped my legs around him tightly, trying to cement him to me while he swung up and down, over and over, like a madman on a rocking horse. I could see the muscles of his neck straining in taut relief underneath his skin. I began to watch him more closely as he sucked my nipples and licked the sweat off my body. He seemed absorbed in a private fantasy, devoid of tenderness or even connection. His performance struck me as more of a feeding frenzy—trying to sate long years of hunger in a single feast. As we went on, my excitement drifted into detachment. I pretended to have an orgasm so that John would come. At his rough, frantic climax, I saw myself as Cassandra Griffin, impaled on the bed with a knife through my heart.

"Great," John said, rolling off me with a grunt.

He kissed me and dozed off. As I lay next to him, I felt the familiar loneliness. His presence now was crude and harsh. The aging man lying next to me now, with his fitful snoring accompanying a restless sleep, was hardly the brilliant lover of my dreams.

I thought of the time one summer, years ago, when John and I had gone swimming together in the ocean off Amagansett and I'd gotten caught up in a riptide. John had a rubber raft. I called out to him to help me.

"Don't panic!" he cried. "Just tread water and let it carry you."

"I'm being carried out to sea!" I screamed. "Swim to me on the raft! Help me!"

"Don't panic!" he yelled.

"Help me, John, please help me!"

He started swimming toward me on the raft but stopped short at the edge of the swirling foam.

"John, please, come get me—!"

"I'll get caught up too . . . Just don't panic—"

"Throw me the raft! Please!"

"It won't reach you. Just relax. You'll drift back in again."

I felt as if a great cold serpent were wrapping itself around me, dragging me out to sea. The more I struggled against it, the farther out it pulled me.

"Listen to me, Faith—float! Just float! Let it take you!"

I reached out for John but he was much too far away. So I did what he said—I floated, just floated, closing my eyes and letting the water take me where it wanted. The tide carried me out so far that John's bobbing raft was just a speck on the horizon. I drifted for what seemed an eternity, certain I was going to die. And then suddenly, just as suddenly as I'd been caught up, I was released. I felt myself being carried back to shore by the slow, heaving motion of the waves. Out of the riptide's grasp at last, I swam frantically to the beach, scrambling up out of the water, collapsing on the blessed sand, exhausted and crying.

I looked up. There was John, standing above me, blocking the sun.

"You see? I told you not to panic."

"You bastard."

He knelt down, stroked me, kissed my face, my hair. I turned my head away, feeling drowned inside.

"There was nothing I could do," he said. "Honestly. You weren't in any danger. The tide comes around again. All you have to do is float with it, not panic. I couldn't have helped you, Faith. Don't you see, you had to do it yourself. I couldn't get to you. You see that, don't you?"

"John," I said finally, turning to him once more, "why didn't you come out and float with me? You had the raft."

His expression flickered slightly. "You want too much."

"Or too little," I replied.

That was one incident. There had been others. Ugly moments where he'd threatened me, even struck me, then repented in a frenzy of passion and regret. I skimmed over them in my mind, glancing at them fleetingly, as if they were traffic accidents involving other people.

John rolled over and got up out of bed. He walked over to the window and stood naked in front of it, his back to me, staring outside.

"John?"

He didn't answer. He lit a cigarette and leaned against the shadowy wall, bracing himself with one hand, head bent forward, his profile outlined by lamplight.

"John?" I said again.

"Hmm?" he replied, after a time.

"What are you thinking?"

"Nothing . . . I'm thinking about your view," he said.

"I don't have a view."

"That's what I was just thinking."

"John?"

"Hmm?"

"Where's your wife?"

"We're separated. I told you."

"What was she like?"

He turned and glared at me.

"I'm not going to answer those questions," he said harshly.

His response didn't surprise me, nor did it frighten me. In fact, he no longer frightened me. I looked at him as I might have looked at some intricate, outdated object, the exact function and purpose of which had been lost over time. Lacking any further investment in him, and no longer compelled by a feeling of danger, I decided to play with him a little.

"It feels strange, doesn't it, John?" I said.

"What?"

"Us being together again."

"Hmm," he replied without conviction.

"Don't you think?"

"What?"

"It feels strange."

"I haven't really thought about it." He sounded vaguely irritated.

"Let me ask you something. Did you ever wonder what it would be like if we got back together?"

"No," he said, glancing out the window once more.

"No?" Despite my newfound detachment, I was vaguely stunned by his response. "You mean you never thought about me?"

"I thought about you. But I'm not a planner."

"A planner?" I repeated, not quite understanding what he meant.

"I don't plan things," he said.

"But when you think about things, don't you imagine how they're going to be?"

"No. I just think about them, that's all."

He faced me directly and squinted his eyes.

"I'm sorry I can't be the way you want me to be," he said.

"What do you mean, John?"

"You want me to think in a certain way, behave in a certain way, say certain things."

"No, John, I don't. Not anymore."

"Oh yes you do."

"All right," I said, playing along. "Let's say I do. Is there something wrong with that?"

"It's naive," he said, turning back to face the window once more.

"Really? How?"

"Because we've just established our connection. We've just done it—"

"By making love—?" I offered.

"That, yes. By being here. Together. This is our connection."

"What's wrong with talking?"

He raked his fingers through his hair impatiently.

"I hate words," he said dryly.

"That's a drawback for a writer, isn't it?"

Closing his eyes, he massaged the bridge of his nose.

"Very funny," he said, clearly unamused.

"John," I continued, "I want to know about you. What you've been up to all this time. All these years I've thought about you, I felt somehow you were thinking about me too. I want to know what your wife was like. I want to know if she reminded you of me. What did she look like? Do you ever see her? Do you have any children?"

I could see him growing more and more irritable. I knew I was getting to him and I rather enjoyed it. John crushed out his cigarette and sat down on the bed.

"Do you want to meet from time to time?" he said casually.

"What do you mean?" I feigned surprise.

"I mean get together from time to time. Like this. Have dinner, you know. . ."

I pretended to think for a moment, as if the idea had caught me off-guard.

"I don't know," I said. "What's from time to time?"

"Whenever we feel like it."

"Nothing regular?"

"No," he replied uncomfortably.

"So," I went on, trying not to sound sarcastic. "Maybe once a month, or once a week, or once a year? Just whenever?"

"We can play it by ear," he said.

"I'm not a musician, John." I smiled perfunctorily.

"Well, listen, I'd like to very much," he said, sweetening his tone a bit, "if you would. Why don't you think about it? I should be going."

I swallowed hard. This was unexpected.

"Going?"

"I have to get home. To pack."

"Pack?"

"I'm heading down to the Amazon for a few months," he went on. "Researching a new book on the rain forest."

"Um . . . What about Tuesday?" I said, trying to restrain myself from an unseemly outburst. "We have a date, remember?"

"Oh, I'm sorry," he replied matter-of-factly. "I won't be here."

"What?"

He cupped my face in both his hands, holding it as if it were a precious object, kissing me gently on the lips.

"You haven't changed," he said.

I pulled away. I really didn't give a damn, but I wasn't going to let him off the hook so easily.

"Let me get this straight, John. You *knew* you weren't going to be here on Tuesday?" I pretended to be incredulous, when, in fact, this was so typical of him. "I mean," I continued, "you just came here to get laid or what?"

"Stop it, Faith."

"I can't believe that was your single motivation. Knowing you, you could get laid a hundred places—"

"Stop using that expression."

"Oh, I beg your pardon. I didn't mean to offend your delicate sensibilities. What I can't figure out is why?" I said.

"Why what?"

"Why bother?" I was genuinely curious.

"I wanted to see you again. I needed to see you again," John replied.

"Why?"

"I don't know why!" he snapped. "Does everything need a reason? You wanted to see me too. Do you know *why?*"

"Yes, in fact, I do," I answered calmly.

My attitude seemed to annoy him.

"Why?" he said, glaring at me.

"You look really annoyed," I said, smiling back.

"Just answer the question, will you?"

"Why I wanted to see you again? Because I wanted to understand why you didn't succeed in killing me."

"Jesus!" he sighed. "We're back to that again, are we?"

"I don't think we ever really got away from it," I said. "I guess I wanted to see why I survived where others didn't. And, in a curious way, I guess I wanted to see *if* I survived, because, you see, *living* doesn't necessarily mean one has survived."

"What the hell are you talking about?"

"It doesn't matter. It wouldn't interest you anyway."

John picked up a sock from the floor. I watched him, fascinated with his catlike movements. He bent down on all fours.

"John?"

"Yes?" he said, from his hands and knees as he retrieved the other sock from under the bed.

"There's something I have to tell you."

"What's that?"

"Stop dressing for a moment. This is something I always wanted to tell you and never really had the courage to."

Socks in hand, he paused, looking at me with renewed interest.

"You love me," he said perfunctorily.

"No, it's not that. I told you that, a lot. It's something else."

"What?" He seemed wary.

I paused a second. For effect.

"John," I began slowly, measuring every word, "I don't think you're a great writer. I never have."

For a moment, he seemed unable to react, unable even to move. He threw the socks on the bed, then reached down and swiped up his shirt from the floor, putting it on in short spasmodic gestures.

"Thank you!" he said coldly.

"You're welcome."

I smiled at him the next time he glanced at me. He nodded curtly, buttoning each button of his shirt with exaggerated precision. Except for his shirt, he was naked from the waist down. His long thin legs looked like two poles under a tent.

"I don't believe you," he said at last, stepping into his pants and pulling them up around his waist. He tucked in his shirt and zipped up his fly. In his wrath, he missed closing the belt buckle the first time around.

"About what?" I said, studying his new awkwardness. It was like watching a specimen fluttering around in a jar. I knew I had him.

"You used to tell me I was a great writer," he said, sitting on the bed to put on his socks.

"People say all sorts of things when they're in love."

He stood up and turned to face me. Dressed, he looked less threatening.

"I am a great writer," he proclaimed. "People all over are finally recognizing just how great I am. I don't really care what you think."

"Oh, well, good."

He hesitated for an instant.

"Just out of curiosity," he went on, "what is it about my writing you don't like?"

"I thought you didn't care what I thought," I replied nonchalantly.

"I don't. I'm just curious."

"All right then . . . In my opinion, it's too safe."

"Safe?!" he snarled. "I risk my neck for my books!"

"I know you do," I replied sympathetically. "But there are no real emotions in them. They're not about people, they're about ideals. And," I sighed, "you're always careful to be so fashionable."

"Fashionable?!" I could feel his anger rising.

" 'Politically correct' is the current expression, I believe."

"Hell hath no fury, perhaps?" he said with a sneer.

I thought about this.

"I don't feel scorned, John," I said, after careful consideration. "Just a little bored. The truth is, it really doesn't matter what I or anyone else says about your writing. In your own heart of hearts, you know you're second-rate. What other people think—for good or for bad—is irrelevant. You're just so angry you're not one of the greats."

I could see the sides of his cheeks moving as he ground his teeth together.

"What if I told you I didn't like your painting?"

I shrugged. "You never told me you *did* like it. In fact, when we were together, you never talked about my work at all, only your own. I was amazed when you asked me so much about myself tonight."

"Clearly, it was a mistake," he said humorlessly.

With that, he grabbed his jacket from the back of the chair and left.

"Thanks for the memories," I called out just before the door slammed.

The next morning in the shower, I heard John leaving a message on my answering machine. When I got out, I played back the tape.

"Faith, John," it said. "Call me, please, it's important. I don't want it to end like this. It can't end like this, do you hear me?" His voice sounded scratchy.

He left a number. When I finally returned his call that afternoon, a woman answered the phone.

"Hello?" she said.

"Is Mr. Noland there?" I asked tentatively.

"No. Who's this?"

"Oh, this is just an old friend. Who's this?"

"This is Mrs. Noland. Who's this?"

I smiled, shook my head, and hung up, thinking that could have been me.

I called Harry later that morning to find out how he was. There was no answer. I kept trying. I finally got hold of him in the evening.

"Fit as a fiddle," he said in a spunky voice, which relieved me. "Oh, and you'll be pleased to know I'm working on our little case. My detective was thrilled to hear from me. I called him up first thing this morning. We're meeting for a drink tonight. Thank you again, dear, for giving me an excuse to get in touch with him."

Harry always sounded renewed when the scent of romance was in the air.

"If you ask me, it's a wild goose chase, but anything for romance. Guess who showed up last night—unexpectedly?"

"Don't tell me—the dreaded Mr. Noland?"

"Typical, huh?"

"Tedious. Well?" he inquired.

"It was a disaster."

"We knew it would be," he said. "How are you feeling?"

"Hungover. But, you know, it's the oddest thing. It's completely unreal, like it never happened. He told me he was separated or divorced, I forget which. He called me this morning, I called him back, and guess who answered the phone?"

"His wife," Harry said knowingly.

"Right."

"And what did you do? Introduce yourself?"

"Hung up, which is what I should have done the very first time he asked me out. Boy, do I feel sorry for her."

"Don't waste your energy. She probably likes it. You did, remember?"

"Do you think people can really outgrow masochism?"

"I think, more likely, they just get bored with it. It's a lot of work. So you're not depressed?"

"No," I said. "I keep expecting to be."

"Frankly, I never did see what you saw in him. He was always such a cold fish in my view."

"He's pretty good-looking, even now. But, God, he's getting old."

"Not my type," Harry said dismissively. "I don't like those ascetic WASPS. I like dark, brooding Mediterraneans, or burly *Mitteleuropa* peasants. It's funny, but I think I've always chosen lovers who looked as if they could take care of me in a severe winter."

"And what, pray tell, would the dark, brooding Mediterranean do with you in a severe winter, I'd like to know?" I asked.

"Take me south, I suppose."

"Now, Harry, I didn't call just to talk about me. Are you sure you're all right? I really, really would take it as a personal favor if you'd go see your doctor tomorrow, or at least sometime this week."

"Faith, my dear, I'm fine. Absolutely fine. Actually, this is a rather good day. I got a present this morning."

"What?"

"No pain whatsoever!" he crowed. "You have no idea what a wonderful gift that is at my age."

The words betrayed his lightness of manner. I was stung once again by the thought of losing him.

"Oh, Harry, I can't bear to think of you in pain. Are you in pain a great deal?"

"Not excruciating pain, no. Just a dull, monotonous sort of thing, like the hum of an air conditioner. You get used to it, but when it suddenly clicks off once in a while, you think—ah, silence—what a relief . . . Anyway, I'm looking forward to seeing Rodney and maybe even having a little fun with our case. You take care of yourself now. Get to know Frances Griffin—I want you to tell me everything about her. And I'll keep you posted."

Toward the end of June I began driving out to The Haven six days a week. In those early days of summer, Mrs. Griffin, trailed by Pom-Pom, strolled over to the ballroom almost every day to watch me work. She would come in sometime during the mid-morning, stand at the top of the stairs, and announce, "I hope I'm not disturbing you."

"No, of course not," I'd say, lying.

The truth was her presence made me rather uncomfortable and unable to concentrate well on what I was doing. I made many more mistakes when she was observing me than I did when I was alone. I hoped this would become evident to her and she would withdraw. On the contrary, however, a mistake gave her the opportunity to open up a conversation with me. She seemed to enjoy it when I had to rub something out and start all over again, or when Pom-Pom got into some mischief with my paints and brushes—anything that took me away from the work at hand and made me available for casual conversation while I cleaned up the mess.

Above all, Mrs. Griffin seemed eager for me to get to know her. I felt as if she wanted me to take even more of an interest in her than she was taking in me. Whenever she asked me a question about myself and I responded, she didn't seem satisfied until I, in turn, had asked a similar question of her. She pouted and sometimes appeared genuinely hurt if I answered her curtly and got on with my work.

Very often, without the slightest encouragement, she would begin to reminisce, recounting some fantastic story, or simply rattling on about the great people she'd known and the grand places she'd been. She had an endless supply of amusing anecdotes about celebrities and socialites, pretenders to thrones and heads of state, artists and intellectuals, most of whom she'd entertained in her heyday. I thought of her forays into the past as excursions away from her loneliness of the moment, and sad attempts to hold on to the glamorous life she'd once lived.

After a while, the stories and the famous people all began to sound alike. She seemed only remotely connected to them, as if she'd been witness to a huge pageant that had passed in front of her without stopping. She rarely mentioned her husband or her daughter. I got the feeling she'd had countless acquaintances and very few friends. The friends were all dead, and the acquaintances didn't seem worth bothering about. She would stay and talk until she got tired. When she left, I found myself thinking about all the things she'd told me, concluding that her life was now as empty as it was privileged.

My work began to suffer as a result of the increased time Mrs. Griffin was spending with me. By mid-July, I'd fallen seriously behind schedule, yet I was reluctant to ask her to stop coming around to visit me. However, my increasingly blunt responses to her questions and my apparent inattention to her stories must have made her realize her presence was too much of a distraction. When she suggested it might be better if she left me alone for a time, I offered no resistance. I simply thanked her for being so understanding. She immediately stopped coming around.

Falling back into my own comfortable rhythm, I worked through the summer, watching the estate bloom into a lush, green paradise. Every day the grounds seemed to sprout new blossoms and leaves. The main house peeked out from behind a proliferation of foliage. Though the temperatures often reached the nineties, it was always cool inside the ballroom. I worked there happily, listening to a chorus of chirping and buzzing outside, thinking occasionally about John Noland, treating my encounter with him as if it had been a bad dream. If he still lingered on in my imagination, it was just as an old lover I'd seen once too often and would never see again. The nostalgia and the longing were gone.

I didn't see Frances Griffin for a long stretch of time, but I always asked Deane how she and Pom-Pom were getting on.

One particularly hot and humid Monday morning he came into the ballroom, looking wilted and visibly shaken. He told me there had been some bad news over the weekend.

"Little Pompy is gone," he announced with tears in his eyes.

I put down my brushes immediately.

"Oh no!" I cried. "What happened?" I thought the poor little dog had been run over.

Deane hesitated slightly, as if it pained him to say what he was going to say.

"Mrs. Griffin gave him away." He hung his head in despair.

"Gave him away? Why?"

"Too many accidents," he said sadly. "He got loose and marked up a chair."

"You're not serious. You mean she gave him away because he peed on a chair?"

"Well, it was Louis Seize after all," he said. "One of her favorites."

The whole thing sounded absurd to me.

"Oh, Deane, I know how fond you were of the little man."

"I told her I'd leash him up with me in the kitchen, but she was worried he'd escape again. I would have offered to keep him myself at home, but I don't have anyone to leave him with."

I could see how upset Deane was. His decision to confide in me made me feel closer to him.

"I'm so sorry, Deane, I really am," was all I could think of to say.

"Yes," he agreed, "it's terrible, a terrible thing."

Deane extracted a large white handkerchief from his back pocket, shook it out, blew his nose, and patted his eyes.

"Anyway," he said, regaining control of himself, "Mrs. Griffin would like to see you."

I followed Deane through the garden, into the house, upstairs to the Chinese Room. He rapped twice on the door. From within, a voice said, "Come in." As Deane opened the door to let me enter, I touched the sleeve of his coat gently and gave him a sympathetic nod, as if to reassure him. He smiled faintly, closing the door behind me. Inside the room, I turned and saw

Mrs. Griffin, wearing an elaborately embroidered silk robe. She was sitting in one of two large carved wooden chairs, staring out the window at the garden below. The sun, streaming in the window behind her, framed her in a strange aura.

"How have you been getting on?" she said without turning toward me.

"Fine, thanks. I'm sorry to hear about Pom-Pom."

"Deane told you?"

"Yes, he did. I think he's quite upset."

"Deane was too attached to that dog," she said.

"He was an awfully cute little thing."

"Far too much trouble," she retorted. "I don't want to talk about him. More importantly—tell me about your work. I apologize for not having been around to see you."

I knew it was pointless to pursue the subject of the little dog any further. However, I was chilled by her apparent indifference to a former love object.

"Well, I think the next phase ought to be finished and ready for your inspection quite shortly," I said. "I'm anxious for you to see the main panel in particular. I've worked hard on the figure of Cassandra. The dress you gave me was a great help."

"Was it? Yes, it's a beautiful dress, isn't it? I had it made for Cassa in Paris. I helped design it because, you see, I was always the best judge of what looked well on her even though she had other ideas. She never showed herself off to her best advantage. She insisted on wearing things that hid her body and accentuated all her weak points. She hated that dress . . ." Her voice trailed off in a current of irritation.

"That's too bad because I think the dress is very beautiful and in her picture she seems to look so well in it."

Her voice a monotone, Mrs. Griffin continued as if she hadn't heard a word I'd said.

"She had no sense of her own style. She had the most awful posture. She didn't walk, she sort of . . . trudged. I was always telling her to stand up straight, stop slouching, look life in the eye . . . Not that she was a beauty, by any means, but when she carried herself well, she looked elegant, regal . . . "

She shifted around in her chair and faced me.

"I'd like you to put that dress on for me one day," she said. "I'd like to see you in it. You have tried it on, haven't you?"

"Yes, as a matter of fact, I have."

"And it fit, of course."

"Yes, it did."

"I knew it would. You're the same size. Tell me, do you like this robe?"

I looked at the rich garment more closely. It was a Chinese Imperial costume made of vermilion silk, loose-fitting, with a high collar and voluminous sleeves. Three fierce, golden thread dragons slithered across a sea of undulating needlework.

"It's amazing."

"It belonged to Tz'u-hsi, the dowager empress of China. Do you know about her?"

"The Boxer Rebellion?" I said, unsure of myself.

"Exactly. She was an absolutely remarkable woman. A genius at the art of statecraft, despite the failure of the Boxer Rebellion. They say that when she was a child she escaped having her feet bound, which made her mobile, unlike the other women of her class. But being crafty, she pretended they were bound so she could sneak around the palace and eavesdrop and no one would ever suspect her. Like many women, she found her real power in feigning helplessness."

Mrs. Griffin rested her head on the back of her chair and continued speaking as if she were in a mild trance. I had seen her in this mode before, and I grew wary.

"They also say she had her son killed so that she could appoint her nephew to the throne, even though he wasn't in the direct line of succession," she droned on. "She didn't love her son. She loved her nephew because she knew she could control him. Do you think it's true that we love the things we can control more than the things we can't? I have three of her robes. She had over ten thousand."

I didn't say anything. I let her go on even though the effort of talking seemed to fatigue her.

"I got this one in China in 1948, just before the Communists took over. Some of the furniture in this room is from the Forbidden City." She made a weak gesture with her hand. "Do you like the wallpaper?"

She referred to the vivid, hand-painted wallpaper depicting myriad scenes of noble life in old China.

"I found it in an antique store in London years ago. Some of the panels are original and some of them I had copied to match because there weren't enough. Can you tell which is which? Go on, walk around, study them, try."

I walked around the room inspecting each panel carefully. The colors, the quality of the draftsmanship, the texture and design of the various scenes were all superb.

"Well?" Mrs. Griffin said. "Can you tell which ones are copies and which ones are real?"

"No, I can't."

She raised her hand and pointed to one wall.

"That's all original. All the panels on that wall. The rest are fakes."

I studied the real wall, comparing it to the others.

"It's impossible to tell the difference."

"If you look really closely, you can see that all the scenes on the fake panels are simply repetitions of scenes on the real panels, mixed up so they don't look too uniform. The artist who painted the fake panels for me had a fit because he wanted to make up his own scenes, from his imagination. But I said to him, 'I don't want your imagination. I want *their* imagination.' He was very offended," she said, smiling. "But in the end, he admitted I was quite right."

"Well, it certainly is an extraordinary room."

Mrs. Griffin paused for a long moment as if she were debating whether or not to tell me something. Finally she said: "It was Cassa's room originally."

I suddenly realized I was standing in the very room in which Cassandra Griffin had been murdered.

"Your daughter's room?"

"Yes. The room in which she grew up. The room in which she died . . ."

Her monotonous voice combined with the gruesome symmetry of events made me shiver. She read my mind when she said: "You're wondering, I suppose, how I can stand to be in here after what happened?"

Her directness made me equally direct.

"Yes, that's just what I was wondering."

Mrs. Griffin began playing with the voluminous sleeve of her robe, stroking it, twisting it around her fingers. Her face was as rigid as a mask.

"For a long time after it happened I pretended this room didn't exist," she said. "I had it boarded up, the door plastered over and painted so it looked like part of the corridor. You never would have known it was here, except from the outside —the dark windows. Even so, I avoided this part of the house.

"But when Holt died and I was left here all alone, I decided it was time to unseal the memories. The ancient Chinese filled their tombs with the essential objects in their lives. I needed to see this room again because there were such objects here. As one gets older, memories become the real furniture of one's life. The only difference is, you can't get rid of the bad pieces. You can't give them away or trade them or sell them off. They continue to surround you. I came to the conclusion that it was better to take an inventory of my memories rather than board them up in locked rooms."

She gripped the sides of the chair with her hands, kneading the smooth wood with her palms.

"I watched them tear down the wall to this room. I felt like they were opening my tomb. I felt the pain here—" With a tiny fist, she thumped the head of the golden dragon on her heart.

"When I walked inside for the first time," she continued, "I nearly fainted. It still smelled of death after all those years. Think . . . Everything strangled out of the air but that terrible smell of death. Who was it who defined insanity as remembering everything at once? I remembered everything about her death in one horrible flash. The terror of it . . . I'm the one who found her, you know. Did you know that I was the one who found her?"

"Yes," I whispered.

"She was lying there—"

Mrs. Griffin pointed in the direction of a long black lacquer table abutting the far wall.

"That's where her bed was. She was lying on the floor, soaked in blood. Her eyes were so wide . . . She looked so young, so astonished . . . I tried to hold her, tried to gather her up in my arms . . . But things are so much heavier when they're dead."

She paused, then said: "May I show you?"

"I beg your pardon?" I said, feeling certain I'd misheard her.

"I want to show you what happened," she replied, articulating each word as if she were speaking to a child.

"If you like."

I let her direct me. I could see that every movement was an effort for her.

"The room's all different now, but if you go and stand just there—"

She lifted her hand and again pointed to the table. I walked across the room.

"I'll show you how I found her."

I stood in front of the long table. Daylight flickered through the bamboo blinds, casting a net of sharp shadows over the room. Mrs. Griffin edged herself out of the chair and walked slowly toward the door. The material of her robe made a hissing sound as it dragged across the floor.

"Lie down," she said, as she reached the door.

"What?"

"Please. Lie down. Just there. In front of the table. Facedown."

She was deadly serious, having become the director of her own passion play. I did as I was told. I lay on the carpet in front of the table, facedown.

"A little to the left," she said. I shifted around until she was satisfied. "Yes," she nodded, "that's right. That's perfect."

With that, Mrs. Griffin left the room, closing the door behind her. I was all alone on the floor, face down in the exact spot where Cassandra had been murdered. Though I was struck by the absurdity of the situation, I couldn't break free of the old woman's singular spell. And, more to the point, I couldn't wait to see what she was intending to do.

Presently, the door opened. Mrs. Griffin entered in her dragon robe and stood immobile for what seemed like an eternity. She was carrying an object of some sort. I couldn't make out what it was. Her hands were hidden in the folds of the robe. Finally, she walked over to me in slow, mincing steps. She knelt down beside me and began stroking my hair with one hand, concealing whatever object she was holding in the other. Her hand brushed against my cheek. It was icy cold. I shrank from her.

"There, there," she said, responding to my involuntary reaction. "I'm not going to hurt you."

I was staring up at her out of the corner of my eye, but the angle made it difficult for me to see her.

"I never meant to hurt you," she said in a low, caressing tone which sounded oddly menacing.

She then withdrew the object she was holding from the folds of her robe and placed it on the floor directly in front of my face. It was a ceremonial dagger shaped like a crescent moon, the hilt encrusted with cabochon sapphires. I held my breath as I stared at the dark stones glinting in the changing light.

"I don't remember if the knife was exactly here," she said. "I think it was, but I'm not sure. This isn't the actual weapon, of course. This one is from my collection. But it was a knife, and I think, I think it was here. I'm almost positive I saw it. I think—oh dear . . ."

She stopped speaking and rolled her eyes back into her head. She seemed disoriented. She held her head.

"Mrs. Griffin? . . . Mrs. Griffin? Are you all right?"

She didn't answer me. She just knelt there, swaying back

and forth, holding her head. I stared at that awful dagger and its light-spangled sapphires. Was Madi the murderer? Or was it someone else? Did she know who killed her daughter? Lying there, I felt the truth was as close to me as she was. I knew that in the end all veneers are scratched away, no matter how carefully they are applied, no matter what craftsman has applied them.

I stayed still for as long as I could. Finally, I rolled over on my back. Mrs. Griffin was staring down at me. She held my gaze; then all at once her eyes flashed as if she'd suddenly seen something terrible. Her skin was parchment pale. She began to tremble. Her fingers flitted around in the air, dabbing at her face, her hair, her robe.

"Oh dear, oh dear!" she cried over and over. "There's been a mistake, there's been a mistake! Get up, please—there's been a terrible mistake!"

I did as she said while she remained on the ground, crouched and trembling. Her panic increased. She picked up the dagger. Her hand shook so violently she dropped it. She began to writhe and shake all over, emitting pathetic little moans. I stood above her, mesmerized by the sight of her, trying to imagine what horrors were racing through that tormented mind of hers. All at once, she shuddered violently and let out a horrible scream. In that second, I saw terror as tangible as that dagger rip through her body. It was a fearful sight.

Still quivering from the force of the seizure, she looked up at me with pleading, unfocused eyes and reached out to me, her arms emerging from the wide sleeves of her robe, frail and brittle. I knelt down to embrace her. Her body felt like a bundle of splinters wrapped in silk. She nestled into my chest, breathing hard. After a while, she calmed down.

"You'll feel better once you've told the truth, Mrs. Griffin. I promise you. You must tell the truth if you know it, for Cassandra's sake."

"Yes," she said in a small voice. "I know."

"You know who killed her, don't you?"

She looked up at me with a perplexed look on her face.

"You know, don't you?" I repeated.

"Oh yes," she hissed. "I know."

"Who? Tell me."

She shook her head. "I . . . I can't."

"Mrs. Griffin, don't you want to bring your daughter's murderer to justice?"

She blinked once or twice. "Justice . . . ?" she repeated absently. "There is no justice."

"Was it Madi? Was it Roberto Madi?"

She closed her eyes, and the faintest hint of a smile gathered around her mouth.

"That's what everyone thought," she said.

"And was it? *Did* he do it?"

"I think . . ." she began, then murmured something I couldn't hear.

"You think what? What do you think?"

"I'm very tired."

I couldn't let go of my prize now. I pressed on.

"Do you think Madi did it?"

I took her silence as a confirmation.

"Yes?" I said anxiously.

"Everyone thought so, I suppose," she said dully.

"But Mrs. Griffin, you know who did it. You do. I know you do. Why won't you say?"

She lapsed into a long silence. Then she said: "Murder can be a very slow process."

"What do you mean?"

"It can happen over years so you don't know it's happening. You want the best for your child. If you see your child in pain, it kills you, and then you realize one day that your child—your innocent child—is already dead."

"Go on—" I said.

"But, you must understand, some people who kill aren't really guilty of murder. They're just carrying out a sentence."

I looked at her askance. What was she trying to tell me?

"Who carried out your daughter's sentence, Mrs. Griffin?"

She covered her face with her hands.

"Leave me alone. Please," she moaned. "Leave me alone."

"You know! I know you do. Why won't you tell me?" I pleaded.

"I don't know anything! Leave me alone!" she cried.

She began writhing again. I held her tighter.

"You must tell me, Mrs. Griffin. You must tell *somebody*. You mustn't die with this on your conscience."

"There is no justice," she said again.

"Why won't you tell me what you know?" I begged her.

"I can't, I can't . . ." she whimpered.

Finally, she closed her eyes and drifted off to sleep. I watched her. Her skin looked as dry as powder, her lips as red as blood. She was a vision of decay. With each breath she took, she seemed to wither away, to shrink into the ornate folds of her silk robe, to sink deep into the embroidered tide. I rocked her back and forth, cradling her in my arms, wondering if she would ever part with her terrible secret.

My latest and eeriest encounter with Mrs. Griffin only whetted my appetite to solve Cassandra's murder. In the meantime, I had my work cut out for me at The Haven. Mrs. Griffin sent word to me through Deane that she had approved my final drawings.

The following week, men arrived to put up the scaffolding. They honeycombed the ballroom with poles and planks. I was there to supervise, as was Deane, who proved helpful in dealing with the workers. He seemed to enjoy the sudden flurry of activity as much as I did. I believed it helped to take his mind off Pom-Pom, whom he still mentioned sadly every now and then. I always liked this part of a job. Deane took to calling the ballroom "the Sistine Chapel," and me, "Miss Michelangelo."

The workers left, and for the next few weeks, I sat perched atop the scaffolding, mixing paint, sketching, thinking about Mrs. Griffin and her strange, sad life. Hanging in the air twenty feet above the cold marble floor, I wondered how the fashionable world would have reacted to the sight of its patron saint crumpled on the ground, weeping and shaking, cradling that sapphire dagger in her arms as if it were a dead child—she, the epitome of style and refinement, the queen of elegance and good behavior?

Every once in a while, I found myself slipping into a daydream about the famous coming-out party. The ghosts of that enchanted night appeared on the floor below me. I could almost hear the distant strains of a dance orchestra playing the butter-smooth medleys that always accompanied such festivities. I imagined Mrs. Griffin sweeping into the ballroom, all ease and sophistication, wearing silk and diamonds, waving a plumed fan over her guests as if it were a magic wand. I imagined Cassandra, slightly awkward and uncomfortable in her satin dress, standing in the receiving line, shyly extending a gloved hand to the society into which she was born a princess, keeping the world at bay, while her mother, the self-invented queen, soaked up the attention and flattery as her due. I imagined Holt Griffin, tall and elegant in white tie and tails, at his daughter's side, proudly helping her make her entrance into his kingdom. A night of promise, with the Griffins above it all, above the ordinary, the ugly, the untoward, suspended in a dream.

What had gone wrong? What was the secret? I felt sorry for Mr. and Mrs. Griffin, for Cassandra, sorry for them all. I wondered if it had ever really been as I imagined it.

Despite occasional fantasizing, I was able to get on with my work, making certain artistic decisions with assurance. Long years of experience had conferred upon me the ease of movement and sureness of stroke which are so essential to the craftsman. The application of paint to surface was now second nature to me. In the mornings, when I was sharper, I worked on the sky. Lying on my back on the scaffolding, I painted with my nose so close to the ceiling I would sometimes touch it inadvertently. Day by day, a heaven emerged, filled with clouds and stars and little cherubs peering down from their celestial nests at the scene on the ballroom walls. I liked fussing over my creations, making sure they looked their best. There was always some detail to go over with my rags and spotting brushes, heightening an effect here, softening one there, hoping to imitate nature with such a degree of perfection that even the suspicious eye would be deceived for a moment.

In the afternoons, feeling lazier, I glided my brushes over the pilasters, niches, and crown moldings framing the body of my work, imitating the rare woods and marbles highlighting the scene. I sat for hours creating faux marbre and faux bois finishes the way others might sit leafing through the pages of a book.

At the end of a day, I was flecked with paint, looking as if I'd been caught in a storm of confetti. I loved the preparation, the smells, the mess of it all. The act of painting gave me a sense of continuity, of pulling the world together somehow, and shaping it into a form I could grasp.

Deane often came into the ballroom and had a cigarette or two while he watched me paint. He never said much. Occasionally, he brought me a cup of tea and a piece of pastry made by the chef, who, not having any grand company to cook for, had taken up baking for the help.

I kept waiting for Frances Griffin to come to the ballroom to see how I was progressing. I felt both relieved and let down at the end of each day when she'd failed to show up and there was no word from her. I knew I'd been on the verge of getting her to admit the truth to me and that the passage of time was a hindrance. Her being such a short distance away was frustrating as well. Sometimes I thought of marching up to her room and simply demanding an interview. But on reflection this seemed pointless. Forcefulness was not the answer. I tried inventing a few excuses to see her on the pretext of needing her advice about this and that. But word always came back through Deane that she was "indisposed." *Indisposed*—a wonderful word, perfectly in keeping, I thought, with the anachronistic atmosphere of the house.

Things went along nicely. I finished the ceiling in less than a month. The men came back to take down the scaffolding. When the ballroom was clear once again, Deane brought the members of the staff in to see my work. They stood in silence as they looked up at my own version of heaven, a navy sky filled with tufted clouds, peering cherubs, dancing stars, and a shimmering white moon. They congratulated me one by one, shaking my hand as they left.

The scaffolding down, I now set to work finishing the revelers on the walls, my "paint-by-the-numbers" phase as I called it. Scheme set, characters in place, all that was left for me to do was fill in the details—the faces, colors, and textures which would bring the scene to life. I particularly enjoyed working on the little visual jokes scattered throughout the murals—a gentleman groping a lady's breast, another dancing with his hand up the folds of his partner's dress, a waiter leering down an ample bustline, a drunken musician slumped over his cello, one dog licking spilled champagne, another peeing on a man's leg, a bird flying off with a large diamond earring—mischievous vignettes, discreetly placed, hardly noticeable at first glance.

Summer drifted into fall. The humid, wilting weeks of August were gradually replaced by a succession of cool, autumn days. Harry and I spoke to one another occasionally, but I was much too preoccupied with my work to really catch up with him. One evening I called him to chat, however, and there was a message on his machine saying that he was out of town and couldn't be reached. This was unexpected and annoying. Harry usually informed me when he was planning to go away for any extended period of time.

On a chilly afternoon, as I was strolling around the garden on a break, I noticed a strange car parked in the driveway, a black Cadillac. When Deane came into the ballroom later offering me a piece of lemon cake and a cup of tea, I asked him who the car belonged to.

"Don't tell me Mrs. Griffin's breaking down and having a visitor?" I said.

"Just breaking down, I'm afraid," he replied, lighting a cigarette. "That was the doctor. They're deciding whether or not she should go to the hospital."

"Oh dear. How bad is she?"

He shrugged. "I don't know. Doctor says he's coming back tomorrow."

"I hope she's going to be all right."

"There's a lot to be said for heart attacks," he sighed wearily. "The last house I was in the lady died of a heart attack. If it was me I'd stay put, take my chances in my own bed, no hospitals."

Deane crushed his cigarette out on the floor, picked up the butt, and slid it discreetly into his pocket.

"Hospitals are where they kill you," he said, leaving.

I got to thinking what would happen if Mrs. Griffin went to the hospital and died without my ever seeing her again. I knew I'd never feel quite right about myself if I didn't make one last effort to pry that secret from her. I sipped my tea and picked over the cake wondering how best to go about it. I figured at this point I had nothing to lose by simply going upstairs to her bedroom and trying to talk to her one last time. I'd refrained from this direct approach before, not simply in the interest of propriety, but because there didn't seem to be a great deal of urgency. Now there was. I thought, the hell with it: this is the moment.

I felt like a mischievous schoolgirl as I sneaked across the garden and ducked into the house, hoping not to be seen by anyone, especially Deane and the nurse. I tiptoed quickly up the grand staircase, pretending to be invisible. On the first-floor landing I stopped to make certain no one was around before hurrying down the corridor toward Mrs. Griffin's bedroom.

The door was slightly ajar. I gave it a gentle push, then entered. The room was dark except for faint edges of daylight around the drawn shades of the windows. Walking to the center of the room, I could barely make out the small shadowy figure lying tucked up in the bed. I heard a distant voice, which startled me. At first I thought it was the nurse calling from the dressing room. Then I realized it was Frances Griffin herself.

"I said who's there?" she whimpered from her bed.

"It's me, Mrs. Griffin, Faith."

"Faith," she repeated drowsily.

I approached the bed, aware of a smell which was both sweet and slightly putrid. The smell of death, I wondered? I gazed down at her wigless head, palish brown with irregular strands of hair shooting out from it, like a coconut. It hardly made any indent on the pillow. Mummylike, her body lay still beneath the bedclothes, neatly wrapped in the linen folds so that no limbs were visible.

"Mrs. Griffin?"

The head bobbed slightly. Her eyes blinked open. She looked startled.

"Who . . . ?"

"It's Faith, Mrs. Griffin. Faith Crowell. You remember me, don't you?"

She blinked two or three more times, as if she were trying to bring me into focus. With some difficulty, she extracted her arm from underneath those tight covers and gave me her hand. I took it. The skin was clammy and cold.

"Water," she whispered, licking her lips, which were shiny white and dry, like two old scars.

I poured her a glass of water from the crystal carafe on her night table. Holding the back of her head with one hand, I pressed the glass to her lips so she could drink from it. The water seemed to refresh her. After a few sips she waved me away.

"Faith . . . Thank you."

"How are you feeling, Mrs. Griffin?"

"What an idiotic question," she said feebly.

I smiled.

"I heard the doctor was here. I was worried."

She was silent for a time. Then she spoke slowly, as if every word were an effort: "Tell me, Faith . . . Am I going to die? Don't lie, please."

"I don't know, Mrs. Griffin. I think they might take you to the hospital."

"To die . . . ?"

I paused.

"I can't say. I don't think anyone can."

She gripped my arm, but so weakly I hardly felt it.

"Stay . . . I'm frightened."

"Of course I'll stay. I'll go with you to the hospital if you like."

My presence seemed to comfort her and she revived a little. "Talk to me. Tell me a story." She sounded like a child.

I wondered if she could really listen to what I was saying or if she just wanted to hear the sound of a voice, any human voice.

"The ballroom is coming along nicely, Mrs. Griffin. I've done a great deal of work since you've been by to see it. I hope I've really been able to capture the spirit of that evening."

"The spirit of that evening . . ." she repeated sourly.

"Well, I hope I have."

She let go a morbid little chuckle.

"I hope you haven't," she said bitterly.

"What do you mean?"

"You've heard of a 'date that will live in infamy'? There was one in this house."

"I don't understand."

"That ballroom was built for her. Especially for her. Every detail, every cornice, every molding . . . I put my life into it. I wanted her to have everything I'd never had—a mother who could give her everything . . ."

"Go on," I said, realizing she was slightly delirious.

"You saw the dress. I gave it to you. Wasn't it the most beautiful dress?"

"Yes. Beautiful."

"You would have worn a dress like that, wouldn't you?"

"Yes, of course."

"Yes . . . It wouldn't have been a hardship for you, would it?"

"No," I said. "Of course not."

"She put it on. She looked beautiful. And then the next thing I knew—it was off. She threw it at me. Threw it at me!"

"The dress?"

"Said it was all for me, not for her. She said I didn't love her, I only loved myself. Can you imagine? Myself? I never thought of myself, I only thought of her. Only of her, from the time she was born. I built the ballroom for her, planned everything for her—for her—only for *her!* She said such terrible things, about me, about her father . . . She kept screaming, 'You don't believe me! You don't believe me!' Over and over. How could I believe her? How could I?!"

Mrs. Griffin started coughing and gasping for air. I tried to steady her by holding her close.

"Please, you mustn't upset yourself," I said, hugging her. "There, there . . ."

I kept stroking her and gradually she became calm. "She never even saw it," she said.

"What?"

"The ballroom."

"What?" I was bewildered.

"She never saw it. Not that night, anyway."

"What night?"

"The night of her party," Mrs. Griffin said. "Cassa never showed up."

I couldn't quite believe what I was hearing.

"Cassandra never came to her own coming-out party?" I asked, incredulous.

"No."

"But the newspapers, the pictures—"

"No pictures of her at the party. Just studio photographs. The evening was conducted without her," Mrs. Griffin said regally. "We told everyone she was ill. I don't think they believed us. I think they felt sorry for us."

"Where was she?"

"Gone. Out of the house," she said with great resentment.

I felt a pang of sadness for the old woman.

"You must have been very upset," I said.

"Holt had been so looking forward to escorting his daughter."

It took a while for me to digest this information. After a time, I said, "Mrs. Griffin, why did you hire me to paint the ballroom? It wasn't a happy memory for you."

She looked at me quizzically.

"I wanted to change it," she said simply.

Suddenly, she hauled herself up on her elbows, saying imperiously, "I do not like things the way they are!"

That effort seemed to sap all her energy. She collapsed back down into the pillows. Tears ran down her cheeks like rivulets in furrowed soil. I was used to intimate contact with her now. It felt perfectly natural to hold her, stroking her head, trying to soothe her.

"Tell me who killed Cassandra."

Mrs. Griffin cried out! "I can't . . ! I want to but I can't . . !"

She raised her arms weakly as if she were trying to prevent something unseen from descending on us.

"Don't worry, you're safe. I'm with you," I assured her.

She was breathing very hard, almost hyperventilating.

"Am I . . . Am I . . . ?"

"What? Are you what?"

"Am I . . . presentable?" she said finally.

"Yes," I answered nonplussed. "Of course you're presentable."

"All right then . . ." she said. "Let's go!"

Before I could ask her where she wanted to go something rattled in the back of her throat. Squeezing her eyes shut, she gripped the sheets and gasped for air, stiffening all over. Her body pressed down into the bed in an involuntary contraction. She exhaled fiercely and went limp all over.

"Mrs. Griffin? Mrs. Griffin?!"

I shook her gently but she didn't respond. I stared at her thinking she must be dead. I couldn't see her breathing. She was so very, very still. I knew I had to go quickly and get help. Feeling slightly disoriented, I stood up and ran out of the room, down the stairs, through the house. Entering the kitchen, I saw the staff sitting around the large dining table having their afternoon tea. At first they didn't notice me.

"Get the doctor!" I said breathlessly.

Everyone stopped and turned to look at me. I repeated myself, louder this time, and more in control.

"Get the doctor. I think Mrs. Griffin's dead."

Deane shot up from the table and bounded out of the room, followed closely by the private nurse. The others just stared at me in stunned silence.

"Where's the doctor?!" I cried.

"Just gone," one of the maids replied.

I left the kitchen and walked back upstairs to Mrs. Griffin's room. Deane was on the telephone ordering an ambulance. The nurse was standing over the old woman, holding an oxygen mask to her face, adjusting the valve. When Deane hung up the phone, he said, "What were you doing up here?"

"I just wanted to say good-bye to her in case she had to go to the hospital."

"You should have asked permission."

"Yes, I know. I'm sorry." I hung my head.

We both focused our attention on the nurse, who, looking somber and concerned, continued to administer the oxygen. Gradually, the folds of the sheets started moving almost imperceptibly as Mrs. Griffin began taking deeper and deeper breaths. Finally, the nurse looked up at us with a nod of encouragement, as if to say, "We caught her in time." We all breathed a collective sigh of relief. Deane turned to me and smiled slightly.

"It's a good thing you were here," he said in a consoling voice.

The ambulance arrived and took Mrs. Griffin to the hospital. Later that evening, Deane called me at home to report that she was resting comfortably but not allowed any visitors. He said she was expected to recover from this particular bout, at any rate, and that she would be home in a few days.

"That's the thing about death," he said. "You can't count on it. It's always quicker or slower than you think it's going to be." On that note, he hung up.

The next day, I went out to the house again and wandered around the ballroom, smoking, looking at my nearly finished mural. For the time being, I'd lost the heart to work on it. It all seemed like a curious sham. I lay down on a drop cloth in the middle of the floor, folded my hands behind my head, and stared up at the ceiling.

What I still couldn't figure out was why Mrs. Griffin had hired me to re-create what had obviously been one of the most disappointing nights of her life. If it were true that Cassandra hadn't shown up for her party and that the ballroom had been constructed for what turned out to be such a hollow event, then why would Mrs. Griffin want to remember it? Was it linked, in some way, to Cassandra's murder? To the secret?

And who was this shadow, Cassandra? Clearly, she was not who I'd first imagined her to be, a shy, innocent girl in a white dress reluctantly obeying the conventions of an insular society. On the contrary, now it seemed she was a powerful personality, defiant, and maybe even a little dangerous. As I thought about these things, I fell asleep.

When I awoke it was nearly dark. All the figures on the wall were as gray as twilight—save one: the faceless Cassandra, prim and stately in her long white dress, still glowing in the fading light.

CHAPTER 11

Their mistress gone, the staff fell into lethargy. Without Mrs. Griffin to tend to they became aimless and demoralized, sitting for hours in the kitchen eating, drinking, and talking. The less work they had to do, the more they neglected their duties. Ill and reclusive as she was during the past few months, the old woman had still been the focal point of all activity.

I saw very little of Deane, who found one excuse after another to do errands outside the house. I, too, became increasingly restless and unfocused, feeling sad about Mrs. Griffin and confused about my work. It struck me as odd indeed that the principal figure in my mural had never gone to her own party. The question gnawed at me day in and day out. Why on earth was I commemorating an occasion that had never happened, at least not the way it was supposed to have happened?

I found myself staring across the garden at the house for long periods of time, wondering if somewhere inside it was the key to Frances Griffin's obsessively guarded secret. The house began to transform itself into a living presence in my life, changing faces in the light, a creature with a hundred eyes and no heart. The more I tried to banish it from my thoughts, the more it occupied them. Finally, one morning I couldn't stand it anymore. I put down my brushes and walked across the garden.

Though it had only been three weeks since Mrs. Griffin's departure, everything inside the house seemed sad and untended. I walked through the rooms slowly, running my fingers over the surfaces of things, glancing through the mail (all bills and circulars), listening to the ponderous ticking of the elegant old grandfather clock. I noticed a thin coat of tarnish creeping over the once-gleaming silver and tiny tumbleweeds of dust growing in dark corners. Smelling of damp and in need of a good airing, the house was heavy with the silence that settles on a place when no one lives there. I wandered around among all the beautiful objects and paintings and pieces of furniture, a collection of inmates in a magnificent prison.

After an hour or so, I began to explore the back halls and corridors which honeycombed the house, hidden passages for the servants. On the top floor, I happened upon a door which had a dark stairway behind it. I climbed up the narrow steps, terrified that one of them would split in two and I would be sent hurtling down to the landing. But they were sturdier than they looked. I reached the top and opened a diminutive door made of cedar. I was greeted by a pitch-black void and the faint aroma of camphor. I groped for a light switch on the wall and found one. I turned it on.

There was a brief flickering overhead; then the place lit up under the cool hue of fluorescent lights. A vast room with no doors or windows stretched out in front of me. It was filled with—I could hardly believe my eyes—clothes! On rack after rack hung countless dresses, suits, and coats, each in its own clear plastic bag. An immense oblong structure in the center of the space was fitted with cubbyholes and drawers to accommodate the dozens of hats, handbags, gloves, and shoes housed there in an orderly fashion. These accessories seemed dated but new, as if they had hardly, if ever, been worn. The hats, for day and evening, rested on individual hat racks. There were dozens of feathery concoctions with veils and trimmings, dozens more of felt or fur. Lined up in a row, they reminded me of a fashionable, decapitated audience.

I opened several of the plastic bags and took a look at the

dresses inside. They were mostly evening clothes—so many, that I wondered if Frances Griffin's entire life had been spent going to parties. Some of them showed such remarkable workmanship they were works of art: ball gowns embroidered as heavily as tapestries, jewel-encrusted dresses glittering in the stark light, fancy dress costumes intricately constructed with hidden bones and stays. I'd never seen anything quite like them before.

I wondered as I browsed through the endless belongings, for whom had she saved them? Cassandra? Herself? A museum? She'd certainly saved things on an awe-inspiring scale. Just at that moment, I felt in some odd way as if she'd saved them for me so that I could understand something about her.

I left the attic and walked downstairs to the basement, where I found yet another collection. The basement was built like a bunker with thick cement walls. Its endless space harbored antiques, paintings, china, silver, old books, and decorative objects packed away in crates, cached under sheets and plastic, or just lying out in full view. There was enough stuff there to furnish a dozen houses, just as there'd been enough clothes in the attic to dress a dozen women.

Having roamed around the house all day undisturbed, I finally went outside and had a cigarette. Sitting out on the lawn, I stared with new eyes at The Haven, which looked bleak, even in the warm afternoon sun. It didn't seem to me to be a home, but a tomb, a pharaonic monument to material life. It was devoid of the casual photographs, cheap knickknacks, and little mementos which mark the moments of a life lived among people. There was no sense of human congress, only of wealth and acquisition. I was sorry for Frances Griffin. It was as though she'd spent her days collecting life rather than living it. She'd buried herself alive among all her possessions. And like the treasures of the pharaohs, only those possessions would outlast her. She left no other legacy.

In the dwindling light, I thought of her alone in the hospital in failing health with none of the things that had defined her and through which she had defined herself. She was at long last being forced to travel inward. And from what I'd seen, the journey was proving unbearable.

I finished my cigarette and went back inside the house. I still hadn't found what I was looking for, but I felt sure I'd know it when I came across it, whether it was an object or a document, a picture or an insight. I went upstairs to Mrs. Griffin's bedroom. The room itself was so pale and musty I had the impression a fog hung over it. It smelled faintly of potpourri. The bed, covered with a rose satin bedspread, looked like a small reflecting pool at sunset.

I sat down for a moment at the dressing table and examined the ivory toiletry set laid out neatly on top of the glass, tracing Frances Griffin's gold script initials on the back of each piece with my finger. Everywhere I looked, I was arrested by vignettes of wit and beauty: a collection of tiny trees and flowers in jade pots, all made of precious and semi-precious stones, artfully arranged on a lacquer table; an intimate grouping of English miniatures hanging from blue velvet ribbons on the wall; a pair of gold candlesticks flanking a carved onyx seal reclining on a floe of diamond snow. Over the mantelpiece hung a famous Renoir, a beautiful young bather with flowing gold hair and seductive eyes, luscious in her youth, a picture I'd seen reproduced so often I couldn't quite believe I was in the presence of the original.

I went into her bathroom. It was the only room in the house I'd never seen. The room was an ice palace of mirrors. Walking in, I was hit by glittering accordion images of myself reflected in a hundred pieces of mirror. There were mirrors everywhere, on the walls, the ceiling, the door—strips of mirror pieced together so seamlessly the effect was to fold and dismember the viewer in countless ways, countless times.

I stood for a moment, disoriented, trying to sort out where I was. I began to walk around the dazzling maze. The room was large, L-shaped, divided by a partition, and because of the reflections, completely unnavigable. I kept bumping into myself. There was no up, down, or sideways, no clear path to anything but myriad images of myself in motion and isolated parts of my body ever diminishing in a thousand reflections. Every time I moved, a thousand of me moved. Sweeping my hands over my head like a dancer, I watched a thousand of my hands sweep over a thousand of my heads in perfect unison, an endless corps de ballet stretching back forever into a cold, clear infinity.

I ran my hands under cool tap water and dabbed my face with refreshing splashes. Suddenly, I wondered what would it be like to take a bath in this room? The thought intrigued me. What would it be like to immerse myself in Frances Griffin's own bathtub, to emulate her in the most private of rituals?

I took off my clothes and stood nude in the middle of the room. The sight of my naked body multiplied so many times over made its flaws irrelevant. It became an object, a thing, a possession of mine.

Filling the tub with hot water, I watched scallops of steam flare up and subside, coating the mirrored walls in an irregular design. I stepped in and slid down the back of the tub until my body was submerged. Little whirlpools swirled around me for a time; then the water was still. I looked up at the ceiling and gazed at my reflection, a bodyless face floating on a bed of wet and tangled hair, a living bas-relief on a flat rectangle of cloudy water. Occasional drops of water fell into the tub, making a light, tinkling sound. I closed my eyes, feeling warm, covered, safe, immune to the cares of the world.

Drifting off to sleep, I dreamed of the Medusa, snake-haired and hideous. I awakened with a start, displacing waves of water all around me. I was frightened because I was beginning to understand how I, too, could be seduced by material comforts. Like the Medusa, they could turn you to stone.

Suddenly I felt a draft. I shivered. Then I saw part of a face reflected in the mirrors. In horror, I twisted around to see who it was. Deane was there peering into the bathroom, looking at me with a dull expression on his face. I reared up, folding my arms over my breasts. I gasped. For a split second, the two of us froze. He looked me up and down, not lasciviously, but as if to say, "What in God's name are you doing here?" I sensed a kind of bewildered outrage in his manner and tried to say something to him, but I couldn't utter a word. Neither could he. He simply bowed out of the room and closed the door behind him. The encounter couldn't have lasted more than five seconds.

Oddly enough, I didn't leap up from the bathtub the moment Deane left. Instead, I settled back down into the tub again, feeling somewhat indignant at having been disturbed. I felt that Deane had interrupted me in a most private moment, and any embarrassment I might have caused him was his own fault. I turned on the tap and ran a new stream of water to warm me. Instead of feeling like a usurper, for some reason, I felt I was supposed to be there.

I continued my bath at a leisurely pace, pouring various unguents and perfumes into the water from the cut crystal bottles on the shelf above the tub. I watched my fingertips become little relief maps of puckered skin. I ran my hands over my thighs and torso. My skin felt as smooth as silk under the milky water. Steam knitted my eyelashes together. With half-closed eyes I watched slivers of sunshine scurry over the water like racing minnows made of light. I felt as if I were floating inside a kaleidoscope. I lay still for a long while, listening to the water lapping against the sides of the tub, surrounded by glittery shapes.

Finally, I rose out of the tub and plucked a thick white terrycloth robe from its hook nearby. Before putting it on, I stood for a moment and stared at myself in one of the full-length strips of mirror. My face was flushed, my skin soft and moist. The tiny lines, the little sunbursts of age around my mouth and eyes, had miraculously disappeared. My hair hung in wet strings, dripping onto a pinkish body glistening with oil. The figure in the reflection looked like that of a young girl. And yet I wasn't a young girl, and would never be again, no matter how long I gazed into those magic mirrors.

I could see how Mrs. Griffin had tried to fill her life with luxury as a substitute for passion, with possessions as substitutes for feelings. Now she was old without having really experienced life, and a terrible anxiety was rising to the surface. What was the secret she was at such pains not to reveal? The secret I knew she wanted me to find out? I discarded the robe and got dressed quickly.

Leaving The Haven that evening, I wondered for the first time if it were possible that Mrs. Griffin had killed Cassandra herself.

When I returned home that night there were several anxious messages on my answering machine from Harry Pitt, imploring me to call him back the minute I got in.

"Harry, it's me. Where the hell have you been, for Christ's sake!"

"Faith? Is that you?" He sounded groggy.

"Yes. What have you been up to? You never told me you were going away." There was a pause. "Harry? Are you there? I have so much to tell you."

"I was sleeping. Sorry. What time is it?"

I looked at my watch.

"About seven," I said.

"Morning or night?"

"Night, for God's sake. What on earth have you been doing?"

"Don't ask. Recapturing my lost youth."

I heard him shuffling the phone around.

"What's up? I hate when you go away without telling me."

"Well," he said, seeming to revive, "I've been with Rodney, and you know what he told me? He said a day hasn't gone by when he hasn't thought of me. Can you believe it?"

"Of course I can. You're very memorable, Harry."

"Thank you, dear, but it's been over eight years."

"A drop in the bucket in matters of the heart."

"Do you know what he said? He said sometimes he thought of telling his wife about us just so he could have someone to talk to about me. Isn't that sweet? He said I'm the one who taught him to appreciate beautiful things. Can you imagine? You should see where he lives, it's so dreary. I never thought he paid much attention to anything I said. But it's very nice to hear that, you know, because so often in life one feels one doesn't leave any impression on people whatsoever."

"So you went away with him? That's where you've been?"

"Yes. To a Holiday Inn, in Montauk. It was both ugly and scenic, heaven and hell, a romantic tour de force," Harry said.

"You've been gone quite a long time."

"Well, then I went on a little buying trip; then I came back; then I saw Rodney again. But, Faith, dear, let me tell you the news."

"What?"

He paused. I knew it was for dramatic effect.

"I have found Roberto Madi. I have found him!" Harry proclaimed.

I sat up immediately. Brush cocked his head to one side, looking at me suspiciously.

"What?!"

"Actually, I didn't. Rodney's nightmare child did it on his computer."

"What do you mean you've found him? Where is he?" I said, not believing what I was hearing.

"Someplace called . . . Broken Ridge," he said with disdain. "In Colorado."

American place names always sounded foreign when Harry pronounced them.

"I can't believe it! God, Harry, you found him! Are you sure it's *our* Roberto Madi?"

"Yes."

"How do you know?" I asked. "There could be more than one."

"There is more than one," Harry drawled. "There are seven—at least that I found. But he's our man for sure."

"How do you know?"

"Because I called them all up on the telephone and said I was a writer doing a book on the Griffin case. The others hadn't the vaguest idea what I was talking about. But this one said, and I quote, 'I never talk about that part of my life,' and hung up."

"So it's him."

"Oh, it's him all right," Harry said with certainty.

"Does he speak with an accent?"

"A slight one, yes."

"I'm coming over for dinner," I announced.

"I don't have a morsel of food in the house. Mr. Spencer ate the last brownie."

"What do you feel like—Chinese or Italian?"

"Chinese—from Foo's, please. Moo shu pork with extra pancakes, shrimp, ginger chicken . . . Never mind, I'll order. You pick it up. Oh, and make sure they put in plenty of—"

"I know, I know," I said, interrupting. "Plenty of fortune cookies."

I was so excited that on my way out I almost forgot to feed Brush. I heard him mewing pathetically as I was halfway down the hall. I went back and put down a plate of food for him.

"Sorry, Brushie, can't be helped!"

I took a taxi to Foo's, a gourmet Chinese restaurant which was right around the corner from Harry. Harry had called up ahead of time and charged a mountain of food on his house account. I lugged the two large shopping bags down the block to Harry's and took the creaking elevator up to his apartment. It jolted to a halt at the ninth floor. The thick gray door lumbered open. I got out and walked down the corridor, looking affectionately at the harsh yellow block wallpaper about which Harry ceaselessly complained.

"Turn right and follow the yellow brick wall," he always joked whenever he gave directions to his apartment to first-time visitors. I remembered back six or seven years ago when he'd tried to persuade his neighbors to chip in with him and change that cell block decor to a stylish burgundy geometric paper. His efforts divided the tenants into two opposing factions which Harry dubbed "the Chic and the Dead." He seemed to love filling his life with inconsequential conflicts. I suppose they diverted him from graver matters.

The door to the apartment opened when I was halfway down the corridor. Harry was standing there with a cigarette in one hand, wearing a red velvet smoking jacket over a green silk caftan, a stocking cap, needlepoint slippers embroidered with his initials, and no socks. His jovial expression and ruddy complexion made him look like a macabre version of Santa Claus. He folded his hands and bowed low.

"Herrow! Good evening," he said majestically, affecting a mock Chinese accent.

"Very funny. Thanks for ordering the food," I said, brushing past him. "There's enough here for the entire People's Liberation Army!"

"You welcome," he replied, bowing again, closing the door behind me.

"Are you going to play Charlie Chan all evening?"

"Sooo serious," he said, following me through the small dining room into the kitchen.

I noticed the table was all set for dinner with Harry's fine blue-and-white Chinese export plates that contrasted so elegantly with the burnt orange walls of the dining room. With Harry, there was no such thing as "the good china." He used priceless plates and real silver whenever he entertained or ate alone. His kitchen was stocked with chipped armorial porcelain and cracked Sèvres plates from the eighteenth century, which, I knew, he routinely used for bacon and eggs or canned tuna fish.

I began unpacking the little white cartons of food in the kitchen and scooping them out into blue-and-white bowls and plates from the service in the dining room.

"I take it back—there's enough food here for *two* armies," I said, scooping out a third shrimp dish—this one with water chestnuts.

Suddenly I heard muffled yelps coming from the vicinity of Harry's bedroom.

"Oh, don't tell me you've got Spencer locked in the bathroom again?"

"In the armoire," Harry said laconically.

"Harry Pitt!" I ran out of the kitchen to the bedroom. "I'm going to report you to the ASPCA! Poor little Spence!"

I turned the key of the carved oak armoire in Harry's bedroom. Mr. Spencer, an imperious, gray miniature schnauzer with a ragged coat and irregular beard, leaped out from the middle of a pile of shoes and started charging around the house, yelping incessantly. I went back into the kitchen and finished preparing the various dishes.

"Have you walked him today?" I said, trying to ignore Spencer's barking and snuffling.

"Five times," Harry moaned. "That dog is a terrorist."

"It's your own fault. You never trained him, poor little guy."

"God knows I tried, but he's an aristocrat from the cadet branch of a near-defunct 'Junker' family—the definition of untrainable."

Soon Mr. Spencer's high-pitched aria of barks got on both of our nerves.

"Can't you give him a Valium?" I said, carrying the last two platters of food into the dining room and lighting the candles.

"How about Seconal? Come here, Spencer," Harry said wearily, laying down a plate of food in one corner of the dining room. "Conquer this bowl of chicken fried rice. There's a good little soldier."

Spencer shut up and began vacuuming up the food Harry had given him.

"What a relief!" I said, sitting down to enjoy our Chinese feast.

Harry and I helped ourselves to large quantities of each dish. Harry opened a bottle of an excellent Meursault, and we settled down to the real business at hand.

Now," I said to Harry, "how on earth did you manage to locate Madi?"

"Just a minute." Harry pointed his index finger in the air as if he were about to scold me. "One thing I cannot bear is eating Chinese food with a knife and fork. Excuse me."

Harry got up from the table, went over to a small English sideboard, and opened the middle drawer. He extracted two pairs of chopsticks and handed one to me. I thanked him and begged him to get on with his story.

"I told you," Harry said, expertly wielding the chopsticks to snag a shrimp from his plate. "It was that little brat of Rodney's. He used his computer to track down all the Roberto and Robert and Bob Madis in the country through their credit cards. Ingenious, no? I never would have thought of it. Of course, Rodney says it's elementary stuff in the gumshoe business. Then I just began calling them all up as I told you. Our Roberto Madi has an American Express Gold Card, if that's of any interest."

I gave up trying to snare a large piece of ginger chicken with my chopsticks and resorted to cutting it into negotiable chunks with my knife and fork.

"Mrs. Griffin's in the hospital," I said, now using my chopsticks to eat the pieces I'd just cut.

Harry looked up.

"Really? Serious?" he inquired with his mouth full.

"I don't know. I don't think she's going to die—not just yet anyway."

Harry carefully spooned second helpings of everything onto his plate and began whittling away at the individual piles. His expertise in this style of eating fascinated me.

"Did you spend lots of time in China, Harry?"

"Hong Kong. Marvelous city. You don't sound very enthusiastic about my discovery, Faith."

"It's not that," I replied absently, thinking back to the afternoon I'd spent at The Haven. "Do you know what I did today?"

"What?" he said, washing down a substantial mouthful of food with a glass of wine.

"I roamed all around Mrs. Griffin's house and wound up taking a bath in her very own bathroom."

Harry stopped eating and raised his eyebrows.

"Why? Were you so dirty you couldn't wait 'til you got home?"

I chuckled.

"No, I just did it to see what it would be like. The butler came in and discovered me. I think he was quite horrified, but he's too well trained to say anything. He walked out. I didn't care. I felt like I belonged there. Maybe I've gotten more brazen in my old age. And before that little incident, I discovered an attic full of clothes, hardly worn, and a huge basement full of antiques and books and objects—all incredibly expensive, all just sitting there for no reason."

"Is that unusual? Cluttered attics and basements? I thought that was *de rigueur* for great houses."

"No, Harry, you should see it. It's beyond clutter. It's acquisitiveness at its height. You've never seen anything like this. Mountains of furniture, a warehouse full of clothes . . . It presents a picture of a woman who can only relate to the world through possessions. This is a cold woman, Harry. This is a woman who can't feel."

"Oh God, modern life with all its feelings. Spare me!" Harry wailed. "We live in the most callous society ever, and all anybody talks about nowadays is getting in touch with their feelings. Isn't it possible for people to just exist and get on with things as they used to do in my day? The world has become one enormous group therapy session. It's a terrible bore. My motto is, 'Thank you for *not* sharing!' "

"But people who can't feel are dangerous, Harry. Don't you know that? And the really dangerous ones are the ones who try to imitate the people who can feel. They're like that poisonous species of mistletoe."

"Mistletoe," Harry repeated, nonplussed. "You mean the Christmas stuff?"

"Well, sort of. But there's a variety of mistletoe out west that attacks a tree and grows on it, imitating its foliage so perfectly that the tree can't tell the difference between the mistletoe and its own leaves. Gradually the mistletoe takes over completely and strangles the tree to death. One of my clients once brought me two sprigs from the same tree. One was mistletoe and one was the real branch. At a distance they look identical. But up close, you can see there's something wrong. The mistletoe leaves are the same exact shape and color as the real leaves, only bigger and more exaggerated. You see, the imitators must exaggerate in order to fool others. Frances Griffin reminds me of that dangerous mistletoe."

"You don't understand, Faith. When you've been at it as long and as successfully as she has, you become the real thing. In America there really isn't any such thing as the real thing because we're all invented to a degree. Society is simply a question of *when* we invented ourselves, not how."

"I'm not talking about her place in society, Harry. I'm talking about her as a mother."

"What do you mean?" Harry said, furrowing his brow, plucking morsels from his plate with his chopsticks and popping them into his mouth.

"Well, I thought about it afterward, and I began to wonder if it might be possible, just possible—and please don't dismiss this out of hand, Harry"—I said, warning him—"that Mrs. Griffin killed her own daughter."

Harry put down his chopsticks and said nothing. He just stared at me.

"It would explain why she goes in and out of these schizophrenic trances," I continued. "That's happened a couple of times, you know. She sort of makes me into Cassandra, and then she wants to apologize for something. For what? I ask myself. At first I thought it was because she knows who did it and she's guilty about not bringing the murderer to justice, you know? I thought it was Madi and for some reason she didn't have him prosecuted. But now I think, maybe, just maybe, she's apologizing to Cassandra—via me—for having killed her. Who knows? Frances Griffin's not the real thing, you said so yourself. She's an exaggeration, an imitation. Imitations want to be perfect, and they want to be surrounded by perfection. Cassandra was far from perfect. It must have grated on Mrs. Griffin."

"No, no," Harry said, shaking his head impatiently. "Not possible. I don't believe it."

"You weren't there. You don't know how she gets. She's utterly tormented, I promise you. And yet, I don't believe it has to do with real feelings. I think it's guilt."

"But, Faith, for a mother to murder her own daughter . . . Now really!" he exclaimed, sounding severely exasperated.

"But that's just it. I don't think she saw Cassandra as a daughter. She saw her as an object. She doesn't see people, Harry. She only sees things. *Things* are what matter to this woman because that's the way she was able to enter society and maintain her position. And that is what really matters to her. The house is a museum, Harry, and she is the curator. There are no knickknacks, no mementos, no photographs—except the one of Cassandra, which is an idealized portrait. So, what if she didn't see Cassandra as a daughter, but as a possession that disappointed her? An extension of herself that embarrassed her? Here's the ultimate motive for a murder, Harry: taste. You offend someone's sensibilities by not being perfect, and they kill you. It's exquisitely pointless, just like Frances Griffin's life."

"Faith, honestly—" Harry sighed, shaking his head.

"I can imagine it. I can absolutely imagine it as far as she's concerned. She's like ice. I feel sorry for her but she's like ice. And her life isn't about people and feelings. It's about possessions and acquisitions and *things*. Her daughter was just another thing—and not a first-rate thing at that. I mean it, Harry, I wouldn't put it past her."

"You have a twelve-cylinder imagination, Faith. I'm not saying Frances Griffin doesn't know who killed her daughter, but I'm saying unequivocally that she didn't do it."

"Maybe not. But it's an interesting idea, isn't it?"

"Interesting and highly improbable."

"Oh, well," I said brightly, "I love my little theories."

"You don't like her, do you?"

"I don't know. I feel sorry for her."

"But you don't like her."

I thought about this for a moment.

"No, I do. Sort of. I'm wary of her. I think there's some hidden agenda there and I can't figure out what it is. I don't know, maybe the father did it."

"What?"

"Killed Cassandra. I just know it was an inside job."

"Now the father I could see," Harry said.

"Why so sure?"

"I told you, I met him once. Now there was ice incarnate. I wouldn't be surprised if you told me he was a murderer."

"Hmm. And we can't forget about Madi," I reminded him. "I must confess I wonder what he's like."

"In any event, both are far more plausible suspects than poor old Frances."

"But she knows who did it," I said. "I know she knows."

"Well, according to her, so does Madi. So why don't we go and have a little talk with him."

"You know, Harry, I'm tempted. I really am. Insane as it is."

"What have we got to lose?"

"Our lives, our sanity. I mean we really are nuts to even think of it . . . And anyway, think of the expense."

"Wait there."

Harry excused himself from the table, rose to his feet with some effort, and waddled out of the dining room. He hadn't been gone five seconds when I felt an insistent scratching at my leg. It was Mr. Spencer, pawing me, looking for a handout. I gave him a piece of chicken from my plate and watched him eat, a laborious effort since he had no front teeth, save one at the dead center of his mouth. When Harry returned, he saw Spencer still fretting over the morsel I'd given him. There were tiny half-chewed bits of chicken all over the carpet.

"He's not supposed to be fed from the table," Harry said snippily.

"Sorry, but he was pawing at me, and he looked so imperious I couldn't refuse him."

"That's a trick he learned when he was a colonial administrator in Africa."

I loved the way Harry invented elaborate lineages and histories for Mr. Spencer, speaking of the little dog as if he were a series of grand persons who had lived in the periods Harry favored as a scholar.

"He's had more teeth out since I saw him last," I observed, bending down to pick up stray scraps of chicken with my napkin.

I heard Mr. Spencer growl.

"Yes. The vet left the one tooth in front in, however—'for cosmetic reasons,' he said. You have to love a vet who leaves one front tooth in a decrepit old schnauzer 'for cosmetic reasons,' don't you? Now, stop all that cleaning-up nonsense and close your eyes," Harry said.

"I beg your pardon?"

"Just do as I say."

I straightened up and did as I was told.

"Is this some sort of joke?" I inquired, my eyes squeezed shut.

"No joke. Now open them," Harry commanded.

I opened my eyes and looked down. Propped up against my wineglass was a long blue envelope.

"What's this?" I said, lifting up the envelope to examine it more closely. I discovered it wasn't an envelope at all, but a ticket folder stuffed with paperwork.

"Two round-trip tickets to Colorado," Harry announced with pride. "Plus a reservation for a rental car, and rooms at the finest—and only, I might add—hotel in Broken Ridge, called, appropriately enough, The Fortune."

I stared at the folder, then looked back up at Harry.

"Why are you doing this?"

"Because, goddammit, now you've got my curiosity up too. Even dear Rodney's intrigued. You have to understand, Frances Griffin is an icon to me. I lived through the scandal. You didn't. I can't imagine anything more fascinating than actually solving this murder. And from what you tell me, we're close. I think this fellow Madi's worth talking to."

"Me too, but what makes you think he'll tell us anything?"

"I don't know. It's worth a try. What have we got to lose?" he said.

"What makes you think he'll even see us?"

"I think if you call up and tell him the truth, he might actually."

"And what exactly is the truth?" I inquired, somewhat puzzled.

"Well, we can call him up—I'll do it if you like—and tell him you've been working on the ballroom for Frances Griffin. Believe me, he'll know what that is. I'll say that Mrs. Griffin is old and ill and we feel—you feel—she's harboring the secret of who killed her daughter. And that she herself told you that, quote, 'Roberto Madi knows the truth.' "

The idea was amusing and intriguing.

"Right," I laughed. "And then he says, 'Golly gee, I'll tell you everything I know just because you asked, and because you're so cute!' Come on, Harry, he's not going to blab anything to us. Can you imagine how many people must have tried to get the truth out of him?"

"You never know," Harry said. "He might. Time's passed. It's been a while, I'm sure, since anyone has talked to him seriously about it. Let me call him. What have we got to lose?"

"Okay, and what happens if Madi himself is the killer?"

"Well, then he probably won't see us. Let's assume he's not the killer. He might very well shed some light on who is. He might have a theory. And even if he doesn't know, you might get an insight into Cassandra or Frances. Let me ask you something, Faith, aren't you curious to meet Madi, to see what he's like, how he looks?"

"Sure I am."

"Well, then, I say it's worth a try."

As I mulled over this convoluted reasoning of Harry's, the idea began to appeal to me more and more. At the very least, I thought to myself, it would be an adventure. And Harry had made it all so easy, getting the tickets and rooms. I did wonder where he'd gotten the money to pay for all the arrangements and I offered to reimburse him.

"All right, but you must let me pay you back for my ticket and hotel room," I said.

"No, no, this is my birthday present to you."

"My birthday isn't for another six months. I'd be grateful if you didn't rush it."

"Don't be so strict," Harry teased. "The trip's on me, and that's that. Shall we go and have our coffee in the living room? I won't be a moment."

"Can't I help?"

"No, no. Too many cooks—"

While Harry was preparing coffee in the kitchen, I wandered into the living room, trailed by Mr. Spencer. I sat down on one of the two chocolate-colored sofas flanking the fireplace and sank deep into its silk velvet folds. As usual, the sconces were blazing with candles, making the room glow like a firelit cave. Mr. Spencer jumped up alongside me on the couch and nestled against my thigh while I thumbed through an elegant book on the painter, David, by a French scholar named Luc de Nanteuil, personally inscribed to Harry on the cover page.

It was always a pleasure to sit in Harry's living room after dinner reading or relaxing. He'd created a wonderful setting out of relatively little, making up for no view and an indifferent architectural space by covering the walls and ceiling with fabric and filling the room with exotic collections of ivory and tortoiseshell objects.

Harry had kept the same general decor ever since I'd known him, though the furniture had changed over the years. He always joked that everything in his house was for sale, including himself. At one time, his living room had been the repository for some of the best antiques I'd seen outside a museum. Harry was never ashamed to brag about the conquests of his great eye—"God's compensation to a fat, ugly man"—as he dubbed it. He loved discovering treasures, especially when they had been overlooked by everyone else. He used to deride his fellow dealers for their lack of expertise, especially the ones who dealt in what he called, "overpriced, overpainted Huey, Dewey, and Louis the Fifteenth copies."

Through the years, however, I saw Harry's collection of great furniture dwindle down to only a couple of good things, the rest having been replaced by decorative mediocrities. Though he never complained about his finances, I gathered that over time Harry had been forced to sell off the best examples of his collection in order to make ends meet. Nevertheless, the apartment, like Harry himself, had managed to retain its original character.

I remembered all the times I'd sat there in that very spot, watching Harry hold court, listening to his reminiscences about art and acquisitions and great eccentrics he had known. Just at that moment, I found myself wondering if Harry had enjoyed his life half as much as he enjoyed the recounting of it to other people. I knew he embellished stories for the amusement of his listeners. By his own admission, he often over-restored anecdotes and regilded personalities so as not to disappoint his audience. But that was Harry. The moment was everything for him, and he wanted to be loved. He had been as good a friend to me as I'd ever had. He knew me better than anyone else, having made it his business to burrow deep inside my emotional life and help me through some very tough times.

I thought back to the time I'd first met him thirteen years ago. Thirteen years—was it that long ago? I could hardly believe it. A mutual friend had taken me to his apartment for dinner, saying that Harry had admired my work, heard all about me, and was anxious to meet me. Apparently we shared some clients in common, a rich young couple who'd hired me to trompe l'oeil their oversized Park Avenue dining room to resemble a Roman ruin and hired Harry to stock it with antiquities.

Though ill at ease at first—coming to a strange apartment to meet a man I didn't know—I was won over almost instantly by Harry, who, by all accounts, was at his most charming and seductive that evening. He was witty without being cruel, informative without monopolizing the conversation, flattering but in no way sycophantic. He wanted to know all about me and my work, but I never once got the feeling he was prying. We discovered many things we loved in common, as well as a shared loathing we had of a certain modern painter whose work was as inferior as it was expensive, and who himself was as pompous as he was untalented. The two of us had poured vitriol on this man for at least twenty solid minutes. I remembered the moment when Harry turned to me and smiled as sweetly as a child and said, "You know, dear, nothing bonds people together as quickly as a common hatred." I laughed and laughed. Our friendship began.

"Are you all right?" Harry cried out from the kitchen. "I'm just getting things together. Won't be a minute."

"Just fine thanks," I called back. "Sure you don't need any help?"

"No, no—rather make the mess all by myself!"

Harry entered at long last carrying a black lacquer tray on which was the coffee, a plate of fortune cookies, and another plate of the chocolate mint twigs and crystalized ginger Harry always served after dinner.

"Oh lord, I forgot the spoons!"

"Not for me," I said, holding up my hand to stop him from retreating to the kitchen again. "I'm taking mine black."

He seemed relieved as he sat down to pour the coffee.

"What beautiful cups." I was admiring the particularly rich gold-and-blue pattern of the delicate porcelain demitasses.

"They're marvelous, aren't they?" he agreed. "They belonged to Tsar Nicholas the Second, poor soul. These are the only two I have left."

"I'm honored. What happens if I drop one?" I said mischievously.

"Then you instantly get deposed and shot."

"But do I get to see the Winter Palace one last time?"

"Not if you break the saucer too," he warned. "What a beautiful family they were, the Romanovs. It's heartbreaking to see pictures of them."

"Beautiful, but dysfunctional," I said.

"Pop lingo rears its ugly head. Speaking of dysfunctional families—are we going to Colorado?"

"Yes, we are," I replied before thinking too much about it. Harry seemed pleased.

"Fortune cookie?" He offered me the plate.

I picked up one of the cookies, splitting it in half in order to extract the little white strip of paper. I read aloud: " 'Congratulations, you are about to solve an old murder.' "

Harry looked at me in utter disbelief.

"You're not serious!" he cried.

"Yes, I am. That's exactly what it says."

"Let me see that," he said, grabbing the paper away from me.

Harry put on his glasses and read the fortune.

" 'Make hay while the sun shines.' You little liar."

"All right, what does yours say?"

Harry split open a cookie and examined the message inside.

"It says, 'Beware of trompe l'oeil artists who lie about their fortunes.' "

"Quite right too. What does it really say?"

"It says, 'The wise man goes unnoticed.' Have another one."

I opened up another cookie and was quite taken aback when I saw the message inside.

"What's the matter?" said Harry, who must have noticed the look of surprise on my face.

"Nothing—just something odd, that's all."

"What does it say? You look like you've seen a ghost."

I handed Harry the little slip of paper, and he read the fortune out loud.

" 'Art is the accomplice of love.' Very nice. What's so strange about that? Not exactly my idea of a fortune, but—"

"That's the exact note Mrs. Griffin wrote to me when I first started working for her. She sent it with a narcissus plant."

"So?"

"So, it's just a bit of a shock, that's all. I thought it was an unusual message then. And now, to find it in a fortune cookie from Foo's, well . . ."

"Maybe she eats at Foo's, who knows?"

"Harry, you don't seem to understand, she never goes out of the house."

"Well, then, maybe it's a saying we all should know," Harry said, dismissing the subject with a wave of his hand.

"You have to admit it's odd."

"Life is odd. But I'll tell you something, Faith—I'm grateful to you."

I lit a cigarette.

"Why?"

"For giving me an excuse to look Rodney up again. I had the best time of my life. Ah," he sighed, "nothing beats romance. Nothing. It's the true Fountain of Youth . . . 'For love, all love of other sights controls, / And makes one little room an everywhere.' "

"Dryden?" I ventured.

"Donne," he said primly.

"Oh yes, of course. 'No man is an island.' I wonder if that applies to women? I somehow doubt it."

"Are you feeling islandish these days?" Harry said.

"Desert islandish."

Harry and I sat in silence for a time while Mr. Spencer snored fitfully, still huddled against my leg. I thought about my life, my "desert islandish" life, as I had dubbed it. I was just now beginning to perceive its arc—the downturn, when everything that is to come is less than what has been before. Was I forever done with romance and adventure, I wondered? Was I going to spend the rest of my days contemplating what might have been instead of looking forward to what could be? Suddenly, I was no longer content with being content. I wanted a new experience.

"Call Madi again, Harry," I said decisively. "I'm ready."

Harry looked sheepish.

"Faith, I must confess—I already have. I called him before I bought the tickets. He's expecting us."

"You wily old bird," I said, somewhat astonished.

"Well, I didn't see the point in buying the tickets if the man wouldn't see us."

"Oh Harry, you never cease to amaze me."

"Don't forget, dear girl," he said gently, "I always have your best interests at heart."

I leaned back on the sofa, chuckling to myself, thinking how wise Harry was. He always seemed to know my mood before I knew it myself.

"When do we leave?" I said.

"Thursday? Is Thursday all right for you? The sooner the better, I say."

"Thursday it is."

"Good!"

"You really are a wily old bird, Harry Pitt . . ."

I crushed the cigarette, but the ash kept on burning. I let it burn.

CHAPTER
13

After I left Harry's, I walked around the corner and stopped in at Foo's Restaurant. I asked the maître d' if a Mrs. Holt Griffin ever ate there. He shook his head, saying the name didn't sound familiar. I tried describing Mrs. Griffin to him, but it wasn't any use. He had no recollection of her. I asked him who made up the fortunes in the cookies. He said he didn't know, that the restaurant purchased their fortune cookies from a large supplier in Brooklyn, and if I wanted the name he'd give it to me. I declined. Perhaps it was just an old saying after all.

That night I tossed and turned until dawn. "Art is the accomplice of love" kept coming back to me like an aimless tune. Brush, a victim of my restlessness, unable to get any sleep himself, slunk off the bed around three in the morning and curled up on a chair. In the morning, with the first bloom of light, I leaped out of bed, made breakfast, and drove out to The Haven. I wanted to put everything in order before I left and to inform Deane that I'd be away for several days in case Mrs. Griffin started asking for me from the hospital. When I arrived, I saw an ambulance parked in the driveway.

"She's home," Deane said, opening the door.

"How is she?"

"Very weak. She wants to see you immediately."

Deane made no mention of the incident in the bathroom the day before, but his manner was cool. The careful camaraderie that had been building up between us during the past few months was gone. He seemed mistrustful around me. I thought perhaps he had a right to be wary of me now. I had, after all, invaded his mistress's most private territory. Nevertheless, I felt no regret for what I'd done. The experience had afforded me an important insight into Mrs. Griffin's character, one that I was having some difficulty dispelling, despite Harry's protestations to the contrary. That bath had been worth all Deane's scorn.

Mrs. Griffin was asleep in her bed when I entered. A thin, cocoa-skinned nurse in a white uniform sat close to the bed, knitting. The soft click-click-click of her knitting needles underscored Mrs. Griffin's irregular breathing. The nurse looked up at me. She had bright brown eyes and a pointed face. Her glistening black hair was pulled back tight in a bun. She reminded me of a bird of prey. I was pleasantly surprised when she opened her mouth and spoke with a soft, musical voice.

"Mrs. Griffin," the nurse said, "your guest is here," gently nudging the old woman to awaken her.

Mrs. Griffin turned toward me. Her startled eyes, pale skin, and a wig, stiff and incongruously dark, all made her look like a macabre doll.

"Faith," she said in a weak, raspy voice, "I've been thinking and thinking of you."

The nurse got up and moved to the other side of the room, leaving the chair by the bed vacant. I sat down. Mrs. Griffin gave me her hand. I took it and held it as a matter of courtesy, though I felt strange in doing so. My new thoughts about her possible guilt made me feel hypocritical.

"I've been thinking of you too, Mrs. Griffin," I said. "You must be very happy to be home."

"I'll be damned if I'll die in a hospital. They're terrible

places. So white and ugly and modern. My idea of hell . . . So tell me, have you finished yet?"

"Almost," I said. "Not quite."

"I'm eager to see what you've done. I want to go now."

"Now? Is that wise, Mrs. Griffin? Don't you think you ought to take it easy for a while—"

Ignoring me, Mrs. Griffin pulled herself up in bed and signaled to the nurse.

"Ellie," she said, "this is Miss Crowell. She's the young girl I've been telling you about."

I was touched and rather surprised that Mrs. Griffin had spoken of me to the nurse. I was also amused to hear myself referred to as a "young girl," especially since I guessed the nurse, herself, was probably several years my junior.

"Hello, Miss Crowell," the nurse said.

"Please call me Faith."

The nurse smiled and repeated my name, "Faith."

"Ellie, get my wheelchair, please. Tell Deane."

Ellie put down her knitting and walked over to the bed.

"Now, Mrs. G.," she said, as if she were addressing a child, "your friend is right. I don't think we want to be getting out of our bed just yet."

"My chair, please," Mrs. Griffin repeated more emphatically. "Now."

The nurse shook her head disapprovingly and left the room. I could see from the expression on her face that she was resigned to giving in to the whims of the old lady, who, even in her weakened condition, was a formidable presence.

"I'm afraid I'm going to have to take a few days off," I said.

"Oh? Just now that I'm back?"

"Well, it's some business I need to attend to. I've been procrastinating about it. But I can't put it off any longer. I'm sorry."

"How long will you be gone?" she asked.

"Not long. Just four or five days. A week at the most. I'll be back before you know it. I promise."

"You must hurry," she said. "I don't have much time left."

She put her hands on her face, patting at it gently, exploring her features one at a time.

"My head feels as if it belongs to someone else. Do I look different to you?"

I decided to lie.

"Yes, you look better. More rested."

"Liar," she said without malice. "Life is very strange, Faith. You'll see. You don't really believe it's happened until it's about to be all over. And even then you think, there must be something else, some final thing to make it all make sense."

"Perhaps the truth is the final thing," I offered.

She turned away.

"I'm going to die soon. That's my truth."

There was something very poignant in the way she uttered these words, as a simple statement of fact, unencumbered by remorse or self-pity. I was genuinely sorry for her.

"No," I said, "you're going to live a long time. You have to. You've got to give another ball, after all." I wanted to lighten up the conversation.

"You think so?"

She withdrew her hand from mine and began fidgeting with the ribbons of her bed jacket.

"I hear you've been exploring," she said.

"What?"

"Deane told me. He tells me everything."

Watching her tie a perfect bow with the ribbons, I realized how naive I'd been to think that Deane would have kept our encounter a secret.

"I'm sorry, Mrs. Griffin. I shouldn't have."

"Oh, don't apologize," she said, aimlessly undoing the bow she had tied so carefully. "I know how curious you are by nature. I knew once I was gone you wouldn't be able to resist the temptation to roam around. It's in your character to want to know things about people. To get underneath their surfaces, if you will. I don't mind. That's why I like you."

"Tell me, do you save everything, Mrs. Griffin?"

"It's not that I save things. It's just that I don't dare throw anything out."

"What do you mean? Why not?"

"I don't know," she said. "I can't part with anything. I wish I could, but it's too difficult. Every time I go to get rid of something, I feel as if I'm throwing out a part of my life. You see, Faith, one day this house will stand as a record of the past. I've endowed it in my will, leaving money for upkeep and a staff. It will be a little museum, a little oasis of tranquility in this terrible world. People will come to visit it, and they will be able to get a sense of what life was like for people who resisted the modern disease of ugliness."

"Really? You intend making The Haven a museum one day?"

"Oh yes. The Griffins are an important part of American cultural history, you know. I believe people will want to know how we lived. That's why your work must be particularly brilliant, Faith, because it will be seen by thousands of people after we're both long gone."

So, I thought to myself, it was immortality that she was after.

"Faith, dear, you do know how fond I am of you, don't you? It's as if Cassa's come back to life. I wouldn't deny you anything."

"That's very kind of you," I said.

"Now don't misinterpret what I'm about to say. I'm not angry, dear. Please don't think I'm angry. I'm rather fascinated. Tell me, what possessed you to take a bath in my bathroom yesterday?"

I could feel my face flush with embarrassment, though, of course, I knew that if Deane had informed her of all my movements, he would scarcely have omitted that one.

"It's such a very odd thing to do," she continued. "Of all the things you could have done—why a bath? I'm curious. Why? Why did you do it?"

"I . . . I suppose . . ." I began, struggling to choose my

words carefully, "I suppose I felt it was somehow a way of . . .
of getting closer to you."

"And why did you want to do that?"

It was difficult to tell whether she was baiting me or whether
she was asking these questions sincerely. I decided I'd better be
honest with her.

"Well, the truth is, Mrs. Griffin, I think you've been on the
verge of telling me something important and dangerous several
times and have stopped yourself for some reason."

"And what, may I ask, does that have to do with taking a
bath in my bathroom?"

"I'm not really sure. At the time, I thought it might give
me an insight into you, that's all."

"And did it?" she asked.

"I don't know."

"Either it did or it didn't."

"Well," I said, feeling uncomfortable, "I think the insight
it gave me might be wrong."

"And what insight was that?"

"That you're someone who cares more about possessions
than about people."

"That's it?" she said, raising her eyebrows.

"Yes."

"It's true, I've found possessions a lot easier to get along
with in the long run," she said. "But that's not the real conclusion
it led you to, is it?"

"Yes, it is," I demurred. "I don't know what you mean."

"I mean you think I know who killed my daughter."

I looked at her, deciding it was not the time to be tactful
or squeamish.

"I do, Mrs. Griffin. Yes, I do."

"Well . . . Why wouldn't I have come forward?"

"I don't know," I said.

She began pulling nervously at stray wisps of hair on her
wig.

"Perhaps you think I did it. Perhaps that was your real
conclusion."

I didn't know what to say.

"The thought did cross your mind," she insisted.

"Yes," I whispered, after a time.

"Well, you're right in a way."

I held my breath. She was silent for another long moment. Finally she said: "I did do it."

I gazed down at her, this strange, wizened little creature who looked as if she barely had the strength to open her eyes, and wondered if my theory was correct, or if she was playing yet another game with me.

"Not literally, of course," she continued, looking up at me with very large eyes.

"Who did, then?"

She blinked several times. "I can't tell you that," she said. "But I will tell you that I share the blame, so, in a sense, I am responsible."

She shook her head from side to side, repeating, "I am responsible, I am responsible."

I stroked her forehead. Her skin felt hot. She reached up, took hold of my hand and kissed it.

"You understand," she said. "I know you do."

"Oh, Mrs. Griffin, please tell me what really happened, please. Please, you must. You must tell someone. You want to tell me, I know you do."

"No, you don't understand. I can't . . . I can never tell anyone. But you must know that I *do* feel for people, not just for possessions. I'm not an evil woman. Yes, I've done many things I regret, and I hold myself responsible for my daughter's death—and not a day goes by when I don't think of her and miss her and want her and feel so guilty about what happened—but still, I'm not evil, and I *am* capable of feeling, I *am!* I want you to understand that, Faith. You must understand that. Promise me you will?"

Before I could answer her, I was aware of someone hovering over me. It was the nurse. She was back. Deane was standing next to her with the wheelchair. They looked like a grim pair of figurines, stiff and proper in their respective black-and-white uniforms.

"Here is Madam's chair," Deane said.

"She can only be out a short time," the nurse said to me in a low voice.

"I don't know if she wants to go out at all," I replied.

"Why are you all whispering?" Mrs. Griffin demanded. "I can't stand it when people whisper."

"Do you feel up to seeing my work, Mrs. Griffin? Deane's here to take you if you like."

"No," she said, dismissing the three of us with a wave of her hand. "I'm tired now. Another time."

Deane and the nurse exchanged little smirks between them as if they had won a battle against me. I felt uncomfortable as Deane wheeled the chair out of the room in that controlled, deliberate manner of his. I was sorry to have lost his goodwill.

"We'll get some sleep now," the nurse said to Mrs. Griffin.

She brushed past me and began smoothing Mrs. Griffin's bedcovers and fluffing up her pillows. Mrs. Griffin motioned her to go away.

"I'm going out to the ballroom now to do a little work. Then I'll be off," I said.

"Wait!" Mrs. Griffin cried. "When will I see you again?"

"Oh, a week. A week at the most."

"Think about what I've told you, please."

"Don't worry. I will. Good-bye."

The nurse closed the door behind me. If I'd ever had any doubts about going out to see Roberto Madi, they were erased by this last visit with the old woman. I suspected Harry was right, that Mrs. Griffin had not actually killed Cassandra herself. But what was so unbearable about the truth that she could not bring herself to tell it almost two decades later on her deathbed? It must be the father, I thought. The distinguished Holt Griffin. He must have done it and for some reason she was protecting him. But why? Why would a father kill his own daughter?

I went downstairs and took the photograph of Cassandra

from the library. I needed it for the final stage of work on the mural. Putting it under my coat to protect it, I walked across the garden. The morning air was cold and damp, the day overcast. I could see my breath dissolving in front of me in little puffs of white mist.

Running up the steps of the pavilion, I opened the French doors and went inside. I looked around. My work was almost finished, the room nearly completed. I felt it had turned out well. This pleased me even more now that I knew Mrs. Griffin intended to make The Haven into a museum. Though I'd always prided myself on being indifferent to thoughts of posterity, I must confess her plan excited me.

I walked around the ballroom slowly, examining each of the panels, remembering the various moments in their creation. They were like my children, and I took pleasure in dwelling on the highlights of their growth and development. I began to imagine the people who might one day visit The Haven. Would some of them wonder, even fleetingly, about the artist who had painted these murals?

The ballroom was no longer the promising empty space it had been when I'd first walked into it in the springtime, all those months ago. Now it was a scene of great festivity. I had managed to capture a moment. There was an air of expectation on the faces of the celebrants straining to catch a glimpse of Cassandra as she entered the room, an enigmatic figure in a white dress, still with no face, holding a bouquet of flowers, stepping tentatively into the center of the gathering in her honor. The moment that had never happened.

I studied the framed picture of Cassandra I'd borrowed from the library, memorizing her features one by one and then together, as they formed the whole of her face. I knew it was going to be difficult, if not impossible, to do her justice from that innocuous studio photograph, so I laid it aside and decided to work from instinct as well as memory. I picked up my palette and brushes and stood at the wall, confronting the blank oval head, and began sketching Cassandra's features as I remembered them. Soon a face emerged. However, it was as lifeless as a death mask.

I started thinking about the sort of expression I might give to this young woman whom I'd never known and who, from what I knew about her, would have hated the idea of being immortalized in this way. I wondered whether to make her looking directly at the viewer, or staring off into the distance. Laughing or talking? Should I capture a fleeting moment, or render her classically, head up, eyes blazing, arms at her sides, as imperious and graceful as a Greek goddess? Should I make her face reflect the pain she was to know later on in life? Or should I make her indifferent to her fate? What attitude, I wondered, would do her the most justice?

I sat trying to compose Cassandra's portrait most of the morning, to no avail. In the midst of all the lively faces, hers kept arriving stillborn. Despite my best efforts, I couldn't get the portrait to live. Rubbing out the features for the fifth or sixth time, I remembered the promise I'd made to Cassandra when I'd first been hit by inspiration. It had been my plan to paint her face at the very end, when the party I'd created for her was ready for her to see. Now the scene was set, but how could I paint her face when I was still missing the final piece of the puzzle: who killed her and why? Until I knew that, I couldn't do her justice. So I put away my brushes and paints and left the ballroom, more eager than ever to meet Roberto Madi.

The next day, I bought a parka on sale at a ski shop in midtown. That afternoon I packed a small bag with the warmest clothes I had, as well as cold remedies, herbal teas, and a first-aid kit. I'd never been to the West before and I imagined it a freezing place of forbidding vastness with few people and fewer comforts.

That night I cooked some chicken and finished what was left of a bottle of Chablis I'd corked and put away in the re-frigerator. After supper I went upstairs and gave Brush to my neighbor, who was fond of cats. She was an older woman with two cats of her own who'd looked after Brush for me on the few occasions when my work had called me away. I kissed him good-bye. I was sad to leave him.

When I went back down to my apartment, I called Harry. There was no answer. I left a message on his machine confirming the plan we'd made to meet at the airport early the next morning. I was terrified I was going to miss the plane, or that he was, or that some calamity was going to befall us both. The logistics of travel so unnerved me that I kept studying my ticket to make sure the date and time of departure were correct and checking over my bag with the gnawing feeling I'd forgotten something.

I called Harry again and again throughout the evening. Still no answer. I left several messages on his machine, the last one of which was the simple, plaintive cry, "Where the hell are you?!" I needed Harry there to guide me. Without his reassuring presence, I had visions of botched reservations, stranded people, mechanical failures, and crashing planes, as if the world outside my own little sphere was a conspiracy of chaos designed to derail even the most vigilant and unobtrusive of travelers.

Just before I went to bed, I ordered a taxi to pick me up at six-thirty sharp the next morning, even though the plane for Denver wasn't scheduled to take off until nine. Harry finally called at ten-thirty, out of breath, with a million excuses for not having gotten back to me sooner.

"All set, old cowgirl?" he said.

"Very funny. Now we're meeting at the ticket counter at eight sharp, right?"

"Right," he concurred.

"And you've got your ticket, right?"

"I've got mine," he assured me. "Have you got yours?"

"Got mine. I bought a parka. I'm bringing herbal tea and antibiotics, and a first-aid kit. I'm trying to think what else," I said.

"How about two six-guns and a covered wagon?" he volunteered.

"I know, I know, I'm just being ridiculous."

"Now I spoke with Mr. Madi again, and he's looking forward to meeting with us," Harry said on a more serious note. "We're going to have dinner with him in the hotel tomorrow night. Apparently he's off on a trip around the world, so we've just caught him in time. He's leaving in a couple of days."

"God Harry, isn't it amazing how this whole thing's working out?! By the way, I have a new theory about the case."

"What?"

"I think the father must have done it."

"Why do you say that?"

"Well, I don't think it's Mrs. Griffin anymore. I think you're right, I don't think she's capable of it. But she admitted to me that she knows who did it and she just can't say who it is. So that sounds to me like it must be the father, doesn't it to you? But the question is why? I mean why would a father murder his own daughter?"

"All I can say is I sincerely hope Mr. Madi will clear things up for us. And now I've got to go."

"Harry, wait. Why do you think Madi wants to talk to people after all this time?"

"I have no idea. We'll just have to ask him. Look, Faith, I've got to get some sleep and I'm not packed yet, and Mr. Spencer is feeling under the weather, so forgive me if I sound abrupt."

"Okay. See you tomorrow. Love you."

"Love you too," he said and hung up.

I tossed and turned all night, fretting over details already attended to. The taxi arrived promptly at six-thirty. I was at the airport by seven-fifteen. I got a cup of coffee, a roll, and a newspaper, and planted myself down in the middle of a row of orange plastic seats opposite the ticket counter where Harry and I were meeting at eight. I became so engrossed in an article in the paper about a major archeological discovery in Umbria that I completely lost track of the time. When I looked at my watch, it was eight-fifteen. Still no Harry. Then I became aware that I was being paged.

"Miss Faith Crowell, please pick up a courtesy phone, Miss Faith Crowell to a courtesy phone, please," said the soothing, disembodied voice over the loudspeaker.

I rushed up to the ticket counter, where a man directed me to one of the airline's phones.

"Hello, Harry?!"

"It's me, Faith," he said in a raspy voice.

"You sound awful. Where are you?"

"Mr. Spencer died."

"Oh Harry, no! Oh no! Oh God, I'm so sorry."

There was a pause. I could hear Harry sobbing on the other end of the phone.

"I can't go with you, Faith. I'm sorry, I just can't. I'm too upset."

"I know you must be. But I can't go all by myself. I can't."

"Why not?" he said.

"Well, I just can't go out there all by myself. What if Madi turns out to be the murderer or something? I just can't. I'm too frightened."

"For Christ's sake, Faith, he's not the murderer, or he wouldn't have agreed to see us."

"I'll tell you what, why don't we wait until you're feeling better, and then we'll go out there together like we planned?"

"Do what you want, but he's going away, I told you. Around the world. It's now or never, Faith. You've got to do this on your own. Listen, you're the one who started it all."

I could feel my heart racing.

"I know, but—"

"Look, my darling, I can't talk now. I'm just too stricken. I have to make arrangements for the funeral. I'm going to have him cremated so I can keep the ashes with me always," Harry said, his voice choking. "I'm sorry I can't go with you."

He hung up. I stood holding the receiver in my hand for

a long moment, paralyzed, wondering what to do. I heard the flight being called over the loudspeaker.

"All passengers on flight 182 to Denver, please proceed to gate 3. The flight is now boarding . . ."

Harry was right. It was now or never. I decided to take that timid, safe little life of mine and throw it up into the air. I banged down the phone and ran for the gate.

14

To my amazement, everything went ahead on schedule. The weather was clear, the plane was on time. I found myself sitting comfortably in the back of a large jet, staring out at the sky, being lulled to sleep by the hum of engines. Now that I was on my way, I relaxed. There was something about being lifted off the ground and going on a quest that gave me a sense of power.

I fell asleep. When I awoke, we were landing in Denver. My connection to Grand Junction was two hours off. I had plenty of time to have a cup of coffee and observe my fellow travelers. A man in a shiny brown suit, wearing cowboy boots and a Stetson, was doing a crossword puzzle. I watched a little boy sucking on a candy bar waddle by while his anxious mother called him back. Every so often, people appeared out of nowhere, hurried on, then scattered like beads rolling into the crowd. I forgot how much I disliked airports, finding this one to be a lively, impersonal place where I felt comfortably lost in the noise and traffic. Finally, a voice announced the boarding of my flight to Grand Junction. I walked to the gate and got on the plane.

As we took off, I pressed my nose against the window and watched the brown-aired city of Denver shrink to the size of a smoky topaz. I read the airline magazine for a while, then lost interest and dozed off. When I awoke, I looked out the window at a horizon rippling with mountains. Fiery sunbeams flitted around the cabin, momentarily blinding me. Then we landed. Stepping out of the plane, I was hit by a curtain of bracing, cold air which made my eyes water. I looked around as I walked toward the terminal. The light was different here. There was a purple cast to the air. Objects in the far distance stood out clearly. I picked up the rental car Harry had reserved for us and started driving the seventy miles to Broken Ridge. According to the map the agent at the counter had given me, it was a relatively easy place to find.

The West was a vast place but not at all frightening, as I thought it would be. The quirky formations of the mountains and the nearly recognizable shapes of the large boulders made the landscape look as if it had been chiseled out of the earth by a lost race of giants. Occasionally I slowed down to look at a shawl of pine trees thrown over one of the great granite slabs in the distance, or a silver stream spilling down the rocks to a hidden valley too deep for me to see. The mantle of royal blue sky was flecked with clouds. On it hung a pale afternoon sun. Once I'd accustomed my eye to the immense scale of things, I was exhilarated by the hard, haphazard beauty all around me. I began to feel like a pioneer, a hunter.

As I drove, the deepening colors of evening descended on the land in successive veils. For a few precious seconds before dark, the dying sun glowed furiously behind the mountains. I stopped the car and watched as red-and-gold flames paled into wispy feathers of light drifting through the air. When they faded, it was night—not the small familiar night I'd known back east, but a big strong night, tattooed with a million stars.

I started up the car and drove on. On the highway a few miles past a big ski resort, there was an exit sign with several names written on it. Broken Ridge was one of them. I got off onto the ramp and headed into the darkness. There were no lights on this road as there had been on the highway. Only my car beams illuminated the faded white dividing line. After fifteen minutes or so, I saw a faint aureole of light up ahead. Soon there was a large sign on my right with a pair of steerhorns on top of it which read, ENTERING BROKEN RIDGE.

I drove through a single street lined with old-fashioned wooden buildings and some parked cars on both sides. Several people were walking around, but there didn't seem to be a great deal of activity. I drove slowly looking for a turnoff to the main part of the town when another steerhorned sign loomed up on my right proclaiming, LEAVING BROKEN RIDGE. The light gone, there was only darkness ahead and a flat wooden arrow attached to a tree reading, SHADOW CREEK—2 MILES.

As far as I could tell, the town of Broken Ridge consisted of one main street, and I'd just driven through it. I turned the car around and drove back, this time very slowly, looking from one side to the other for the Fortune Hotel, where Harry had booked our reservations. I drove up and down the street a couple of times without success. I stopped alongside a passerby, rolled down my window, and called out to him.

"Excuse me, could you tell me where the Fortune Hotel is?"

"That's it down there with the blue lights," he said, pointing to one of the buildings near the center of the street. A pair of blue lanterns hung on either side of the door.

"That's the hotel?" I said.

"They got rooms, yeah."

He walked on. I drove up to the hotel, parked the car, and got my suitcase out of the trunk. Walking up the wooden steps to the entrance I noticed a small brass plaque above the door which read, FORTUNE. A man on his way out wearing jeans and cowboy boots, reeking of liquor, held the door open for me as I stepped inside.

The lobby was a dimly lit place filled with heavy Victorian furniture, paintings of the Old West, and framed "wanted" posters. Several people were milling around, a couple of whom stared at me as I stepped up to the desk to register. One, a tall, strikingly handsome woman talking to two men, seemed to take a particular interest in me. She had straight blond hair down to her waist. Her face was tan. She was wearing a long denim skirt, a suede coat with fringe dangling from the sleeves, and red lizard cowboy boots. It was my impression she whispered something about me to her two companions as I came in. I tried not to pay any attention.

I heard music and laughter coming from the next room. The Fortune, in particular its bar, seemed to be the center of whatever activity there was in Broken Ridge.

There was no one behind the desk. There was, however, a bell next to a framed handwritten sign reading, PLEASE RING FOR SERVICE. I tapped the top of the bell lightly with my palm. After a moment, the blond woman walked over and stepped behind the desk.

"Hi," she said, smiling broadly. "How're y'a doin?"

Up close, she looked much older than I'd first thought her to be. Her features were youthful, but her skin was deeply lined and mottled. It looked oddly patched together. I guessed she was somewhere in her mid-forties, whereas from a distance she looked as if she might have been in her late twenties. She had the air of an aging flower child.

Opening an old-fashioned register, she handed me a pen.

"If you'll just sign in, please."

She looked at my signature.

"Oh, Miss Crowell. Your room's been prepaid, and I understand Mr. Pitt's not coming."

"No, that's right," I said. "I'm supposed to be meeting someone here for dinner."

"Uh-huh, well, there's the dining room," she said cheerlessly, closing the register and taking a large key down from a board.

"How late do you serve dinner?"

"Nine. But you can get a hamburger or a taco up 'til we

close at two. Welcome to The Fortune. I'll show you up to your room."

She came around the front of the desk and picked up my bag. I followed her up the staircase, running my hand along the wide oak banister. We walked up two flights of stairs. She turned down a corridor on the second landing. The wallpaper was patterned all over with brownish roses, on which wood-framed old prints, mainly catalogue illustrations from the nineteenth century, hung in groups of four.

"How old is this hotel?" I said, as we continued down the hall.

"Oh, the original part dates back to about 1880. They built it during the mining boom. Then it got abandoned. Someone converted it into a private house in the fifties. My ex-husband and I bought it and two of the neighboring houses in the seventies and turned them back into a hotel. There's literature about it in the room. The reason it's called Fortune is because the original owner built it with the stake he made mining."

"You've done a great job restoring it," I said.

"Oh, well, you know—my ex-husband was a carpenter with a Ph.D. in philosophy. You don't know the meaning of the word *obsessive* until you've met a carpenter with a Ph.D."

She unlocked the door and switched on the light, revealing a large room, painted pale yellow, decorated with nineteenth-century pictures of ladies of fashion. A big brass bed took up most of the center wall. Alongside it an old-fashioned pitcher and basin rested on a nightstand. There was a pine armoire in one corner and a writing desk in another, on which hotel literature as well as picture postcards of the region were laid out neatly on top of the blotter. Everything was fresh and clean.

"No room service," she said, putting down my suitcase on the luggage rack at the foot of the bed. "Breakfast is served from six to eight-thirty sharp. The bathroom's in there. So holler if you need anything. My name's Sally."

"Sally," I said, as she was leaving, "you must know most of the people around here, don't you?"

"Every single one. Dyin' for a new face."

"Have you ever heard of someone called Roberto Madi?"

"Bob Madi? Sure. I was just talkin' to him when you came in. That who you're havin' dinner with?"

I felt the blood rush to my head. I'd seen him and I hadn't known it.

"Yes," I said, trying not to betray my excitement.

"Bob, you sneaky bastard, never sayin' anything. 'Course he's always here. Always at the bar 'til closing time. You a friend of his?"

"Uh, not exactly. We have some friends in common."

"Okay, so just lemme know when you come down. I'll point him out to you," she said as she closed the door behind her.

I unpacked, freshened up, and changed clothes. I stared at myself in the blotchy old mirror inside the armoire door. There wasn't a trace of fear or apprehension in my expression. Though I had no idea how I was going to approach Roberto Madi or what on earth I was going to say when I did make contact with him, I nevertheless left the room confident of my mission. Walking downstairs, I shivered once or twice. I felt Cassandra's ghost was hovering around me, guiding me and protecting me from harm.

Sally was nowhere to be seen when I reached the lobby so I went into the bar by myself. It was a large room decorated with cowboy memorabilia and Indian artifacts, dimly lit by gaslight wall sconces which had been electrified. A jukebox played softly in one corner. A few diners were scattered around the room at the round tables covered with red-and-white-checked tablecloths. I sat down, lit a cigarette with the candle in the middle of the table, and looked around the room.

Four men were standing at the long oak bar and I knew immediately which one was Madi. It wasn't that I remembered seeing him talking to Sally on my way into the hotel or that I'd had a specific image of him in my mind. No, I just knew who he was.

Madi turned and looked at me. I assumed that Sally had told him of our conversation. I didn't flinch. I looked back at him and smiled.

He appeared to be somewhere around forty-five, though I knew from the newspaper accounts he was older. He had thick dark hair he wore on the long side combed straight back. He was medium height, and he showed his lean body to advantage in tight blue jeans and a checked shirt, opened one button too many at the neck. He was extremely handsome. I could see where he must have been dazzling as a young man. He had darkly glittering eyes, a straight nose with nostrils flaring slightly over a strong, full-lipped mouth. With his smooth olive complexion, he might have passed for a number of nationalities— Spanish, Italian, even Arab. There was something feral about him. He began ambling toward me, drink in hand. When he reached my table, he stood still for a couple of seconds without saying a word, looking down as if he were ready to either lick me or pounce.

"Miss Crowell?" he said.

I detected the accent Harry had mentioned. I nodded and motioned for him to sit down.

"Mr. Madi?"

I held out my hand and he shook it, holding it a little longer than necessary. He kept staring at me. There was a moment of awkward silence.

"So," I said self-consciously, "you're Roberto Madi."

He chuckled. "No one has called me that in years."

"What?"

"Roberto."

"What do they call you?"

"Bob. What do they call you?"

"Faith."

"Faith, as in faith, hope, and charity?"

"Or as in 'ye of little faith.' "

"How do you do, Little Faith? Would you like a drink?"

"Thank you. I'd love a glass of red wine, please."

"Red wine is not the best thing to have here unless you get a bottle. Permit me."

He got up from the table and went over to the bar, giving me a bit of time to think about this first encounter. I thought I'd pegged his accent as Italian, but I still wasn't quite sure. He was much gentler than I thought he'd be when I first saw him. He didn't seem to have an edge to him. On the contrary, there was something sweet about him, even endearing.

He came back to the table with an open bottle of wine, sat down, and poured us each a glass.

"To mischief!" he said, raising his glass.

I raised my glass in turn, he clicked it, we both drank. The wine tasted warm and soothing and, on an empty stomach, went straight to my head.

"How's the wine? A bit acid, no?"

"No, it's fine, thank you."

"Wine is usually mediocre in this part of the world. They don't know how to order it because they don't like to drink it. Beer, yes. Wine, no. So . . . where is Mr. Pitt?"

"Well, his dog died and he was just too upset to come."

"How sad," he said.

"Yes, it's very sad. Mr. Spencer—that was the name of his dog—Mr. Spencer was like a child to him. He was shattered."

"Oh, I understand that well. My wife loved animals more than she loved people. She trusted them like she could never trust a human being. I think she was right."

His manner was direct and disarming.

"When you say your wife," I began, hesitating slightly, "you mean Cassandra?"

"Sandy, yes."

"You call her Sandy? Her mother calls her Cassa," I said.

"She is Sandy to me," he said firmly, keeping his eyes fixed on me. "Forgive me if I am staring at you, but you are very like her."

"Am I?" I shifted in my chair, nervously sipping my wine.

"How old are you?"

"Thirty-nine."

He looked genuinely surprised.

"I would not have put you at more than thirty-two or -three. Honestly."

"Whenever people say 'honestly,' I know they're lying," I said.

"Yes, but you like men who lie, no?" he teased. "And anyway, I am not lying."

I couldn't help smiling.

"So, you are working for Frances," he continued, pouring both of us some more wine.

"Yes, I was hired to trompe l'oeil the ballroom."

"Ah, the famous ballroom," he said with contempt. "Trompe l'oeil, how appropriate. And what design have you chosen?"

"Well, it was built, as you know, for your wife's coming-out party, so I've just tried to re-create the party, with her at the center."

He put down his glass and lowered his eyes, remaining silent for a long moment. When he looked at me again his face had grown sad and serious.

"Why did you come to see me?"

"I came about Cassandra."

"What about her?"

I continued on in a slow, measured voice.

"Mrs. Griffin says that you know who killed her." I paused. He said nothing. "I think Mrs. Griffin knows, but she won't tell me. I want to find out."

"Why?"

I thought for a moment. "I'm not sure exactly. But it's not just curiosity," I assured him. "For some reason, I feel a kind of bond with her."

"With Sandy or with Frances?"

"With Cassandra. I can't explain it. I feel as if I owe it to her."

"How did you find me?" he said.

"I didn't. Harry Pitt did. He tracked you down through your credit cards. Didn't he tell you?"

"Oh yes, I suppose he did mention something about that . . . So Frances tells you that I know the truth?"

"Yes."

"I am surprised she didn't tell you that I did it," he said, smirking.

"What?"

"We are not fond of each other, Frances and I. I am sure you understand that. When the crime happened, reporters, journalists, writers—they followed me around the world always asking the same things: Did you kill your wife? Was it a conspiracy? And Frances did nothing, nothing at all to dissuade them from the thought that I had done it. Finally, it got to be too much. I said to them, let me ask you something: What do you expect me to say to you? Hmmm? Yes, I murdered my wife, and because you ask me, I will tell you. '*E troppo*,' you know? Too much." He shook his head and drained his glass.

Of all the reactions I could have gotten from Roberto Madi, this was the most unexpected and ingenuous. He seemed completely open about the subject—tired of it, in fact. His attitude made me wonder what on earth I had expected him to say or do. Suddenly, I was a hunter without any weapons.

"So, Frances sent you to me to sort everything out."

"Oh no, she doesn't know I'm here."

He nodded as if he were skeptical.

"You are a brave girl to come out here all alone."

"Well, I thought I was coming with Harry, but—"

"The dog," he interrupted.

"Yes."

"I will tell you something. I am beyond caring what anyone thinks anymore. I loved Sandy very much. She was my life. So let them think what they want."

"Mr. Madi—"

"Bob, please," he corrected me.

"Bob," I said, "do you know who did it?"

He stared at me intently. "Don't you think if I had done it, they would have prosecuted me until I was dead? Believe me, poor people, unlike some others in this world, cannot get away with murder."

"Who can?"

He shrugged. "Ah, well—"

"You do know who did it, don't you?"

He leaned in, folding his hands together.

"And if I did know, why would I tell you? My dear, what has possessed you to come here like this? Why do you take such an interest in this old, old story? I am sure that a beautiful woman like you has much better things to do."

I wasn't used to being referred to as "a beautiful woman" and I was slightly taken aback. I was sure it was just his polished manner—a trick of the gigolo trade—but he nevertheless made me feel as if he really meant it, and I enjoyed that.

"Won't you at least tell me about her? How you met? What she was like?"

"I am sorry," he said with mock arrogance, "I never give interviews on an empty stomach!" Then he smiled broadly. "Let me take you to dinner."

"Why not?" I said, feeling flattered. "What shall we order?"

"Christ, not here!" he cried. "The food here is atrocious. We'll drive over to Snow Lady. It's only a few miles from here. There is a very good Italian restaurant there, run by friends of mine. It's open late. We'll have some pasta and a little more wine and I will tell you my life story. And then you will tell me yours. Come—I am hungry."

He got up from the table and held out his hand to me. I nodded and let him help me up from my chair. He guided me out of the bar, back through the lobby. We walked outside into the November night. I followed him to a small lot behind the hotel where his jeep was parked. He opened the door for me and I got in. He was very courtly, very correct, yet I kept waiting for some dark aspect of his character to reveal itself.

As Madi drove, he made polite conversation.

"Have you ever been to Snow Lady?" he said.

"No, this is the first time I've ever been out west."

"It always amazes me how Americans do not travel in their own country," he said. "It's the most beautiful country in the world, and yet they always want to go to Europe before they explore their own land."

"I guess you're right. I've been abroad five times, and I've never been out here. I think I was always a little afraid of the West. I must say, I think I was wrong."

We drove in silence for a time. The road was dark. I stared out the window at the blackness on either side. We seemed to be taking the back routes.

"Where are you from?" I said.

"Italy."

"Where in Italy?"

"Milano. Do you know it?"

"I've never been to Milan, but I love Italy. God, I adore it, especially the Veneto. I don't understand why on earth you'd ever want to live here if you were born there. I'd stay in Italy for the food alone, never mind the art."

"Europe is too old and decadent," he sighed.

"America's quite decadent these days, don't you think?"

"Oh yes, but America's decadence is wonderfully naive, like the decadence of youth. In Europe, we are so old and so cynical. We've seen too much. Our decadence has lost its energy. We have completely surrendered to it, whereas you Americans are still capable of struggling against it. You want to be pure, whereas Europeans simply accept corruption as a fact of life. It's such a bore in Europe because there is no real social theater like there is here."

"Is that why you came to America—for the social theater?" I said facetiously.

"No."

"Then why?"

"I married Sandy."

"Where did you meet her?"

"In St. Moritz."

"What were you doing there?"

He turned to look at me for a second.

"How much are you pretending not to know?" he said.

"What do you mean?"

"It's quite well known, the story of how I met her," he said. "Lowly ski instructor meets great heiress. You do not know it?"

"Just parts of it," I replied. "Not the details."

"You really are a brave girl to come all this way not knowing anything about me."

"Maybe." I shrugged.

"Brave and foolish."

I suddenly felt very foolish—and vulnerable. There I was, out in the middle of nowhere, speeding along dark roads with a person I had once suspected of murder.

"I like that," he went on. "It is so typically American. You dive into the water without looking to see if there are any rocks."

"Some of us dive even though we do see the rocks," I said.

He smiled at me as he was driving, putting me more at ease.

"Who is this Mr. Pitt who was supposed to come with you?"

"He's a friend of mine. An antique dealer."

"Why is he interested in this case?"

"Because of me, primarily. But also because he knew of it. He met Mrs. Griffin years ago."

"So you persuaded him to come out here with you?"

"Actually, it was more the other way around. He persuaded me. He thought a little adventure would be good for me. He was the one who talked me into working for her in the first place."

"How very considerate of him," Madi said, sounding slightly sardonic.

"It's true, I was becoming too isolated. Working for Mrs. Griffin has been an amazing experience. But that's enough about me. I want to know how you met Cassandra."

Madi didn't answer until a few moments later when we turned onto the main highway.

"I grew up in poverty," he said, almost as if he were talking to himself. "I thought poverty was the worst thing in the world. Then I met Sandy, so beautiful, so sweet, so rich . . . But I never met another human being as tragic as she."

"In what way?" I said, moved by his evident feeling.

"In every way you can imagine." He shook his head. "She was like a wounded bird. Every night she had terrible dreams. She would wake up screaming and I would hold her until she fell back to sleep. We understood each other's pain."

"You think love is based on pain?" I asked him.

"The greatest love, perhaps, yes. But not all love is great. There are other kinds of love, much more comfortable, which are based on other things. Unfortunately, they are not the ones that interest me."

I glanced at him out of the corner of my eye. His face was weaker in profile, less handsome.

"Sandy and I came out here for our honeymoon. She is the one who introduced me to the West. She hated the East. She hated anything that was cluttered or constricting."

"She must have loathed The Haven," I said, recalling the stifling grandeur of that great house.

"The Prison. That is what she called it."

"Why did you come back east to live?"

"We did not. We lived out here. We built a house together. I live there now."

I was rather surprised to hear this as I'd always assumed Cassandra had lived in New York.

"So you were actually living out west when—?"

"*Ecco!*" he said interrupting, "The great Snow Lady."

The lights of the resort town shone up ahead.

"You must be hungry," he said.

"Yes, as a matter of fact, I am. I haven't eaten all day."

"Good. I enjoy seeing women eat."

"What's that supposed to mean?" I looked at him askance.

"You worry too much," he grinned. He leaned in close so that when he spoke, I could feel his breath on my cheek. He patted my hand.

"You're a very serious girl, you know that? Very, very serious."

I didn't pull away. His hand felt warm on my skin. I understood how Cassandra would have been attracted to him. I was beginning to be attracted to him myself.

15

We drove into Snow Lady, a resort wrapped around the base of a mountain of the same name. Madi played guide as we toured the twinkling town, driving around prefabricated chalets and quaint streets that were too well thought out. There were carved wooden signs for everything from ski lifts to rest rooms to restaurants. The town looked as if it had been assembled all at once from some mammoth kit—the full-blown fantasy of an inferior architect, stocked with gingerbread buildings which were a combination of Austria and Disneyland. Lack of age and history made Snow Lady a bland, uninteresting place meant only for skiing, shopping, sleeping, and eating. Without question I preferred the comparative seediness of Broken Ridge, and apparently, so did Madi.

In a mock guide's patter, he pointed out various "uninteresting points of interest," as he called them, and related the history of the place, which was built by a group of developers in the mid 1960s who went broke just before America resumed its love affair with the West in the early 1970s. Then speculators moved in and made a killing.

"Now it is impossible to buy a place here for less than a half million dollars," he said. "I never come here except to eat. Everything is too luxurious and too boring."

Madi parked the jeep and we walked to Roffredo's, a tiny

Italian restaurant tucked behind some ski shops at the base of Snow Lady Mountain. He was greeted enthusiastically by the proprietor, and we were seated at a corner table with a dramatic view of the mountain. Lights sparkled across the slope where a motionless ski lift hung, a drooping string of black stones.

We settled in. Madi ordered a bottle of Chianti and the pasta special for both of us. I was eager to learn more about his relationship with Cassandra, but I was also aware of a connection forming between the two of us. Once or twice I caught him staring at me with the same intense curiosity I thought I'd detected in Mrs. Griffin the first time I met her.

"Why are you looking at me like that?" I said.

"You remind me so much of Sandy," he said simply.

"That's what Mrs. Griffin said."

"I'm not surprised. You could be sisters."

"How old would she be now? Thirty-nine, forty?"

"Forty, just turning forty-one. Her birthday is in December. And you are thirty-nine you said."

"Thirty-nine, just turning a hundred."

He laughed.

"When I asked you that before, you answered me immediately. Most women are not so candid about their age."

"Why be coy about a fact?" I asked.

"Because facts are generally irrelevant, so why not?"

"What do you mean?"

"A fact is merely an event: it happened, it didn't happen. It is the perception of an event which is more important than the event itself. If you look and feel much younger than your age, the fact of your age is meaningless."

"Did you ever kiss the Blarney Stone?" I inquried.

He laughed again. We both did.

"So, as you say: cut the bullshit, right?" he said.

"Right."

"I like you, Faith." There was with a new sincerity in his voice. "I really do like you. It's rare for me to like a woman. I love them, I hate them, but I rarely like them."

"You were going to tell me how you met Cassandra?"

He leaned back, finished his glass of wine, and poured himself another.

"You must understand," he began with a sigh, "Sandy is my life, my obsession."

"Was."

"Was. Is. Same thing."

"Tell me again where you met her?"

"St. Moritz."

"You were introduced to her?"

"She was on a ski trip. I was her guide. I came round to pick her up at her hotel. When I asked her what sort of program she wanted to follow, she said, 'I want to follow you.' " He smiled wistfully, seeming lost for a moment in the recollection.

"How old was she?"

"Nineteen."

"Did you have any idea who she was when you met her?"

"What do you mean?"

"Had you ever heard of Holt Griffin?"

"*Non! Certo non!*" he cried.

"When did you find out who she was?"

"When it was too late. The great Holt Griffin," he said bitterly, shaking his head. "What a monster."

"In what way?"

Madi lit a cigarette and polished off still another glass of wine.

"In what way?" he repeated. "You don't want to know."

"Oh, but I do," I said emphatically.

A puff of smoke curled into his nostrils. His eyes grew cold and distant. He bit his lip.

"What, exactly, do you know of him?" Madi said.

"Not much really. Except that he was very grand and rich, from an old family. Supposedly very elegant. Possibly bisexual—at least that's what Harry Pitt told me. Now that I think about it, there isn't one picture of him in the house. That's odd, isn't it? I have seen photographs in newspaper clippings, but I don't have a very clear impression of him."

"I will tell you one story about him," Madi said, narrowing his eyes.

"Go on, please."

"Holt named one of his racehorses after Sandy. A filly—Cassa Mia. When Sandy was twelve, Holt took her out of school one day and flew her in his plane somewhere where Cassa Mia was racing—Louisville, I think. He made a big production, introducing her to the trainer, letting her pat the horse in its stall before the race. She watched the race from a private box."

"Sounds good so far," I said.

"Wait," he said, holding up his hand. "Cassa Mia did not win the race. When Sandy said she wanted to go back and see the horse again, Holt announced that he had had the poor animal shot. He told Sandy, 'That is what happens when those that belong to me do not obey.' "

"My God," I gasped. "I can't believe it. Shot for no reason? Are you sure the horse didn't go lame and had to be put down?"

"No—listen to the rest," Madi said. "They spent the night in Louisville, and the next day, all the way home, Sandy was in tears over this horse. But when she got home, what was the first thing she saw?"

I shook my head, unable to imagine what was coming next.

"The horse," Madi said. "Cassa Mia."

"What?" I was incredulous.

"Yes. Cassa Mia. She was fine. Holt never had her shot at all. In fact, he gave her to Sandy as a present."

"I don't understand."

"You see, he wanted to show Sandy his power, to let her know he had the power of life and death over the horse . . . and by extension, over her."

"Jesus, what a story."

Madi snickered. "That is nothing."

"I can't believe it," I said. "Where the hell was Frances?"

"Terrified, probably. Everyone close to this man was terrified. No—I take it back—everyone who depended on him for something was terrified of him."

"What do you mean?"

"You were fine if you did not want anything from him, or did not need him. Then, as I understand it, he could be very generous—a great friend, a great benefactor. But God help you if you did need him. And God help you even more if you were related to him."

"I wish I could remember his picture in the newspaper better."

"He was very attractive, very elegant, and sophisticated. Always dressed perfectly, but understated, like an English gentleman. And quite disarming. With not a bad sense of humor. Even I liked him when I first met him," Madi said grudgingly.

"Do you think Frances loved him?"

"Certainly she loved his money and his position."

"But not him?" I pressed.

"I do not think she could separate the man from what he represented, and she worshipped what he represented. After all, he made her what she was. Before him, she was nothing. Holt was the one who started her real education in collecting, in society. Then, as often happens, the student surpassed the teacher."

"Did Cassandra love him?"

"He was her father. Daughters love their fathers, do they not?"

"Did he kill her?" I said without thinking.

Madi averted his eyes and shook his head, but I knew there was something more he wanted to tell me, just like Mrs. Griffin. I was sure they both knew the truth about Cassandra's murder, and Madi struck me as a battle-weary mercenary on the verge of defection. I felt in time I could get him to talk.

"So what happened after you met Sandy?" I said, deciding to pursue a gentler course for the moment.

"We got married." He seemed relieved by the new tack.

"In Switzerland?"

"Yes. Then Sandy took me back to America, and for the next year her father tried to have the marriage annulled."

"Really? Why?"

"Let us just say, not for the reason everybody thought."

"What did everybody think?"

"That I was a poor boy with no background. A fortune hunter."

"And that wasn't the reason?"

"Not the real one, no."

Madi stared at me hard as if some part of him were hoping I'd intuit the true cause of Holt Griffin's vindictiveness. I couldn't imagine what "real reason" he was talking about, though I began to suspect it had something to do with Cassandra's death. He continued:

"Of course, it was a ridiculous tactic on his part. His opposition only made us come closer together. It's incredible how much you remind me of her," he said, staring at me harder.

I ignored the comment. "What about Frances? How did she feel about you?"

"Frances was also afraid of the monster."

"The monster being Holt Griffin?"

He nodded.

"Did Frances like you?" I asked.

"She did not want to, but I think she did. I think she was pleased that I made Sandy happy."

"Why do you hate her now?"

"Because . . . I hate her. Now I think I hate Frances more than Holt," Madi said, shaking his head.

"But why?" I kept pressing him. "What happened? Something to do with the murder. It is, isn't it?"

"For that you will have to inject truth serum," he said. "And there is one more. One I hate even more than I hate both of them."

"Who?" I was fascinated.

"No. I will take these things to my grave."

I sipped some wine and wondered what secret he was keeping. Clearly he knew who killed Cassandra, just as her mother knew. I no longer believed it was he who had done it, but he was certainly part of the cover-up.

"What was Cassandra really like?" I said, after a time.

"Look in the mirror," he replied.

"Seriously—I've seen one picture of her, but her mother says it doesn't do her justice."

"No, her pictures were terrible and she hated having her photograph taken. She was too animated to capture in a single moment. I took some movies of her. In the movies you can see how beautiful she is. Especially when she is laughing."

"Do you still have those movies?"

"I have saved everything to do with her."

"Really? Her clothes?" I said.

"Yes, though she did not have many. She hated clothes."

"A reaction against the mother?" I offered.

"Of course. And I will tell you something amusing," he said. "Her clothes were all solid colors—never a pattern. She used to say to me, 'Roberto, I can never wear prints because my mother tells me my face is too busy.' "

I laughed. "So she was quite funny and self-deprecating."

"Oh yes, she had a wonderful sense of humor," he concurred. "But she was shy. She did not show that side of herself to many people. Like you, I suspect, have sides you do not show to many people."

I let the comment pass, for the way he said it presumed a flirtation between us I was wary of encouraging. I didn't want to get off the subject of Cassandra.

"Did she have a lot of friends?" I inquired.

"No. Her father isolated her, you know. He was afraid."

"Of what?"

"Of losing her. Tell me, Faith, are you afraid of losing anything?"

"I don't know. Sometimes I think I'm more afraid of what's been lost." I replied.

Madi reached over and took hold of my hand.

"Now you are just like Sandy," he said softly.

I didn't take my hand away. I looked past the candle flame between us into his clear, dark eyes, focused intently on me.

"I have never remarried, nor have I had another long relationship," he said.

"Why not?"

"As you just said—because of what was lost. You make me think of her more than any woman I have met."

His eyes swelled with tears. I reached out to him with my other hand. We locked hold of one another across the table.

"I can't explain it," I said, "but I've felt so close to her all these months. It's as if I've become her avenging angel. I have the feeling she's been guiding me. I thought I'd come out here to solve her murder, but now—"

"What?"

"I don't know—maybe it was more to solve my life in some way."

"In what way? Tell me, Faith."

He looked at me tenderly, and, for a moment, I read into that look an unspoken suggestion that he might be part of that solution. Then I thought, "Oh God, Faith, you're really getting carried away!"

"I wanted to know why I survived and she didn't," I went on. "She would have been around my age now, had she lived, and I felt there was somehow a connection between her death and my survival. I thought it might have had to do with my escaping from a destructive man before it was too late."

"What man?"

"Oh, first my father, who ran off before I ever knew him. And then others with whom I could relive that abandonment again and again because it was familiar and compelling. One in particular."

"Who?" He seemed interested.

"No one. Just somebody." I was anxious to get off the subject.

"But you survived," he said.

"Maybe," I responded, with a weak smile. "Sometimes I'm not so sure."

"Who was the one man in particular? Tell me."

"Oh, just somebody—a writer."

"He was cruel to you?"

"Not on purpose, I don't think. I think he was just being himself."

Madi let go my hands and edged his chair around the table in order to be nearer to me. He stroked my cheek gently with the back of his hand.

"Such lovely, soft skin," he said as he pushed my hair behind my ear to reveal more of my face. "And such delicate little ears." He leaned over and kissed my neck.

Over another bottle of wine, our faces softened by candlelight, Roberto Madi and I drifted toward that timeless universe for lovers where there is nothing but a look, a touch, a shiver of the heart. The world narrowed down to the two of us, and finally, to the sensations that the slightest physical contact between us produced. Everything and everyone else became an intrusion or an amusement, put there for us to dismiss or embrace as the mood took us. We were, as the Buddhists say, not two and not one, but a different entity governed by our attraction to one another. By the end of dinner, having drank too much and said too much in too short a time, we both knew we were going to be lovers.

When we left the restaurant, well past midnight, it was colder and darker outside. Madi put his arm around my waist as we walked to the car. We said nothing. We got in and started driving. The car was freezing inside and took a while to warm up. Madi pulled me to him but it was difficult to nestle close to him in the jeep, the seats being separated by the gearshift. I stayed as near him as I could, paying no attention to where we were going. The night skidded by on either side of us. I closed my eyes, letting a floating feeling of intoxication take hold of my body.

After a time, I felt the car vibrating a bit, as if we were on rougher terrain. I sat up and looked out the window. We'd turned off the main road down a rocky trail with tall, black trees on either side.

"Where are we?" I said groggily.

"We are going to my house. Is it all right?"

He looked over at me for a split second. I stared straight ahead without speaking. The car was bouncing up and down now, and I gripped the dashboard to keep from being tossed around.

"I am sorry, the driveway is a bit rough. I keep it this way to discourage visitors," he grinned.

"How far is your house from Broken Ridge?"

"Three miles as the crow flies. Longer, of course, to drive."

He shifted the car into low gear, and we headed up a steep hill. Suddenly the road leveled off, and we were on smooth ground. I could see the distant outline of a ranch house crouching against the sky. A single porch light glowed in the night. When we reached the front door, Madi got out and came around to my side of the car. He opened the door and took hold of my hand more firmly than he had done in the past. I felt woozy as he led me up the steps of the porch. He was weaving slightly, and I could tell the alcohol was getting to him too.

The exterior of the one-story house was simple and rustic, built with rough-hewn timber. Madi opened the front door and switched on a light close at hand, nearly stumbling as he did so. I was freezing and grateful to get in out of the cold. As I entered, Madi pulled me into him and we stood hugging one another for a long moment. I thought he was going to kiss me. I wanted him to kiss me. I held my ground and looked up at him without turning away.

"Faith is what I need," he whispered.

He leaned in, brushing his lips against mine. His breath was hot and reeked of wine. I suddenly realized how crazy the whole thing was—I'm drunk, he's drunk, neither of us really has a clue what we're doing. I'm out here in the middle of nowhere with a man I hardly know and whom I once suspected was a killer. These thoughts lanced through the alcoholic fog, breaking the spell. When he began to kiss me, I shied away. His passion flared up. He clamped his lips down hard on mine and gripped my shoulders. I let out a little gasp of pain and tried to withdraw, but he wouldn't let me go. I jerked my head around, trying to stop him from kissing me.

"Stop!" I cried. "That hurts!"

He let go suddenly and raised his hands. For a moment I thought he was going to hit me, but he grabbed his hair and pulled it in anguish. I remained still, barely breathing. He was staring at me. I felt my face flush with fear. I touched my lips with my fingertips. They felt tender, bruised.

"Forgive me," he said, excusing himself abruptly and leaving the room.

Still drunk and now fearful, I began to tremble. I wondered if Madi might indeed be the murderer. His absence gave me a much-needed opportunity to calm down, catch my breath, and look around.

I found myself standing in an enormous room with bare oak plank floors, sparsely furnished, centered on a huge stone fireplace. The great log walls were bare except for four antique Indian chief's blankets nailed up evenly across them. A beaten-up leather couch and some canvas deck chairs were grouped around the fireplace. Some antique Indian pots and baskets were scattered here and there, along with a few other artifacts—a Kachina doll, a Peruvian flute, a spear. There was sleek, black, state-of-the-art electronic equipment—an elaborate sound system, a huge television, a VCR, along with tapes, compact disks, records, and movie cassettes neatly organized in fitted wooden compartments.

It struck me as a completely male room. There was no softness, no artifice, no attempt at decoration. I could imagine Madi holed up there for days with nothing except controlled electronic contact with the outside world. As I looked around, I thought how I could get to that spear, if need be. I wished to God I weren't so drunk.

When Madi returned, he was holding a joint in one hand and a videotape in the other. He put the tape down on top of the television.

"Remind me to show you this later," he said, offering me a puff of his joint.

"What is it?"

"Weed."

"No, I mean the tape," I said.

"Later." He held out the joint again, motioning me to take it. I shook my head. He walked to the middle of the floor and stood there, inhaling deeply. He was spacing out—slurring words, moving carelessly, dropping ashes on the floor. He didn't seem to notice or care.

"So—what you think? Just like The Haven, no? This was our answer to her parents. Can you see Frances Griffin here— even for a day, an hour? She would kill herself." He laughed, steadying himself against a table. "I have changed nothing. Everything is the way it was when Sandy was here except for that junk over there." He pointed to the electronic equipment. "She used to tell me it was the only time in her life she had ever been happy . . . Have a puff of this shit—it's fantastic!"

"No thanks," I demurred. My head was spinning.

Madi finished off the joint and ferreted out a bottle of brandy stowed in a makeshift bar inside one of the stereo cabinets. He poured himself a shot, which he downed, letting out a little gasp of air after he'd swallowed it all in one gulp.

"Brandy?" he said, offering me the bottle.

I shook my head. That was all I needed.

This time he swigged some directly from the bottle and, taking it with him, went over and plunked himself down on the couch, sinking into its soft leather folds.

"Come, sit here with me." He patted his thigh.

"May I have a look around?" I said, not wanting to go anywhere near him.

I walked around the room slowly, aware that he was watching me, aware of the clunking sounds my footsteps were making on the bare wooden floor. I wondered what he was thinking as he sat there stoned, drinking his brandy, looking at me. I wondered how many women had been in that house, what his life had really been like since Cassandra's death.

I peered inside a darkened room. In the gloom, I could make out a large mattress strewn with blankets and pillows shoved up against one wall. There was a small lamp on the floor next to a stack of magazines and newspapers. Nothing else. No phone, which was what I was really looking for.

"The master bedroom?" I said, half-joking, turning around.

Madi had crept up so he was standing directly behind me. I jumped.

"Do not be so nervous," he said in a voice laced with innuendo.

I edged away from him. He didn't follow me. He just leaned against the door and watched me.

"Sandy was a vagabond," he said. "She hated anything to be permanent."

"What about you?"

He didn't answer. His eyelids drooped shut, then snapped open a couple of times, as if he were making an effort to stay awake.

"I really ought to be getting back," I said.

He sauntered over and picked up the videotape he'd left on top of the television.

"Don't you want to see this?" he asked.

"I'm not sure."

Madi bent down, pressing the tape against the mouth of the VCR. The machine inhaled it smoothly, making a soft whirring sound. He went over and sat on the couch, beckoning me to come sit beside him. I pulled up a chair instead, careful to maintain a good distance between us. This seemed to amuse him. Chuckling, he shook his head from side to side and muttered something unintelligible under his breath.

Using a remote control, Madi clicked on the television set. A blank gray screen bloomed in front of us for a few seconds before bursting into the colors of an autumn day in the mountains. The camera glided across a ridge teeming with golden aspen trees. Suddenly, the screen filled with the image of a young woman laughing. I recognized her immediately: it was Cassandra, lying on a blanket, surrounded by the remains of a picnic on the grass, dressed in jeans and a red sweater. There was no soundtrack. I studied her as she played in front of the camera, alternately shy, indignant, and mischievous. Madi was right. Her lively, shifting expressions made her far prettier than she appeared in the formal photograph in her mother's library.

She kept burying her head in her hands, laughing and making faces, motioning the cameraman to go away. She hid, she pleaded, all to no avail. Finally, she shook up a bottle of soda, playfully threatening to spray the cameraman. The camera backed off slightly but not enough. She let go her finger from the bottle. Drops of liquid spattered the screen, the camera turned topsy-turvy, the screen went black, the film switched to another scene.

This time Cassandra was sitting alone under a tree reading a book, apparently unaware she was being filmed. Occasionally, she pushed her hair out of her eyes with a sweep of her hand. The camera stayed on her an inordinately long time. I looked over at Madi.

"She was beautiful," I said. "I wish I'd known her."

He didn't answer me. He continued staring at the television and drinking from the brandy bottle. All at once he bolted up from the couch and went into his bedroom. I, in my drunken haze, continued to be mesmerized by the tape of Cassandra, and wanted to see it through to the end.

The scene on the video abruptly switched to black-and-white images. The camera was stationary, focused on an unmade bed. The film was grainy, the scene harshly lit. A round, whitish shape filled the screen, then disappeared. This happened several times. I couldn't make out what it was at first. Then I realized it was a pair of bare buttocks, moving in and out of the frame. The view changed. Cassandra, nude, smoking a cigarette, draped herself across the bed, her small, round breasts firm on her chest. Smiling and smoking, she beckoned to an unseen person in the room. A naked man with a lean, muscular torso slid down on top of her, his back to the camera. She teasingly offered him a puff of her cigarette. Craning his neck for the puff, he turned his head to one side and I recognized him: it was Madi, looking younger, fitter, with a moustache and longer hair.

What gradually unfolded was a movie of Cassandra and Madi making love. Like a sexual handmaiden, she offered herself up to him in different positions. He stroked her, licked her, played with her hair, sucked on her nipples, devoured the insides of her thighs. Growing more frenzied, she straddled him, reared up on top of him, ran her hands down her own body, eyes closed, sculpting its curves with her fingers. With a look of intense concentration and solemnity, she slid her hands from her body onto his, as if she were a high priestess sharing her magic energy with him. Toppling her with a stroke of his arm, he scrambled on top of her and fucked her violently, drilling her to the mattress.

Watching them, I felt disgusted and titillated at the same time. I wanted to turn away, but I was riveted by the two of them bucking and writhing on the bed, oblivious to the camera. As their passion intensified, Cassandra looked as if she were fighting for her life, scratching and flailing, needing to be free. Madi was unrelenting. I kept thinking of John Noland and myself, of the scenes of our passion, fueled by anger.

The screen went gray. The movie was over. I continued to stare at the blank set, feeling dizzy and vaguely sick. I was afraid to move for fear I'd throw up. I wanted to leave the house, get back to the hotel, have a bath. I wanted to put on a thick flannel nightgown, climb into bed, pull clean white sheets up over my head, and go to sleep.

I heard a noise behind me. I didn't turn around.

"Why did you show me that?" I said somberly.

"Why did you look?"

He flung a manila envelope down in my lap. I didn't touch it.

"What's this?" I asked.

"Open it."

"No."

"Open it!" he demanded.

I took a deep breath and opened the envelope. I slid out a photograph. It was upside down. When I turned it over, I gasped in horror. I couldn't believe what I was seeing. It was a

gruesome black-and-white police photo of Cassandra's murdered body, taken at the scene of the crime. She looked like a
marionette splayed out on the floor. I stared at the twisted head,
the blood-soaked nightgown, the expressionless features, the
open eyes staring at nothing, the pale lips, the slack jaw, the
tangled hair. I saw my own face in hers. My heart was beating
with fear.

"Look at her."

"Please—" I said, pushing the picture aside.

Madi grabbed it and held it up close to my face. I could
feel his hot brandy breath on my neck. He reeked of liquor.

"Look at her!" he wailed.

"I—I see her," I said.

"You remember I told you I hated someone more than
Holt Griffin, more than Frances Griffin?" he hissed.

I nodded, too frightened to utter a word.

"You know who that person is?"

I shook my head. My mouth was dry.

"Myself!" he groaned.

With that, he flung the picture away and clamped both his
hands hard around my shoulders. I let out a scream, wriggled
free, and sprang to my feet, out of his grasp.

"I want to go back to the hotel!" I cried.

Madi looked at me with wide, uncomprehending eyes. His
face was bloated. I could see he was stoned and drunk.

"C'mon, baby . . . spend the night," he said, slurring his
words, collapsing onto the couch. He heaved a sigh and passed
out.

I had to get out of there. I put on my coat and crept to the
door, fearing I'd wake him up. Where were the car keys? Had
Madi left them in the ignition? Had he put them in his pocket?
I couldn't remember. We'd both gotten so drunk. I reached for
the doorknob and turned it slowly, trying not to make any noise.
The door opened. A current of freezing air shot through me;
it had a momentarily sobering effect. I ran outside to the jeep,
yanked open the door, and hurled myself into the driver's seat,
praying the keys would be in the ignition. They weren't.

My head was swimming. I couldn't get the police photo-graph of Cassandra out of my mind. I decided it was too risky to go back inside the house. At that moment, Madi seemed more dangerous than the bitter cold. I was going to make a run for it.

Jogging down the long driveway, I imagined that Madi had somehow awakened and was coming after me. The notion ter-rified me so much that at one point, thinking I heard his jeep starting up, I jumped off the side of the road, slid down the embankment, and hid in the thick of the trees.

The night was tomb black. Now I really began to feel the cold—an Arctic chill that stung all over. Even in my intoxicated state, I knew if I stayed out too long, I'd freeze to death. I knew I had to keep moving. I scurried back up the embankment and ran down the road, scanning the dark shapes of the night, trying to get my bearings.

Finally, I reached the highway. Disoriented, I chose a di-rection and started walking. After a few minutes, I saw the headlights of a car in the distance. As it came closer, I could see it was an old Chevrolet. I flagged it down. I had no choice. The car slowed to a halt.

"Need some help?" asked an elderly woman, rolling down her window.

"I'm trying to get to Broken Ridge," I said, relieved.

"You're headed the wrong way. Broken Ridge's in the other direction, 'bout five miles."

I asked if she'd mind giving me a lift to where she was going so I could get to a phone and call a taxi. This idea amused her so much she started laughing.

"C'mon, get in. I'll take you," she said.

I thanked her and climbed into the passenger seat. She turned around and we began heading toward Broken Ridge.

"Dangerous being out at night by yourself," the woman said.

"I know," I replied. My head was pounding.

"Where're you from?"

"New York."

"City?"

"Yes."

She nodded as if to say that figured. We drove in silence the rest of the way. When we reached the hotel, I was grateful but too tired and hung over to say anything more than a brief thank you. She seemed to take it in stride, driving off into the night.

I climbed the stairs to my room, bone weary. I kicked off my boots, dropped onto the bed, and fell asleep with all my clothes on.

The next morning I was awakened by a series of sharp, staccato rings. Half asleep, I fumbled for the phone next to the bed. For a moment, I wondered where I was and how I'd gotten there. Hearing the voice on the other end of the line, however, I remembered everything.

"Faith," the voice said, "are you all right? Faith?"

It was Madi. I didn't know what to say. Scenes of the previous night rushed through my mind.

"Faith, please—are you there?"

"I'm here," I said, after a long pause.

"Faith, I am so sorry. Please forgive me."

I didn't answer. I thought of the moment when he'd kissed me and I shuddered. I waited for him to go on.

"I was drunk. I know how much I must have frightened you," he continued. "But you should not have left. It is very dangerous to be out alone at night."

"So I was told."

"How did you get back to the hotel?"

"Roberto," I said impatiently, "why are you calling me? Are you afraid I'll tell people about you? I won't."

"Please," he said, "will you let me see you?"

"What's the point?"

"You do not understand. Please—I have something that I must tell you." He sounded desperate.

"No," I replied, but with less conviction.

The thought of seeing him again frightened me, and I wasn't eager to prolong the conversation. Yet I sensed he meant me no harm.

"Please, listen," he said with urgency in his voice. "I want to tell you the truth. I *must* tell you the truth."

"Why?" I asked, wary, but interested.

"I lost my head last night, not just because I was drunk, but because you remind me of her. You brought back all the old memories. I thought things had changed. I thought I had learned to live with myself, but I have not. Please, Faith, I ask you to give me another chance. This time, I will tell you everything you want to know. Please, please . . ." he begged. "It is time for the truth."

"Where are you?" I said at last.

"Downstairs, in the lobby," he replied. "I am waiting for you."

Exhausted and hung over, I undressed and ran a bath. Before stepping into the tub, I studied my face in the mirror. The skin on my mouth and cheeks was chapped, burned raw by the cold. I looked pale and drawn—and older. The last veil of youth had lifted, exposing the deeper lines of middle age. I could see my skin sagging toward decay. I ached as I sank down into the hot tub. I closed my eyes and let my body go limp while my mind made lazy, incomplete connections.

Had I been right from the beginning, I wondered? Was Madi, in fact, the murderer? Or was it Frances? Or Holt Griffin? Which one? Or was it someone else entirely? Clearly, the cover-up—and there had been a cover-up—had eaten away like lye at all those involved in it over the years. I was so close now. I kept repeating to myself over and over, what shall I do with the truth, Cassandra? What shall I do with the truth?

After my bath, I packed and dressed and went downstairs. Madi was in the restaurant, seated at a table in the corner away from the small lunch crowd. He saw me come in and immediately stood up. I walked over to his table and sat down. He looked haggard and hung over. His face was sallow and unshaven, his eyes sunk in dark circles. He had a stale smell about him. I glanced at his drink.

"Don't worry, it is only a Virgin Mary," he said, with a feeble grin, holding up the glass to reassure me. "Or what the English call a Bloody Shame."

He had a certain charm about him, even in this state. I couldn't help but smile. A waitress came around to the table. I ordered a large orange juice and some eggs. After she'd gone, Madi and I sat across the table from one another, staring at each other, without saying a word. Finally, he cleared his throat and spoke.

"I . . . I am so sorry about last night." His voice was throaty and full of pain. "Can you forgive me?"

I lowered my eyes, without answering. He continued:

"You remind me so much of her. It has been years since I thought about any other woman in this way. It was too much. There are some ghosts that will not leave you alone. As you get older, instead of gradually fading, they become more clear. Can you understand that?"

I looked back up at him. His eyes seemed to be searching my face for some sign of empathy. The waitress came back with my orange juice. Madi ordered another Virgin Mary.

"How did you manage to get back?" he said, pulling out a cigarette.

"I managed."

Looking genuinely remorseful, he said, "Was I terrible?"

"Don't you remember?"

He shook his head. "I am an expert at forgetting."

Just at that moment, despite all the implied cynicism in the remark, he reminded me of a little boy.

"You were drunk," I said. "Let's just leave it at that."

Madi lit the cigarette and inhaled deeply, seeming to savor the smoke in his lungs.

"You were going to tell me the truth?" I went on.

"Oh yes, the truth," he said. "I want to make a confession, yes. I was brought up a Catholic. What about you?"

"My mother was a Presbyterian. My father was a deserter," I said.

"What is that?" Madi inquired.

"A bad joke. Never mind. Please go on."

"So you have never made confession?" he said.

"No."

"Confession in church is simple. You go to a priest, you say your sins, you do your penance, and you are absolved. But there are some sins for which you cannot atone, no matter how sorry you are. Those sins you live with, and your penance is your life," he said gravely.

"And what are your sins, Roberto?"

He hesitated for a moment, then said in a trembling voice: "I let her be killed."

I felt my chest constrict, my face grow hot. In that instant, I imagined him idly watching someone plunge the knife into Cassandra's heart. He must have sensed my revulsion because he reached across the table with his hand in order to reassure me. I recoiled.

"Not literally—!" he cried.

"Who did it? Who?"

"I will tell you, I will," he said. "But you must understand that I feel I am the one who is responsible."

"What do you mean, Roberto? Please tell me."

He spoke slowly.

"I am responsible because . . . I let her go back to the house . . . I let her spend the night under the same roof with that monster—"

"What monster?" I said, riveted by his intensity.

"Even though I knew what he was and what he might do to her," Roberto continued.

"*Who*?!"

"Holt Griffin," Madi said without taking his eyes off me. "The great Holt Griffin."

"Her father?"

"Her *father*," he spit out the word. "Her *killer*."

I believed him. I'd suspected it.

"But why? *Why* did he do it?" I was fascinated.

"The great collector, the great philanthropist, the great gentleman—the legend, Holt Griffin!" he said contemptuously. "That is what the world saw. But what the world sees is very different from what is true."

"Why, Roberto? Tell me," I begged him.

"I will. I trust you. Holt Griffin killed Sandy long before he actually stabbed her," he said.

"What do you mean?"

"I mean this—" he said, his eyes hard. "Her father took her virginity when she was eleven years old."

"My God. He raped her?" I held my breath.

"Worse. He seduced her. Enslaved her. Became her lover," Madi groaned.

"No!"

He nodded.

"My God—" I was completely stunned, yet there wasn't the slightest doubt in my mind he was telling me the truth.

I thought of Mrs. Griffin.

"Did her mother know?" I asked.

"Who knows what she knew or when she knew it?" Madi said. "She did not want to know it. It would have meant giving up too much."

"But she must have known. Or at least she must have suspected."

"If she knew, or if she suspected, she said nothing. Then Sandy finally told her, to her face."

"When?"

"The night of the famous coming-out party," Madi said.

"So *that's* why Cassandra didn't go!" I gasped.

"Yes, it will interest you, especially. The night of that party Sandy refused to put on the dress that had been made for her—because it was white, she said."

I thought of myself standing in front of the mirror in my

bedroom, enveloped by the creamy satin of Cassandra's debutante dress.

"Sandy told her mother that she would be a hypocrite to wear a white dress," Madi continued. "When she refused to put it on, Frances became furious with her, screaming at her that she was ungrateful and selfish to ruin this great party being given for her. Then Sandy told her mother everything."

"What did Frances do?"

Madi sipped his drink and lit another cigarette.

"She refused to believe Sandy. They confronted Holt," he went on. "But, of course, Holt denied it. What was he going to say? Yes, I have been fucking my own daughter for eight years? Sandy was screaming and crying. She refused to go to the party, and ran away from the house. But the party went on without her, with Holt and Frances greeting their guests as if nothing had happened."

"Dear God," I said, shaking my head in disbelief.

"I am told," Madi said dryly, "that the evening was a great success."

"How could they?" I wondered aloud. "How could they do that?"

"The show must go on, as you say." Madi crushed out his cigarette in disgust. "I have the taste of ashes in my mouth."

"I wonder if Frances knew all along?"

"You think not?" he said, looking at me wide-eyed. "I think she must have known. But, in any case, the daughter chose an inconvenient time to tell her. The most important thing that night was the party, not the past."

"Didn't anyone ask about Cassandra that night?" I said. "I mean, didn't anyone wonder where the hell the guest of honor *was?*"

"I am sure that they did," he said. "But I am also sure that Frances and Holt made up some acceptable excuse for her absence. People do not care what is really going on beneath the surface. They are like mosquitos flitting over a pond."

Now everything made sense—why Cassandra hadn't come to her own party, why Mrs. Griffin wanted the ballroom done up, why she seemed so anxious to confess something to me, why I'd been given the white dress.

"What happened after that?"

"Sandy ran away for a while. Then she came back."

"She came *back*? Jesus, *why*?"

"It was what she knew. Life goes on. You would be surprised what people can learn to live with," Madi said, sounding defeated and bitter.

"God almighty," I said, reflecting on this. "Think how guilty Frances Griffin must feel. It must be intolerable for her."

"She'll survive," Madi said, curling his lip.

"I don't know. She certainly wants to assuage her guilt now."

"You think so?" he inquired, without real interest.

"Yes. I was trying to figure out why she wanted that ballroom all done up so she could relive a moment that never actually happened. I think you're right. I think she did know the truth all along and couldn't face it. By redoing the ballroom, maybe she's trying to redo the memory in some way," I suggested.

"I have no pity for her," Madi said.

"No? I do."

"Why? If you know something evil is happening, and you do nothing to stop it, then you become an accomplice, no? You are just as responsible," he said.

Madi grew more nervous, fidgeting with the objects on the table—the glasses, the salt and pepper shakers, the unlit candle.

"When we got married," he continued, "I made Sandy promise me she would never spend another night in the same house with her father. He was still madly jealous of her. I could see it because he was doing everything to end our marriage. He told people I had been in prison—which was a lie—that I had married Sandy for her money—which was a lie—that I planned to kill her—which was the biggest lie of all." Madi held up successive fingers for each item on the list. "I loved Sandy with all my heart and soul!" he cried, banging his hand on the table. "I have never loved another woman like that! And I never will!

That is why I was so upset last night. You do forgive me, don't you?"

I nodded. Madi smiled feebly, took a deep breath, then resumed.

"Holt was trying to have me deported, and thanks to his powerful friends, he might have succeeded. I told Sandy we could move to Italy and have a life away from America, but she wanted to live in the West, out here, in our house. Finally, she convinced me she had to go back and visit her father, to plead with him to stop all the persecution, to let us live in peace. But I would not let her go and see him alone."

As Madi spoke, I imagined the scene at The Haven that night. All the characters in the drama were clear in my mind, including the elusive Holt Griffin, who now stood out in terrifying relief.

"We went to the house for dinner," he began. "It was the four of us—Frances, Holt, Sandy and myself. I remember Holt very well that night. He was at his most charming, telling all kinds of stories about the war and his days in the diplomatic service. He was more reasonable with me than he had ever been. But I could not listen to him. I could not stand the sight of him, knowing what he had done to Sandy." Madi's intensity fascinated me. He hunched over and lowered his voice.

"After dinner, Sandy took me aside and said it would be better if I left the house so that she and her mother could persuade Holt to stop all the immigration nonsense against me. She knew that if I stayed there, I would do something we would both regret." Madi bit his lip. "That was the moment when I could have changed her destiny, and my own. I can see myself so clearly in that moment. I did not want to go, but Sandy convinced me it was for the best, that she could not reason with her father if I was there. I was such a fool. I listened to her. I left the house."

Madi rubbed his hands over his face, kneading it hard. He raked his fingers through his hair like he was trying to pull it out. I watched him squirm as he seemed to relive the terrible memory.

"I left her with the monster that night—as I had vowed I never would do," he continued. "The next morning I came back . . ." He paused for a long time, then whispered, "She was dead."

He stopped speaking and wiped his eyes with the napkin. I waited for him to compose himself.

"How did it happen?" I said, after a time.

"I believe that Holt came to her room in the middle of the night, to attack her again. When she tried to defend herself, he . . ." His voice trailed off. "Frances told me," he said, resuming a second later, "Frances *swore* to me that he did not kill her on purpose. She swore it was an accident, that the knife had been on a plate of fruit by Sandy's bed and that somehow, in the struggle . . ."

"Do you believe it was an accident?"

He shook his head.

"No."

"What do you believe?" I asked.

"I believe he did it on purpose," Madi said gravely. "He did not want anyone else to have her."

I thought about this for a moment.

"Roberto, why do you suppose Frances told you he did it? You weren't there. Why didn't they lie to you like they did to the police?"

"Because I knew too much," he said, as if it were obvious.

"I see. And when did Frances finally tell you the truth?"

"Two days later. When the police were beginning to suspect something."

"Were they beginning to suspect Holt?" I asked.

"I think so," Madi nodded. "But it was difficult for them. You must understand, Holt Griffin was a formidable figure, a friend of presidents and judges. Do you arrest such a man for the murder of his own daughter? What motive could he possibly have for such a crime? There was no motive—unless I told them what I knew."

"Right. And where was Holt during all this?"

"In his room, under sedation. I never saw him," Madi said.

"And Frances?"

"She was handling everything, as usual," he said bitterly. "At that moment, the most important thing was protecting the position of the family. She would have sacrificed everything for that, including justice for her daughter. And she did."

I sat across the table, staring at Madi as he finished his drink. I could see he was a beaten man.

"Roberto," I began gently, "you loved her. Why didn't you go to the police yourself? Why didn't you turn Holt in if you loathed him so much?"

Madi sighed and looked away. "Frances offered me money," he said. "The income for my life on five million dollars."

"What about Cassandra's money? You were entitled to that. Wasn't it enough?" I asked, trying not to be accusatory.

"Sandy's money was all in trust until she was thirty. On her death it went back into the estate. There was almost nothing for me," he replied frankly.

"So you sold her out."

"Yes," he said. "You know the thirty pieces of silver? Well . . . there you have it." He blinked back a tear.

There was something so pathetic about Roberto Madi in that moment that I didn't want to press him. Yet I was curious how he'd managed to reconcile the depth of his emotions with the tawdriness of his actions.

"And through the years, you never wanted to come forward?"

"Of course," he said, looking at me as if I were mad. "But I did not."

"Why not?"

"Because, I told myself that nothing I said could bring Sandy back to me. I told myself no one would believe me anyway. But the truth is . . . the truth is I had grown used to the money. I liked being rich."

"But you don't live like a rich man," I observed.

"No," he grimaced. "That is the joke."

"So you never told anyone the truth? In all this time? Not a single soul?"

"No one," he said solemnly. "You are the first."

"Why me?"

He hesitated. His voice changed to a more matter-of-fact tone.

"Because of my behavior last night. I feel badly. I don't know. You are so much like Sandy, and I realize my emotions are still very strong. Perhaps I thought a confession would make me feel better," he said.

"And do you feel better?"

"No." He smiled and shook his head.

We sat in silence for a long time. Gradually, I became more aware of the sounds of the restaurant—the other diners talking, the clinking of plates and glasses. A jukebox in the corner was playing a jangly country-western tune. My eggs finally came, but I wasn't hungry anymore. I took a couple of bites and pushed the plate away. I lit a cigarette.

"Imagine if people really knew the truth," I said.

"They would not believe it," he shrugged. "And if they did, they probably would not care."

We both smiled sadly.

"How did Holt Griffin die, I forget? A heart attack, wasn't it?"

"A heart attack?" Madi snickered. "Holt had no heart to attack."

"Isn't that what it said in the paper? Now I vaguely remember."

"Holt Griffin died of an overdose of drugs."

"You're kidding."

"The only thing I am not clear about is whether or not he did it on purpose." Madi said.

"You mean, he may have killed himself?" I said, stunned.

"Possibly. I suspect so. But you cannot tell with drugs."

Roberto Madi looked at me with a kind, but somewhat pitying expression.

"My dear Faith," he said, "when will you understand that nothing—*nothing*—is what they say?"

"Poor old Frances," I said. "What a life."

"She chose it," Madi snapped.

"Maybe. But she wants to confess everything now and absolve herself. I know she does."

"Confess what?" Madi said irritably. "That her husband was a monster? That her child was doomed from the beginning? That her whole life is nothing but ashes? She will never tell a soul the truth. She will never bring down the great name of Griffin. She has dedicated her life to being Mrs. Holt Griffin. It is the only thing she has. Her immortality depends on it, on him—even now."

"She wants me to know," I objected. "I know she does."

"Then you must ask yourself *why*," Madi said mysteriously.

"What do you mean?"

"Why would she want you to know? You do not find it strange?" he probed.

I thought for a moment. "She wants the release of a confession, like you," I offered. "She's old and sick. She doesn't want to die with it on her conscience. She needs to talk about it with someone."

"But why *you*?" Madi said. "She could confess it to a psychiatrist, or a priest."

"What are you getting at?"

"This Mr. Pitt," he went on, "you are close to him?"

"Yes, very," I replied. "Why?"

"Ask him then."

"Ask him what?"

"Talk with him," Madi urged.

"I fully intend to. But what do you mean, Roberto? What are you trying to tell me?"

He leaned back and folded his arms.

"I do not know," he said thoughtfully. "But there is something, I promise you."

He reached out for his pack of cigarettes, but none were left. He crumpled up the empty package into a little ball, tossing it on the table where it began to crackle open.

"Why did she pick you for this bizarre project of hers?" Madi continued. "Have you ever really thought about it?"

"Yes, as a matter of fact, I have. Look, I'm roughly the same age Cassandra would have been, a little younger. I'm an artist, which means that even though I'm outside Mrs. Griffin's world, I can understand and appreciate it. I think I remind her of Cassandra—"

Madi was shaking his head as I spoke.

"I doubt it," he said.

"Why? You said yourself I remind you of Cassandra."

"That is not the point." He waved his hand dismissively.

"What is?"

"I will tell you what I think," he said.

"Please do."

"I think there is a hidden reason for you to be in that house, and that you must find out that reason. You forget, Frances is very suspicious of people," Madi said. "She does not let them come into her life so easily."

I thought back to the early days when she'd had me followed and when I suspected she was spying on me.

"What reason could there be?" I asked, genuinely perplexed.

"I do not know," he replied. "As I said, it is strange. Tell me, how did she find you in the first place?"

"Well, she said she read an article I wrote on Veronese."

Madi let out a hoot. "Come now!"

"But she had read it," I protested. "We discussed it."

"That is no reason for her to take you into her life, believe me," Madi said.

"Oh, and I'd also done some work for a couple of people she knows," I recollected.

"So she had her secretary call you up?"

"No. I've never met her secretary. She just dropped by my studio one day, out of the blue."

"Herself?" Madi asked, narrowing his eyes.

"Yes."

"Unannounced?"

"Why, yes."

Madi began to laugh.

"You find that amusing?"

"I find it astonishing," he replied. "It is not like Frances to go anywhere without being announced. She is too insecure to do anything by herself. She is not a real aristocrat, you know. She married her position. She was not born into it. The ones who are not born into it are always too frightened to do anything by themselves. They need an army of secretaries and servants to deal with the world for them. They think by being removed from people, it makes them more grand."

"She's not like that," I said, defending her.

"I know her better than you do," Madi pointed out. "And besides, after Sandy died, Frances never left the house at all, for any reason."

"You don't know that," I said. "You haven't been in touch with her for years, have you?"

Once again, he hesitated.

"No."

"So, you see. Maybe she's changed," I said, wanting to prove my point.

"No one changes. Circumstances change, and then people appear to have changed," Madi observed. "Faith, believe me, I know Frances. She never does anything without a reason, an interior motive."

"Ulterior motive," I corrected him.

"Whatever."

"Roberto, what do you think she's up to?"

"I have no idea, but I suspect you will find out," Madi said ominously.

"But if it's not about Cassandra, what on earth could it be?"

"Faith, I like you very much." He reached across the table. I let him take my hand. "Whatever it is, I urge you to be careful."

"What about you, Roberto? If she finds out you told me about all this, you'll lose the money, won't you?"

"The money was never really mine because I never enjoyed it," he sighed. "I do not care who knows the truth now. Nothing matters to me anymore. Nothing at all. I am going away in a couple of days, and I do not know when I will be back."

"Where will you go?"

"Wherever," he said, gently tracing the tendons on the back of my hand with his finger. "It does not matter. I will try to find a place that feels different from all other places. But I do not think that will be easy. For me, everything is the same."

We sat in silence for a while, listening to the laughter of the nearby diners underscored by a lively jukebox tune. What an incongruous setting this was.

"Well, I should be going," I said, getting up from my chair. "Good-bye, Roberto."

He got up. We shook hands. He leaned over and gave me a kiss on the cheek.

"When we are young and strong and proud," he said in a faltering voice, "we all set out to do a great battle with life. Most of us lose, and no one really wins in the end. God bless you, Faith. And do not forget what I told you—be careful."

17

I left Broken Ridge that afternoon and took the next flight from Denver back to New York. The cabin was nearly empty. I had a row of seats all to myself. I closed my eyes and thought about Madi, about Cassandra, about the tape of them making love. Suddenly, like the brief cut of a horror film, an image of Cassandra being stabbed through the heart by her father flashed through my mind. I snapped open my eyes and lurched forward, stifling a cry.

There was no doubt that Madi had told me the truth. I had an image of him leaving the bar, hunched over and defeated, a sad man, far less potent than he'd first appeared to be. I thought about his admonition to be careful. Gradually, however, he receded in my thoughts as I began to concentrate more and more on Holt Griffin—the man of the world, the monster of private life.

Who was Holt Griffin? Was he really as charming, attractive, and erudite as people said? Surely, he must have been. How else could he have fooled everyone into thinking he was a person of great probity and honor? Or perhaps he was not as fine as people said he was, even on the surface. Perhaps people had made allowances for him because of what he seemed to represent. His position in the world was such that everyone wanted to believe the legend. And yet, there must have been some who

sensed the uncomfortable truth about him and who had declined to come forward either out of loyalty or fear, or the hope
that they would one day be included in his circle.

I wondered, had I met Holt Griffin, what I would have
thought of him. Would I have been seduced, like so many others, by his looks, his elegance, his knowledge, set against that
brilliant background of wealth and culture? Or would I have
somehow seen through to the core of the man? Would something, some telltale sign, some peculiarity in his expression or
his manner, have given away the evil twist in his heart? I liked
to think I would have recognized the man for what he really
was.

His actions had been evil. Of that there was no doubt. Yet
was he thoroughly evil, someone of no conscience whatsoever?
Or was he himself the victim of one direly misplaced passion?
Holt Griffin had died of an overdose of drugs, Madi said. I
wondered, as Madi did, whether he killed himself on purpose
or out of carelessness? Can such a person be forgiven?

I thought of Cassandra and the misery she must have en-
dured. I remembered a job I'd had once, working in a nineteenth-century dinosaur of a house in upstate New York where
I'd been contracted to touch up some murals. Over the gigantic
stone fireplace in the great hall was an inscription carved in
marble: WEALTH HATH NO SWAY. At the time, it had made me
chuckle. I could almost see the self-righteous robber baron
who'd commissioned it as a perverse atonement for the excesses
of his life, of which that fifty-room Queen Anne Revival house
was an egregious example. For some reason, I thought of this
in connection with Cassandra. It seemed to explain agony in
the midst of luxury: WEALTH HATH NO SWAY.

Finally, there was Frances Griffin. Only now did I begin to
fathom the depth of her guilt and the pain in her life. Who was
this strange old survivor, and what did she want from me? I
suspected Madi was right. There was some ulterior motive in
her having chosen me to paint the ballroom. But what?

The plane landed at eleven o'clock, New York time. I took
a taxi into the city and reached my apartment before midnight.

I called my upstairs neighbor, whom I knew to be a night owl. She came down to deliver Brush. He was happy to see me. I tried calling Harry, but there was no answer. I left a message on his machine to please call me the minute he got in, no matter what time it was. There was a strange message on my own answering machine from a Mrs. Edna Grubek. I called the number she'd left, which turned out to be the Howard Johnson's motor lodge on the west side. I asked for Mrs. Grubek, but she'd had her phone turned off for the night. I left my name and a brief message that I was returning her call. I thought it was most likely a wrong number.

I got into bed with some of the newspaper clippings I'd collected on the murder. Brush curled up alongside me as I went through them. I was only interested in the photographs this time, for I knew the articles themselves were mostly fiction. I lined up the pictures of Holt, Cassandra, and Frances, and stared at them for a while. The grainy image of Holt Griffin was in some ways the most interesting. I found it fascinating how completely he'd fooled the world into thinking he was a great gentleman. He certainly appeared the part, but his patrician good looks, clean and sharp, gleaming with achievement, now seemed to me as sinister as an unsheathed hunting knife.

Cassandra looked so pathetic to me now, like a scorched sunflower. She resembled her father more than her mother, which must have titillated the narcissist in him. I could see where he might have looked upon her as a younger, female version of himself and found her irresistible.

However, the photograph of Frances Griffin disturbed me most. I recognized her clear, cold gaze looking out at me from the youthful face in the newspaper. Her eyes hadn't changed with age. They were unsoftened, undimmed. They still wanted something.

I thought back to one of our early meetings, when Frances Griffin had said to me, "One day I'll need all your compassion." I remembered the phrase. It had struck me as odd at the time. I still wondered what she meant. Finally, overcome by fatigue,

I put the pictures aside, intending to close my eyes for just a moment.

When I woke up it was early the next morning. The clippings had all slipped to the floor and the light was still on. I got out of bed, anxious to get to The Haven as soon as possible. I heard the telephone ringing when I was in the shower. Hoping it was Harry, I ran out of the stall and grabbed the phone.

"Yes!" I panted, dripping wet.

"Hello, Miss Crowell?" said a woman with a midwestern accent on the other end of the line.

"Yes, who's this?"

"My name is Edna Grubek." Her voice was slow and deliberate.

"Oh yes. You called before."

"Yes." She hesitated. "I'm Harry's sister."

"Harry Pitt?"

"Well, yes," she said.

I felt a queasy feeling in my stomach. I knew something was wrong.

"Where is Harry? I've been trying to get in touch with him."

After a long pause she said, "I'm afraid Harry is no longer with us."

I was seized by dizziness. I sank down on the bed and clasped the sheet to my naked, wet body.

"What?" I heard myself say. "*What?*"

"Yes," she continued. "He passed away the day before yesterday in the morning. Heart attack. Bang—just like that."

"But I spoke to him—" I said, recalling my last conversation with Harry from the airport.

"Listen, my poor husband was talkin' to him on the phone when it happened. His dog died and he was real upset. If you ask me, I think that's what did it. I came in soon as I could get a flight. Now I'm here getting things sorted out. We're flying him back home to Cincinnati for the funeral. I just got rid of the dog."

She went on talking, but I didn't hear her. I just kept imagining Harry in front of me, hearing his voice. I couldn't believe I was never going to see him again.

"So, can you come over to Harry's apartment and pick it up?" I heard the woman say.

I had no idea what she was talking about.

"I said, can you come over to Harry's and pick it up?"

"I beg your pardon?"

"The picture."

"What picture?"

"The one he left you. The one I've just been telling you about. It's not too big."

"I'm sorry. I'm afraid I've lost track."

"That's okay, honey. You're upset. It's understandable. I'm upset too, even though Harry wasn't, well, you know, much a part of the family. Thing is, I'm leaving tomorrow morning first thing, and I hate carting this darn thing over back to the motel with me and leaving it down at the front desk."

"What . . . what is it?"

"I just told you, honey, it's this old picture Harry left for you. It's all crated up. You're the only one he left anything to, 'sides me and Joe, of course. Sorry it's such short notice, but could you come over and get it?"

"Where are you?"

"I'm over at Harry's. I'll be here all day packing things up."

"Packing things up?"

"Yup. Was here all yesterday, most of the night. My oh my, there's a lotta stuff."

I suddenly had a hilarious vision of Harry, dead, propped up on one of his silk pillows, staring glassy-eyed, as this incongruous-sounding relative packed his life away in plastic garbage bags in front of him.

"Where exactly is Harry?"

"Well," she plodded on in her twangy voice, "the remains are at the airport. I'm taking him back home with me. Joe and I thought it was the Christian thing to do, you know."

"I'll come over now."

I threw on some clothes and raced downstairs. I hailed a

taxi, got in, gave the driver Harry's address, and sat back on the torn, black seat. As the cab jerked along the streets, I squeezed my eyes shut, trying to remain calm. I arrived at Harry's building in a short time and took the elevator up to his apartment as I had done so many times in the past.

I rang the doorbell. An older woman wearing green-rimmed harlequin glasses and a tan polyester pantsuit opened the door. She was neat and pleasant-looking, with strong features and an aura of stocky good health about her. The thick lenses of her glasses made her brown eyes seem disproportionately large and slightly bulging. Her short, tightly-permed gray hair had a bluish tint to it. She was holding a sheaf of plastic bubble-wrap in one hand along with some masking tape.

"Hello, I'm Faith Crowell," I said.

"Edna Grubek. Come in, come in. Thanks for coming over. 'Scuse my appearance, won't you?" she said, smiling, patting her hair. "I've been sorting things out all day. My Lord in heaven, my brother has more stuff than a pack rat."

I couldn't believe this was a relation of Harry's, no less his own sister. Harry had never talked openly about his childhood, but sometimes he alluded to it in vague, derogatory ways. Early on in our friendship, I'd made a concerted effort to delve into his past. I asked him where he'd come from, how he'd grown up, who his parents were, if he had any sisters or brothers. The subject clearly pained him.

"Please," he said softly in the middle of my interrogation, "if you don't mind, it's not a time I care to think about."

In that moment, I saw all of Harry's apparent sophistication suddenly melt away, revealing the sad, lonely little boy that was his core. I never broached the subject again, and I learned to avoid making even the most casual inquiries into his prior history. He never volunteered anything. Throughout our friendship, however, I noticed he had a fascination with people who had managed to eradicate their pasts and become something else—Frances Griffin being a major case in point. He would speak about them in oddly contradictory ways, admiring them and denigrating them at the same time, as if he couldn't make up his mind how he felt about them. I suspected this was because he couldn't make up his mind how he felt about himself and his own self-invention.

So this was Harry's sister, I thought, as I followed her down the long corridor toward the living room. She appeared to be his opposite in every way, from her style of dress to her voice, down to her gestures, and the way she seemed to view the world. From the looks of it, her clothes had been chosen for function rather than fashion. I wondered how Harry would have reacted to her outfit, particularly the white shoes with green laces and the little handkerchief dripping from her breast pocket, patterned all over with ducks and guns. Also, Mrs. Grubek's ungrammatical twang was a far cry from Harry's clipped, faintly English accent. One or two comments she made about Harry's career led me to suspect she viewed art as little more than expensive wallpaper. ". . . All that fancy stuff he went broke on" was one of her more pointed references to Harry's career.

She might have sturdier values than the ones that guided Harry, but there was no question with whom I would have preferred to spend an evening. Harry was fun and had a profound appreciation of art and great craftsmanship. I doubted the same could be said of Edna Grubek. If they were from the same family, how on earth, I wondered, had Harry managed to transform himself so completely into the esthete he was?

Walking behind her, I recalled the many happy times I'd spent in that apartment. Just before entering the living room, I hung back for a moment, closed my eyes, and conjured up my favorite image of Harry, wearing a brocade dressing gown, cigarette smoke flaring from his nostrils, drinking red wine, holding court. Harry had designed the perfect stage set for his invented self. It was hard for me to believe that he was no more, and that his passing had little effect on the world beyond the dispersal of some goods.

I had quite a shock when I entered the room. The fabric had been torn away from the walls. The tented ceiling hung down in huge pieces of cloth, its tattered insides exposed. The chandelier was gone—only the chain remained. The furniture had been pushed into two piles on either side of the room. There were packing crates and boxes all around, some sealed up with masking tape, some with their contents bulging out. The carpets were rolled up, revealing a splintery, dried-out wooden floor underneath.

"Sorry 'bout the mess," Mrs. Grubek said. "Some people from the building came to see the apartment and they wanted to take a gander at what was back of all that junk on the walls. Good thing they did 'cause we discovered a leak. Now let me see, where did I put that darn crate? Lordy me, I had it right here."

I watched her as she rummaged around the room. The more I studied her, the more she reminded me of a thinner version of Harry. The closely set eyes, the large forehead, the mouth turned down at the corners giving a slightly hangdog look to her expression—all were diminished versions of Harry's fleshy features.

"Sure is a bitch getting all these loose ends tied up in no time," she said, apropos of nothing in particular. "Oh, here 'tis."

She pulled out a small crate from behind one of the round tables covered with a drop cloth, lifted it with some effort, and presented it to me.

"There you go."

"Thank you."

"We're selling most of this stuff. It should help a little."

"If you have a problem with funeral expenses or anything, I'd like very much to contribute if I may. Harry was very dear to me," I said.

"Oh, no thanks. We'll manage. Always have. But that's a kind offer. No, my Joe's a saint. He helped support Harry for the last couple of years even though, well, you know . . ."

"No. What?"

"Even though he didn't approve of Harry's, well, persuasion," she said, pursing her lips slightly.

I felt she was trying to be as tactful as possible. Nonetheless, I found myself rising instinctively to defend him.

"Persuasion," I said. "You mean that he was gay?"

She blushed.

"Oh listen, dearie, when it's up to me, I say live and let live," she said apologetically.

I could see she meant well. I smiled at her and nodded. She seemed relieved.

"Anyway," she continued, "if you want to come out to the funeral, we're having it the day after tomorrow in Cincinnati. You're more than welcome."

Part of me wanted to see Harry properly laid to rest. Another part wanted to attend simply out of curiosity. But I decided I was better off not going. I very much wanted to remember Harry the way I'd always known him, the way he'd presented himself, the way he wanted to be remembered. I had the sense that were I to go out and unearth the roots he'd spent a lifetime burying, I would somehow be disloyal to his memory.

"That's very nice of you," I replied, "but I don't think I can."

She shrugged as if to say, "suit yourself," and started to walk out of the room. I followed her, carrying the crate. It wasn't heavy, but quite bulky. Mrs. Grubek opened the front door. She offered to help me downstairs with it but I declined.

"Good-bye," I said. "Forgive me for not shaking hands."

"Good-bye, Faith. Thanks for coming over. Saved me a trip."

"Thank you. God bless Harry."

"Amen."

We looked at each other for a brief moment. Then she closed the door.

On the way home in the taxi, clutching the crate, I thought about Harry, and about death. Harry was still there for me in my imagination, more vivid than ever in some ways, now that I knew I was never going to see him again. Yet, at the same time, he was gone forever. It was as if some part of my life had come to a halt when I wasn't looking. I'd moved on, suspecting nothing, expecting to turn around and see my friend at my side the next moment. And then he wasn't there. He had stopped, and I had gone on. Was death that simple?

When I got home, I put the crate on the kitchen table and examined it more carefully. The lid had been opened and nailed shut again. I pried it open gently with the claw of a hammer. Brush sat on a chair and looked on as I took the wooden cover off the box. The picture was small, measuring about a foot by a foot and a half, wrapped in newspaper, nestled in a pile of excelsior. I lifted it up out of its packing with the utmost care. Bits of the excelsior floated to the floor. While Brush jumped down from his perch to play with them, I carried the still-wrapped picture into the living room and placed it on the couch. I felt certain that Harry had left me some kind of message.

I tore back the newspaper slowly, not wanting to look too closely at the painting until the whole of it had been revealed. Having stripped all the newspaper away, I stepped back and stared at the picture for a long time. It was an old-master portrait of a mother and child. The mother, wearing a sumptuous brocade dress, encrusted with pearls and jewels, was seated on a green velvet divan dandling a rather plain-looking little girl on her knee. The little girl, simply dressed in white silk, was holding out a flower to her mother. The frame was hand-carved and gilded.

The more I looked at this charming, innocent pair, the more I began to see how very odd they were. Everything about them seemed slightly off-kilter, as if the artist had meant for this vision of apparent wealth and familial piety to somehow disconcert the viewer.

When I stepped up to inspect the canvas more closely, I saw that both the mother and the little girl were composed of a conglomeration of seashells made to look like parts of the body. Every aspect of their respective anatomies—eyes, nose, mouth, hair, hands—was a different shell, brilliantly chosen, exquisitely painted, and artfully arranged to assume human form. It was one of the most remarkable trompe l'oeil works I'd ever seen. I doubted there was another like it.

There was no signature on the canvas. I turned the picture over to see if there might be some indication of the painter or a date on the reverse side. The slatted wooden back had only one thing on it—a yellowing label with something written on it in faded brown ink. I took it to the desk and examined it closely under the lamplight. It read: "Property of Harry Pitofsky, Jan. 1976." Harry Pitofsky. Harry Pitt.

I went back into the kitchen, where Brush was still chasing pieces of excelsior around the floor. I rummaged through the packing to see if there was a note from Harry. There was none. I couldn't imagine what he meant by leaving me this painting, except that it was an exquisite work of trompe l'oeil which he knew I'd appreciate. The mother-daughter theme seemed a bit strange, given that my mother was dead and that I had no children of my own. But Harry obviously had his reasons.

That night, as I lay in bed, the painting propped up on my bureau so I could look at the shell people, I thought about the fragility of existence. I thought about Harry, about my vanished family, about Cassandra, the Griffins, and the loss of love in life, and finally allowed myself to weep.

CHAPTER 18

I stayed inside my apartment for the next few days, lost in the lassitude of grief. I ordered my meals in from take-out places in the neighborhood, browsed through old art books, watched television, read some, and slept a lot. Brush stayed closer to me than usual, perhaps sensing I needed his companionship more than ever. At times I felt Harry's spirit hovering around me. I talked to him out loud, reminiscing, telling him how much I missed him. I stared for long periods of time at the curious painting he'd left me, trying to decipher the message, if there was one. I thought about the ballroom—how I was going to finish it, and when. My desire to see Frances Griffin and confront her had waned in the wake of Harry's death.

One evening, a week later, when I was toying with the idea of going back out to The Haven to finish my job, the phone rang. Instead of letting it ring and having my answering machine pick up, as I'd done for the past few days, I answered it myself.

"Hello?" I said tentatively.

"Faith, it's Frances Griffin."

I sat up.

"Mrs. Griffin, I was just thinking about you. How are you?"

"I've missed you, Faith. When are you coming back to me?"

"Well, I thought I'd come out tomorrow," I said, feeling this was something I wanted to get over with as soon as possible. "I still have some work left to do."

"Yes. And we have a great deal to talk about. I look forward to seeing you." She hung up.

I got up so early the next morning that even Brush had a difficult time rousing himself to have breakfast with me. I was on the road by seven-thirty.

It was a cold, dreary day, pale and monochromatic. A light rain turned into a fine drizzle, then stopped. Gray clouds rolled over the horizon. I sped along the highway, thinking about the first time I'd driven out to The Haven last spring. The vibrant colors of that day had intensified my excitement at the prospect of working for Frances Griffin. Now, as I approached it, I saw no beauty left in the house or its grounds. It looked more like an asylum rotting in the middle of a geometric wasteland. The woman who lived there was no longer a queen, but a lonely old invalid whose life had been a model of deceit and tragedy.

I pulled into the courtyard and got out of the car. The cobblestones were still slippery from the rain. Deane opened the door as if he'd been expecting me. He mentioned nothing about my having been away, nor did he offer any word of welcome.

"Mrs. Griffin is in the ballroom," he said flatly.

I wondered how she knew what time I'd be arriving.

Deane showed me through the house but did not accompany me the rest of the way. He opened one of the French doors in the living room and waved his hand in the direction of the ballroom. His manner was as chilly as the weather.

I stepped outside and walked across the garden. The country dampness crept into my bones. The grounds seemed smaller without foliage to lend them perspective. I passed by the wisteria arbor, whose tangled vines looked like petrified snakes weaving in and out of the trellises. The bright flower beds were gone. In their place, tidy patches of brown earth marked the withered grass.

The steps leading up to the ballroom were as slippery as the cobblestones. Once inside, I saw Mrs. Griffin sitting by herself in her wheelchair in the middle of the floor, a fur blanket tucked around her legs. She turned toward me as I came in.

"Oh, Faith—" she said, "you're here . . ."

As I walked down the steps, I glanced around at the completed murals. Whether or not I'd managed to create a work of art was a judgment better left to posterity, but I believed, at the very least, I'd done the job I was commissioned to do. I'd made the room come alive. I almost expected to hear soft strains of music and muted conversations. I was struck once again by the haunting figure of the faceless girl in the white dress occupying the center panel. She anchored the scene beautifully, easily holding her own as the centerpiece of the ball. The only thing left for me to do was to paint in her face.

Mrs. Griffin now seemed to embody all the sadness I was feeling about life at the moment. Her wig sat so low on her brow it looked like a hat. Her makeup was a little too heavy and a few razor-thin lipstick lines pricked the outline of her mouth. I didn't hate her or feel particularly sorry for her. But I still felt she was up to something, and I'd run out of patience with her game, whatever it was.

"Mrs. Griffin, why did you choose me to paint this room? Why am I really here? I would like to know."

She flinched slightly.

"What do you mean?" she said.

"I mean why me, of all people?"

"I told you—I admired your work."

"No, that's not it."

"Why, yes it is," she replied.

"No!" I cried, hearing my voice ricochet around the empty room. "That's not the reason!"

She looked at me sheepishly.

"What is?" she said, like a child.

"I don't know, but I'll tell you what I think."

"Go ahead—"

"You didn't choose me to paint this ballroom. You chose this ballroom because I could paint it."

A dark smile passed across her face like a fleeting shadow. She took a deep breath. I knew I'd hit my mark.

"You wanted me here for some reason," I said. "If I'd been a plumber, you'd have had me out here to fix a sink."

She laughed nervously.

"I'm serious," I went on. "It wasn't my work you wanted, it was me." I paused. "Am I wrong?"

Her body stiffened, then relaxed suddenly. She let go a sigh of relief.

"No," she said at last. "You're not wrong."

I stood over her, nodding like the victor I imagined myself to be.

"Then why, Mrs. Griffin? Why me?"

She looked up at me with a new softness in her expression. She beckoned me to come sit by her.

"Please, pull up that chair," she said.

I positioned my sketching chair close to her and sat down. She smelled strongly of perfume, yet, once again, I detected a stale, off-putting aroma underneath.

"Are you warm enough?" she asked.

"I'm fine, thank you," I replied brusquely.

"Calm down," she said, patting my hand.

I felt tense and tried to relax.

"I'm sorry, Mrs. Griffin. I'm just upset. I'm upset about a lot of things. A lot of things don't make sense. And there are other reasons—personal reasons I won't bore you with."

"What reasons? We must be honest with each other now."

Her manner was gentle and conciliatory.

"Well, the truth is, a really close friend of mine's just died and"—I felt my eyes beginning to brim with tears—"and I just feel very, very low at the moment."

I was trying hard not to cry.

"Poor old Harry," I heard Mrs. Griffin say.

I looked up.

A shock went through me.

"What did you say?"

"I said poor old Harry."

"Did you *know* Harry?" I asked.

"Oh yes." She looked at me pointedly.

I shivered slightly.

"Wait—Harry Pitt—the antique dealer?"

"Yes, dear. Harry Pitt. Harry was a very old friend of mine. Here, take this."

She pulled out a lace handkerchief hidden in the cuff of her sleeve and handed it to me. I declined it, extracting a tissue from my pocket instead.

"An old friend?" I said, dabbing my eyes. "Harry told me he'd only met you once or twice years ago, very briefly. That you bought a commode from his shop and then asked him to get some things for you at auction."

"Yes," she said, hesitating. "Well, you see, that's what I told him to say."

I could feel the blood rushing to my head.

"You *told* him?"

"Yes, my dear. Oh my, my," she said, wringing her hands together. "I thought surely you would have guessed by now."

"Guessed?" I said, staring at her in amazement. "Guessed *what?*"

"That we know, *knew* one another, Harry and I."

"No," I heard myself stammering. "I-I didn't guess."

"Perhaps that's just as well," she sighed. "You're not suspicious. That's good. But, you see, Harry and I go back a very long time. He's been my best friend in many ways, as he was yours. I shall miss him more than I can say." She smiled sadly.

I shook my head from side to side, not believing what I was hearing.

"What are you talking about, Mrs. Griffin? What are you saying?"

"My dear, this shouldn't alarm you so. I see you're becoming very agitated, but there's no reason."

"But why wouldn't Harry have said something? When I asked him about coming to work for you, all he said was that I should do it. He never said he knew you. In fact, he was always asking me about you, as if you fascinated him."

"He was asking you about me to find out what you thought of me."

"I'm very confused, Mrs. Griffin. I want to know what's going on," I demanded.

"Yes, dear, I understand that, and I'm going to tell you the truth now," she said in a measured voice. "Harry did know me. He knew me well. I met Harry Pitt just after Holt and I were married. What he told you is true—I did walk into his shop and buy a commode from him. I could see from the things he had there that he had an extraordinary eye, so I asked him if he would deal privately for me, without anyone knowing. In fact, Harry was responsible for some of the greatest acquisitions of my life."

I shot up from my chair.

"Why didn't he tell me?" I cried.

"Oh, it was essential our relationship remain absolutely secret so that when he bid for things or purchased them from other dealers, they wouldn't know he was acting on my behalf. Otherwise the prices would have gone up or they might have used my name somehow. You know how people are. And anyway, I don't like people knowing too much about me or the things I acquire. It's none of their business."

I felt as if the ground was shifting under me.

"So . . . Harry knew your husband?"

"Yes, of course. Though Holt never had much use for him. Holt didn't like gay men. They threatened him."

"And Cassandra?" I said, knowing the answer already.

"He adored her. She used to call him Uncle Harry whenever he came àround. I would have made him her godfather, but Holt objected. And, anyway, it would have given our relationship away."

She blinked twice, innocently. I began pacing around the room.

"Why did he lie to me? Why?"

"I'm afraid that was my fault, Faith dear," Mrs. Griffin said, following me with her eyes. "I thought you'd be shy about coming here if you knew the whole truth all at once. Harry and I discussed it endlessly, and we agreed that it would be better to let you find things out for yourself. That way you could come to a gradual understanding."

"Understanding? Of what?"

"Of me, of course. You remember when I said to you one day I'd need all your compassion. Well, you see, now I do."

I whirled around, glaring at her.

"Why?!"

She lowered her eyes.

"If you are to love me as a daughter, you must understand me, and forgive me."

"Love you as a daughter?" I said, mystified.

"As you know too well, my own daughter died. And I feel somewhat responsible. But I can't help that. That's in the past. And now I want a daughter, you see. Another one, to replace the one I lost. I need one. I need you."

I was speechless. I let her go on.

"A couple of years after Holt died and I was all alone, Harry convinced me that I should think of adopting a child. Do come and sit by me, please."

"I prefer to stand, thank you."

"You think I'm the wickedest woman who ever lived, don't you?" she said, theatrically.

"No, Mrs. Griffin. I don't know what to think."

"Please, come . . ." she said, indicating the chair next to her.

I walked over and sat down beside her once more.

"I told Harry I was too old to adopt a child. He explained to me that he didn't mean an infant. He meant an adult. Of course, finding someone—the perfect person—was a problem. But then, finding the perfect anything is a problem, I'm sure you'll agree."

I nodded, too riveted to speak.

"Roberto Madi," she said, changing her tone of voice. "Tell me what you thought of him?"

My God, Madi—I'd nearly forgotten all about him.

"You know I went to Colorado?" I said.

"Know, my dear? I *sent* you there."

"You sent me?"

"Well, it wasn't that difficult because you were so curious. All Harry had to do was push you a little. He called me when his little dog died. He was very upset he couldn't go with you. He was worried, he really was. In fact, the very last conversation I had with him was about that."

"I see."

"I assured him Roberto was completely harmless and that he would do as he was told. But Harry was a worrier. Tell me," she asked, "didn't you find it strange that Harry located Madi so easily, and that Madi was suddenly willing to talk after all these years?"

I thought back on it as she pointed it out. Of course, it seemed ludicrous. I was angered by my own gullibility.

"I guess not," I sighed.

"Never mind, you're just like Cassa. Sophisticated in some ways, ingenuous in others. It's charming. As I told you, you're not suspicious by nature, which is good. Suspicious people always wind up alone."

"Please go on."

"I spoke to Roberto after your visit to his house," she continued. "He told me a little bit about what happened. You shouldn't have left like that. It can be very dangerous out there alone at night."

"I was frightened," I said.

"I don't blame you. I was very annoyed with him for showing you the police photo. Of course, then he started accusing me of things, as usual, saying I was responsible for sending you there in the first place. The old litany—everything's my fault," she said, sounding annoyed.

"Did you tell him to show me the movies?" I inquired.

"I don't know anything about any movies, and I don't want to know," she snapped. "But I told him to tell you the truth about what happened. About Holt and everything. You understand now why I could never have told you those things myself."

"Yes, I do."

"Roberto's very emotional. He carries on so. But don't let that fool you. He's also very practical," she said with contempt. "Why do you think he's kept his mouth shut all these years?"

I shook my head.

"Because I'd have cut him off in an instant if he'd told anyone. And no matter what he says about not caring about money, I assure you he wouldn't have liked that," she said.

"No, I suppose not."

"Anyway, to get back to what I was saying, he couldn't get over the resemblance between you and Cassa. You know, I think he was quite taken with you. Even though I don't like him and I know the feeling is mutual, I'll always have a soft spot in my heart for him because he loved Cassa so dearly. I instructed him to tell you everything. I thought it would be better coming from a third person, though I'm sorry he got a bit carried away."

"You instructed him?" I was still trying to get this all straight.

"Don't you see, Faith, it's a measure of my love and trust for you that you've been permitted to learn these things? These are things that no one else in the world knows, except for myself, Roberto, Harry—and now you. Dear Harry's gone. That leaves only us three, and Roberto doesn't really count."

I glanced at her gnarled fingers weaving in and out of the fur of her blanket. She was looking around at the walls. Her skin was translucent in the flat winter light.

"You're almost finished here, I see," she said.

"Mrs. Griffin, why on earth have you gone to all this trouble?" I asked.

"Because I don't want anything fake or second-rate in my life. I only want real things, the best things . . . So," she continued brightly, "just the face of the girl left to paint."

"Tell me something—"

"Anything," she replied eagerly.

"If Harry knew you long before he knew me, was he the one who told you about me?"

She looked at me with a puzzled expression.

"What do you mean?" she asked.

"I mean was it my article on Veronese or your other friends or Harry who told you about me?"

"It was Harry, of course. He gave me your article."

"So you knew about me long before I knew anything about you?" I said.

"Why yes, my dear," she replied in a sympathetic tone. "But I don't think you quite understand."

"What do you mean?"

"Harry became friends with you *because* of me. He *found* you for me."

"*Found* me for you?" I couldn't imagine what she was talking about.

"Faith, Harry adored you. Please don't ever think he didn't. But he'd been looking for you for a very long time, and when he met you, he knew that you were the one."

"The one?" I repeated.

"You were the perfect one to replace Cassa," she said matter-of-factly. "He'd heard about you, you see," she went on. "And you fit the bill perfectly. First of all, you were around the age Cassa would have been had she lived. You were alone in the world. You were an artist with a great sensibility and an appreciation of beauty, which is so important to me. It all seemed right, so Harry arranged to meet you. I believe some mutual friends brought you to his apartment years ago, did they not?"

"Yes," I whispered.

"He told me he couldn't believe it when you walked in the door that night!" Mrs. Griffin said jubilantly. "He called me up right after you'd left, going on and on about how much you reminded him of Cassa. He was so excited. He said the resemblance, the demeanor, the enthusiasm—everything was uncanny. He was beside himself with delight. And then as he got to know you, he grew to genuinely love you. He told me you could have been Cassa's sister you were so like her—including your attachment to difficult and unworthy men, such as Mr. Noland."

"You know about John too?" I said, absolutely stunned.

"I made it my business to know everything there was to know about you, dear," she said in a kindly way, as though there was nothing odd about this. "Harry and I used to joke that you were so much like my daughter, you might have been an illegitimate child of Holt's," she giggled. "It was all too perfect, like the will of God, don't you see?"

"Tell me something," I said, trying hard to digest the notion that Harry had initially befriended me in order to "acquire" me for Mrs. Griffin. "Why did you wait so long to meet me? I met Harry over thirteen years ago."

"Well, to be perfectly honest with you, Faith, dear, there was one other young woman we were considering."

I swallowed hard.

"You're kidding!" I said.

"Harry knew she wasn't right." "But she was a little less independent than you are, and at first I felt she might be more amenable to the task."

"So what made you decide on me?" I asked politely.

"Time," she said, smiling. "We watched the two of you over a period of years. For that matter, Harry took a cursory look at some others as well, but they wouldn't do at all. You see, we had to be sure that our final choice was the sort of person who could appreciate all this—" she gestured in the direction of the house, "and handle it correctly when the time comes. It became clear to both of us that this other young woman—who shall be nameless—was not equipped in the way you are to take on such a position in life. Oh, she was a sweet enough girl, but ultimately unsatisfactory for reasons I won't go into. You, on the other hand, have all the prerequisites, Faith. Harry observed your character year in and year out, and he and I both concluded that you were perfectly suited for this . . . place."

"I see," I said, nodding.

"Faith, I'm old and rich and dying," she went on, without

apparent emotion. "I've lived a sinful life for which I need to atone. Some time ago, I thought that if I could make things up to Cassa, I'd be forgiven in God's eyes—perhaps even in my own. But that's impossible, because Cassa's dead. I need to make things up to someone in my old age," she said, staring at me intently, her eyes looking bluer and colder.

"I need a companion whom I can love and trust—not a *paid* companion, of course," she said with distaste. "A paid companion is a fake, and I only like real things, as you know. I need a child—a daughter—someone who will love me and find it in her heart to forgive me and accept me as I am, even knowing everything about me."

I let her take hold of my hand.

"That first day I came to see you in your studio, I knew Harry had found you for me. I knew you were the one. In fact, I wanted to tell you right then and there."

"Why didn't you?"

"I don't know. Well, I suppose I had to get to know you, to see if I liked you," she said, as if this made perfect sense.

"To see if you liked me?" The thought amused me.

"Well, I loved you right away, because you reminded me so much of Cassa, but I didn't know if I was going to *like* you. You see the difference, don't you? I must confess, I didn't like Cassa very much, though I loved her deeply. If I hadn't liked you, I wouldn't have chosen you, because I think when one is acquiring something as important as this, one should get exactly what one wants."

"Oh. Yes, I can see that you would feel that way," I said.

"Everything must be exactly right in this kind of delicate matter. Otherwise the thing has little value."

I knew she was using the word *right* in the way that curators and dealers use it, to describe the authenticity of a piece of furniture.

"And if I hadn't been *right*," I said, emphasizing the word, "what would Harry have done? Looked for someone else?"

"No," she said, leaning back in her chair. "We agreed I was

getting too old for him to start the search all over again. It's such a long process. If you hadn't worked out, I'd have given up the idea entirely. But, you see," she went on, oblivious to my growing amazement, "I do like you, *and* I love you, Faith. And I know you and I will be very happy together in the time I have left."

She paused as if she were waiting for me to return the compliment.

"Mrs. Griffin," I said, clearing my throat, "what exactly is it that you want from me?"

She glanced at the faceless young woman in the mural, then looked back at me.

"Faith, you are to be the most important acquisition of my life. You are to become my daughter."

I recalled the trompe l'oeil painting of the mother and child Harry had left me. There it was: the message from the grave.

"What does that mean?" I asked her.

"Well, it means you'll come and live here, that all that I have will be yours one day. That you will forgive me and take care of me until I die."

"Forgive you? For what, Mrs. Griffin?"

"For Cassa . . . for all my sins . . . Think how I felt all those years, Faith," she said softly. "Think how I felt."

I suddenly had a vision of this woman sitting alone in her bedroom, paralyzed with fear and denial while her ghastly husband abused her daughter nearby. Mrs. Griffin must have known, I thought. They all must have lived in a hellish symbiosis with one another, locked into that terrifying secret, unable to confront it, unwilling to break the pattern.

"I'll atone through you," Mrs. Griffin went on, sounding hopeful, "by doing everything for you that I should have done—that I wanted to do—for her."

"Do you honestly think you can atone for your daughter's death through me?"

"I . . ." she stammered, "I hope so. I'm hoping it will make some difference in how I feel. I feel so badly now." She coughed away the catch in her throat. "Oh dear, oh dear," she said, shaking her head. "These moments are never what one imagines they'll be, are they? Prick them and they burst—all empty."

"Just out of interest, Mrs. Griffin," I said, purposely ignoring the melodrama of the moment, "was Harry supposed to get a commission on me?"

"Seven hundred and fifty thousand dollars," she said simply, "upon my signing the adoption papers."

My eyes widened in disbelief.

"Oh, Faith, you mustn't be too hard on Harry," she pleaded. "He was a dealer, after all, and acquisitions were his business. I know he needed the money, but that aspect of it had nothing to do with his feelings about you. He'd come to love you very much, and I know he thought he was doing you as much of a favor as he was doing me."

"I'm sure he did," I said, trying to hide the skepticism in my voice.

"As Frances Griffin's daughter, the world will be yours," she said grandly. "Look around you, my dear. You'll inherit all this one day."

I knew what she meant, but all I could see were the painted figures on the walls, and the faceless portrait of a girl who'd been abused and murdered by her own father.

"All this," I repeated dully.

"I know it must be a shock to you," she said.

"Yes, it is."

"But is it so wrong for me to want a daughter for the final part of my life, Faith? Is it? Is it so wrong to want you?" she said plaintively.

"No, it's not wrong," I said, feeling completely defeated by the truth. "It's just sad."

"Sad? Why sad?"

"I don't know. I guess because it shows how lonely people can be, that's all."

"Yes, how true. The human condition, loneliness. And yet now, two lonely people have found each other and can give each other comfort. Hmm? Don't you think?"

"I don't know."

"Well, I do," she said briskly. "And since I'm older than you, and wiser, you must trust my judgment. The sooner we get all this settled, the better. My lawyers have prepared the papers. Once you agree, we'll petition the court. It shouldn't take too much time after that. Meanwhile, I'll have Deane help you move out of your apartment. You can keep whatever you like from it, of course. We'll put it all somewhere. You'll move out here with me. You can have your choice of rooms. The ballroom can be your studio. Later this year, provided I'm well enough, we'll take a trip somewhere—wherever you like—Europe, South America. I'll buy you anything you want. We'll have such fun, looking for wonderful furniture and paintings together. I'll introduce you to everyone as my daughter—my daughter, Faith Griffin."

She patted my hand, beaming at me. I didn't know what to say.

"How does that sound, hmm?" she pressed.

"Forgive me, Mrs. Griffin, I just, um . . . I have to think about it."

She frowned.

"What is there to think about?"

"There's quite a lot actually. Please, I need some time."

She looked genuinely astonished.

"But why? Your own mother's dead. You're alone in the world, like I am. Look what I'm offering you, Faith. And," she added, as if it were the final flourish to the bargain, "I don't have long to live."

"Please, Mrs. Griffin, I must think about it."

"All right then," she said. "Give me your answer tomorrow."

CHAPTER 19

That night, alone in my little apartment, I sat on the bed, stroking Brush, mulling over the events of the past few days. I still couldn't quite believe that Harry, whom I'd loved and trusted all those years, had always been working secretly for Mrs. Griffin, that his friendship with me had been predicated on an elaborate scheme. I thought back on many of the moments and confidences we'd shared, wondering if they'd been genuine, or if Harry had cultivated our relationship with an eye to his commission.

Seven hundred and fifty thousand dollars . . . The figure seemed absurd and arbitrary, making me overpriced and undervalued at the same time. Three quarters of a million dollars for a surrogate daughter. I wondered how on earth they'd arrived at that particular figure. How much negotiation had been involved? Was it a flat fee or a percentage of the amount they thought a daughter was worth? Would the sum have been different for the other woman had she been picked? Was she worth a million, or, perhaps, only six hundred thousand? It was so strange. I wondered briefly if poor old Harry had collected any of the money in advance to pay for expenses. No wonder he'd entertained me so well over the years, I thought somewhat bitterly. After all, I was an investment.

Now lots of little things began to make sense. The gift of the dress, Harry's subtle urging that I accept Mrs. Griffin's commission, his resourcefulness in finding Madi, his insistence I go out to Colorado to see him, not to mention the fortune cookie from Foo's. And Rodney? Had all that business about Rodney been a sham? Harry knew full well I had a soft spot in my heart for romance and would have encouraged him to use my interest in finding Madi as a ploy to contact his old lover. Naturally, I'd never expected him to produce any results, but when he did, it seemed too fortuitous a coincidence not to act on. Now, however, it was obvious that Rodney had nothing to do with it. Harry had invented the whole story, following Mrs. Griffin's instructions to make uncovering the whereabouts of Madi look plausible.

My mind drifted back to the early days of our friendship when I'd confided to Harry on an almost daily basis about my trials with John Noland. I remembered how we discussed my difficult childhood, how Harry had managed to pry out the innermost secrets of my heart. He'd made himself available to me at all hours to talk about my problems. He must have been comparing me to Cassandra every step of the way and reporting back to Mrs. Griffin. The miracle was that I never once suspected any motive on his part other than kindness.

Try as I might, I couldn't bring myself to hate Harry for what he'd done. I didn't feel betrayed so much as I felt let down by him. I wondered, had he lived, would he eventually have told me of his involvement with Mrs. Griffin? Or was this a secret they would have kept between themselves forever?

Every aspect of our friendship now seemed tainted by my knowledge that it had started under false pretenses. Yet, I was certain that Harry had loved me and been a genuine friend. I kept reminding myself of what Mrs. Griffin had said: that he believed he was doing me a great favor by arranging my adoption by one of the richest and most elegant women in the world.

Other thoughts crossed my mind as I made myself and

Brush some dinner. I wondered if Roberto Madi had known all along about Mrs. Griffin's plan. I suspected not, for it was he who warned me to be careful, that she was up to something, and I should be on my guard. I decided that Madi had simply done what he'd been told to do and gotten carried away in the process, reliving old memories. I wondered where he was now. Had he really left to go around the world, or was that a ruse as well, to get me out there on their timetable?

I had no appetite. Brush licked some of the scraps off my plate and seemed surprised when I didn't shoo him away. I poured myself a glass of wine, lit a fire, set to contemplate the biggest decision of my life.

All that money, all those beautiful things . . . I could see pieces of gold dancing in the flames. The paintings alone were enough to make me think of selling my soul . . . And what was her price? Not that much. A couple of years—maybe less—with a woman I mistrusted, true, but mainly felt sorry for, and might possibly grow fond of. Would it be such a terrible life being her companion? She'd pamper me, confess her sins, confide her fears and longings. And in return, I'd live at The Haven in the lap of luxury with my own studio, under no pressure to make a living. I'd comfort her in her last days and try to grow to love and understand her as a daughter. Then, afterward—of course I'd always be waiting for the afterward—I'd be rich. What a life I could lead! Buy anything I desired, help other artists, travel everywhere, live surrounded by treasures, never having to worry about money or security again. All very tempting. Yes, I thought, why not? What were a couple of years compared to all that privilege and ease of mind, not to mention the good I could do?

I thought of my own dear mother and wondered if she'd approve? Yes, I thought, of course she would. She'd encourage me to do it. She'd always wanted the best for me, and Frances Griffin was indisputably the best of a certain tradition. It was not a question of Frances taking Mother's place in my heart. It was simply a matter of expediency, of opportunity, of luck.

"Do you want to be filthy rich, Brush? Hmm?" I said to the little cat, curled up by my shoe in front of the fire.

I began to look around my apartment, mentally going over the things I'd discard, the things I'd keep. The little brass hourglass Harry had given me for Christmas—I'd keep that. I'd keep all the things Harry had given me. My shabby couch—would I keep that? It was so comfortable. No, I suppose that could go. My needlepoint samplers, my botanical prints, the quirky little Victorian chairs with the tattered fringe, my dog's-head andirons, the coal scuttle I used for dried flowers, the books I'd collected over the years . . . They weren't things of much value, but . . . I caught myself before I finished the thought. Was I falling into Mrs. Griffin's trap? Was I too dependent upon the possessions I'd accumulated? Why not just walk out clean and unencumbered?

But as I looked around more and more, I realized just how fond I was of my little nest and how sorry I'd be to leave it. Small and insular as my life was, it was the life I'd chosen and fashioned for myself. I felt an allegiance to it. It gave me a sense of dignity. I thought of my trompe l'oeil business and the good reputation I'd built up over the years . . . Over the years . . . I began to think about time and feel its passing as I'd never quite felt it before.

The flames in the fireplace died down while the clock on the mantel counted off seconds in barely audible ticks. I followed Brush's soft, rhythmic breathing, watching his little stomach gently rise and fall over and over again. I looked at the backs of my hands. The veins were more pronounced, the skin more wrinkled. There were strands of gray in my hair. The slackness around my eyes and mouth was more obvious. My face had lost the careless strength of youth. I found myself tiring more easily. A good night's sleep didn't resuscitate me like it used to. I needed glasses for reading, and my digestion had started rebelling against the occasional overindulgence.

The fruit was just about to turn overripe—but not quite yet. I was in the middle of my life, where time is the most valuable capital. Who knows? I might still meet the love of my life . . . Or develop into a great artist. There were so many possibilities. In that moment, I realized I couldn't afford to squander even a minute by putting my life on hold to bind myself to Frances Griffin as a supporting player in her sad drama.

The following morning, I drove out to The Haven. Mrs. Griffin received me in the conservatory, a large glass-enclosed room filled with potted plants and Indian and Victorian porch furniture. She was wearing a red silk dress and a colorful chiffon scarf. She looked pretty, rejuvenated in fact, as young and vital as the first day I'd met her. The moment I entered the room, she danced up to me like a young girl and threw her arms around me.

"Oh Faith, Faith!" she cried. "I'm so happy to see you! Now that you've had your little think, have you come to your senses?"

"Yes, I think I have."

"Good."

She looked quizzically into my eyes, sensing perhaps what I was about to tell her.

"Why so serious?" she asked. "I hope you've thought about all the fun we're going to have. I've been making plans all night. I can't wait to show you my world and all the things I loved when I was young. I'm going to indulge you, you know."

"Mrs. Griffin," I began hesitantly, trying to choose my words carefully, "I've given the matter a great deal of thought, and, well, even though I'm very flattered by your offer, I don't feel I can accept it."

She appeared uncomprehending.

"I beg your pardon?"

"I'm afraid I'm going to have to decline."

She released me and backed away.

"You're joking."

"I'm afraid not."

There was a slight pause, then she cried: "Don't be absurd!"

"I'm sorry."

"But you can't be serious. If you like, I'll give you more time to think about it."

"That won't change anything, Mrs. Griffin. My answer's still going to be the same. I'm sorry. I really am. Believe me. And I'm very grateful to you for the offer."

"Give me another chance. Do you understand that I'll give you anything you want?" I heard the panic in her voice.

"That's very, very kind of you. But I don't want anything."

"You must want *something!*" she pleaded.

She stood staring at me as if I'd just slapped her. I felt terrible having let her down so.

"Look," I began in an effort to say something to ease her evident pain, "you were right about me. I am too independent. I'm sorry. Maybe you can still get this other girl, whoever she is."

"I don't want her," she replied petulantly. "I want you."

"Look, Mrs. Griffin, this doesn't mean we'll stop being friends. I'll come out and visit you. Often. Really I will."

"It's not the same thing."

She sank down onto one of the antique rattan chairs whose back was shaped like a huge fan.

"Why?" She glared at me defiantly. "Why don't you want to be my daughter?"

"I really can't explain it to you. I'm not sure I can explain it to myself."

"You disapprove of me?"

"No."

"Of my methods? You feel I put you through too much, is that it?" she said.

"No, not at all."

"Don't lie to me," she warned.

I could feel her becoming angry.

"I'm not lying. It's nothing you did. I promise."

"My God—I'm offering you a kingdom! Are you mad?"

I shook my head. "Maybe."

"I'm not giving you another chance, you know," she said in a threatening tone. "If you say no today, that's it. Do you *understand?*"

"Yes. All right," I answered uncomfortably.

She bowed her head and was silent for a long moment. Then she looked up at me, her pale eyes glinting with rage.

"You stupid little bitch!" she hissed.

I was so taken aback by the remark that I burst out laughing.

"What's so funny?"

"Your reaction," I said.

"How the hell do you expect me to react?!" she shrieked.

Her tone of voice, her face—everything about her was suddenly hard-edged and bitter, full of fury and scorn.

"I don't know," I replied. "I suppose I didn't really think about it."

"That's because you're all alike. You never think about anyone but yourselves."

"Who's all alike?"

"All of you! Never mind!"

I wondered whom she meant.

She sat, head bowed, fidgeting with her scarf. Neither of us spoke for a while.

"Well, Mrs. Griffin," I said, finally breaking the silence, "I'd better go out to the ballroom and finish up my work."

"Do you realize just how much of my time you've taken? How long I've spent on you? Years! *Years!*"

"I better go."

I started to leave the room, when she suddenly let out a terrible cry.

"Ooooh! Damn you! Damn you! I'm ill and alone!" she wailed, bursting into tears. "And there's no one left!"

She started sobbing. I couldn't take my eyes off her. God, what a pathetic sight—little gray streams of mascara trickling down her wrinkled cheeks, lipstick caked in the corners of her mouth. She raised her hand to her head and tore off her wig, hurling it across the room.

"God damn you!" she screeched. "God damn life!"

The air reverberated with her cries. She heaved a final sigh, then crumpled back down into the chair.

"I'm sorry, Mrs. Griffin. I truly am."

"That's not good enough." She waved me away with her hand.

"It's the best I can do."

Her moment of agony passed, and she seemed to regain control of her emotions. She drew herself up imperiously and pointed to the wig, which was lying on the floor under a small settee where she'd thrown it.

"My wig," she said. "Get it for me."

I knelt down and picked it up, then walked over and handed it to her. She grabbed it from me, hit it once or twice as if she were knocking off dust, and put it on. Extracting a small mirror from her pocket, she refitted it, tucking in stray wisps of hair. After she was through, she straightened her dress and composed herself.

"You haven't finished your job here," she said coldly.

"No."

"What's left?"

"Just the face of the girl."

"Finish it now."

"Yes, all right."

"I'll tell you exactly how I want it done," she said. "Come with me."

We left the house by the conservatory door and walked to the ballroom by another, less-traveled route. Mrs. Griffin took the lead. I wondered that she wasn't freezing wearing only a light silk dress. I offered her my coat, which she declined.

"But you'll catch cold," I said.

"Never you mind about me," she replied angrily.

Inside, her wheelchair and fur blanket were waiting for her in the middle of the floor. She descended the steps and made herself comfortable in the chair, pulling the blanket up around her.

I prepared my palette and brushes, feeling her eyes on me every moment. I approached the figure of the faceless girl and stood in front of it for a long time without moving, concentrating on the blank head, imagining Cassandra's face then my face, intermingling within the precincts of that smooth white oval. As I raised my brush to begin painting Cassandra's face from memory, the old woman called out to me.

"Come here!"

I walked over to her wheelchair.

"You're not to paint Cassandra's face."

"But she's the centerpiece of the room," I said. "She's the whole point."

"You're not to paint her face," she said firmly.

"Fine. Whose face do you want me to paint?"

She extracted a small rectangular object from beneath her blanket. At first I thought it was a frame. Then I realized what it was.

"Look here," she commanded me. "This face. This is the face I want."

She turned the object around and held it up to me. It was the mirror she had used in the conservatory to adjust her wig. My face was reflected in it.

"Me?" I said, bewildered. "You want me to paint *my* face?"

"Yes. If it's the only thing I'm to have of you."

"I-I don't know—"

"This is a commission," she interrupted. "You will do as I say."

Now *this* was the Frances Griffin of legend—the steely, exacting woman who was accustomed to imposing her will on the artists and craftsmen in her employ.

"Of course. Whatever you like . . . May I borrow the mirror?"

She shoved it into my hand. I walked back to the easel and took up my palette once more. I looked into the mirror and then began to paint. As I sketched my own face in the oval, I felt as if I'd somehow stood outside my life all these years and was now, at this moment, about to break into it. I shaped and shaded the features, taking pains to present a fair account of the countenance I knew so well. Every once in a while I glanced back at Mrs. Griffin, who sat as still as stone, watching me paint. It was a long, arduous process, getting the expression just right.

Having applied the last stroke of paint, I put down my brush and palette and stepped back to view the work. But even before I'd had a chance to reflect on what I'd done, I heard the old woman's voice echoing through the room.

"Not good enough," she said.

I turned around.

"I think it's the best I can do."

"Then you'll have to do better than your best if you expect to get paid."

I bit my lip.

"May I ask what's wrong with it?"

"It has no life or depth. It's a picture without being a portrait. The modeling is flat and without interest. It's a mediocre representation, nothing more."

I turned to look at the face again. She was right. The face *was* flat and without interest.

"I'm afraid I just don't know how to make it any better."

"Rub it out. Start again. This time, concentrate on the expression first. Don't be so worried about the features. Life comes through expression, not through representation."

I did as I was told. I rubbed out the face and began all over again.

"Start with the eyes," she counseled dispassionately. "Go behind them before you paint them. Make them see, but first decide what they're looking at."

I knew what she meant. As I'd painted them before, the eyes had been dull, blind to their surroundings.

"What are they looking at?" she asked.

"You, Mrs. Griffin," I said without turning around.

"Good."

Soon a pair of eyes emerged as vivid and alive and knowing as any in real life. I turned around to see if Mrs. Griffin approved.

"That's better," she nodded. "Now the structure. Start with the bones, the skull. You must learn to paint underneath the surface of things if you ever want to do more than cartoons and faux finishes. Facility is no substitute for depth," she said sharply.

I began sketching in the nose, cheeks, mouth, and chin over the outlines of a skull. I tilted the head, to give it a slightly inquisitive air. Gradually, I put flesh over these bones, building it up, layer upon layer, a painstaking exercise. When I'd finished, I turned around to her again.

"Now concentrate on the mouth. That's where you tell a great portraitist from a merely competent one."

As my brush swept and darted here and there, deepening every feature, informing the expression with plasticity and life, I heard the old woman occasionally muttering under her breath, "That's better . . . Much better . . . No, try again . . ."

Under her exacting tutelage, I became inspired and really began to paint. I knew for the first time what it felt like to work with my heart as well as my hand. The face I painted had weariness and wonder, sophistication and innocence, courage and fearfulness as parts of the whole. My portrait reflected both the soft light of tolerance and the harsh glare of truth. I neither spared nor condemned myself in paint.

I lost track of time. It was the middle of the afternoon when I finally put down my brushes. I looked at the woman I'd created with pride. For the first time, I knew I'd succeeded in painting beneath the surface as well as on top of it. At last I was an artist, not simply a craftsman.

Mrs. Griffin had fallen asleep in her wheelchair. I walked over to her and nudged her gently.

"Mrs. Griffin, it's done."

The old woman awoke fitfully.

"Oh!" she cried out, disoriented.

"It's finished, Mrs. Griffin. Look."

She gazed at the portrait. The figure on the wall was no longer that of a faceless girl, but of a woman on the brink of middle age. She was staring straight at Frances Griffin with a look of candor and forgiveness. She looked as if she were beckoning to the old woman, about to take her hand and guide her through the crowd to a place where they could be alone together. A daughter reaching out to the mother she loved.

Mrs. Griffin sat silently for some time, staring at the portrait. I stood by, waiting for a word of praise, a compliment, a comment. She offered none.

"Tell Deane to come and fetch me. I'm cold and tired," she said in a monotone, closing her eyes.

She pulled the fur blanket up around her neck and seemed to doze off.

As I walked across the garden to get Deane, I paused to look up at the great house. The Haven and everything about it was like a stage set constructed for the peculiar play in which I was an unwitting main character.

I found Deane in the pantry, overseeing the polishing of the silver.

"Mrs. Griffin would like to come inside now," I said.

He looked at me with scant acknowledgment and put on his overcoat. The nurse, who was nearby in the kitchen, followed suit. The three of us went outside. I trailed behind as the two of them made their way to the ballroom to fetch their charge.

Mrs. Griffin said nothing to any of us as we entered. She stared straight ahead without speaking as Deane and the nurse hoisted her in her wheelchair up the marble steps to the main landing. They wheeled her out the door. I watched the sad little trio make their way across the barren winter garden until they were out of sight.

After I packed up my paints and put everything in order for Deane to clean up, I spent some time alone with my masterpiece, looking at it closely, admiring it—especially the portrait of myself. It was good, really good. The best thing I'd ever done by far. I couldn't wait to come back and photograph it for my records. I was proud to have been the creator of this work, prouder still that it would one day be seen by the public when the house became a museum.

Outside the ballroom, I put down my paintbox and sketch pads and lit a cigarette. I thought of the chain of orchestrated events which had led me to this moment. It was Frances Griffin,

not I, who was the trompe l'oeil artist here. She had created a
real trick of the eye.

I had one last drag of my cigarette. I dropped the butt on
the ground, crushing it out with my foot. I didn't bother picking
it up. I left it there intentionally, to disintegrate on the pristine
winter lawn.

As I was loading up my car to drive back to the city, Mrs.
Griffin unexpectedly emerged from the house and walked toward me, signaling me not to go.

"Mrs. Griffin," I said, running to meet her.

"Faith, dear . . ." she said, tenderly putting her hand on
my cheek. "Forgive me. I'm afraid I've been harsh with you."

"No, please, don't apologize—"

"I have, and you must excuse me. It was the disappointment, that's all," she said.

I felt my heart reaching out for the old woman once more.

"Mrs. Griffin, I hope we'll be friends."

"Yes," she said, with a sad look in her eyes, "I want you to
always remember me."

"Of course I will! Of course, dear Mrs. Griffin . . ."

I was touched by her fragility.

"I'm afraid I failed to compliment you on your work," she
went on. "The portrait you've done of yourself is—well, it's
magnificent." I felt a little thrill go through me. "More than I
could have hoped for," she continued. "Is it, do you think, the
best thing you've ever done?"

I thought for a moment, then replied with conviction.

"I do, Mrs. Griffin. And I think it's quite possibly the best
thing I ever will do." She nodded in agreement. "And I have
you to thank for it," I said. "It's all because of you, because you
drew it out of me."

"Well," she said tenderly, "I'm happy I was able to help you
in some way. It's so gratifying to aid an artist in a great creation."

"Do you think it's great, Mrs. Griffin? Because that's all I
really care about—if you think so," I asked, hanging on her
response.

"Oh yes, I think it is great," she said nodding.

"And I'm glad it's here," I replied, "I'm glad it's going to be with you."

"Yes." She paused. "I'm sorry things with us didn't work out another way, but that's life, isn't it?"

"I will come and visit you, I promise. I do so want to keep in touch."

She gave me a radiant smile. She looked restored. It was amazing, I thought, how quickly she could alternate between vigor and exhaustion.

"You're sure you won't change your mind?" she said, as though she already knew my answer.

I shook my head sadly. "No, dear Mrs. Griffin, I can't."

"Well then," she sighed, "that's that."

"Good-bye," I said.

"Oh, no!" she cried. "It's not good-bye—not yet."

"What do you mean?"

"You must come back tomorrow so that I may give you the final payment you deserve. You will come back tomorrow, won't you?"

Though I was quite happy to collect so promptly the rest of the money she owed me, I was much more eager to photograph my masterpiece for my book.

"Of course I'll come back tomorrow," I said. "And may I bring my camera equipment? I always photograph everything I do."

"Yes, indeed!" she beamed. "Please do. Please bring all your equipment. I know you'll want a record of this wonderful work of art."

I could see how genuinely pleased she was with my efforts. She seemed so docile and understanding at that moment, as if she'd forgiven me for refusing her offer.

"Well, Faith, dear," she said, kissing me on the cheek. "It's getting cold and late. Good-bye . . . until tomorrow."

She turned and walked back into the house, hugging her shoulders to keep warm.

All the way home, I kept wondering if I had, in fact, done the right thing after all, or if I'd been a fool not to accept Mrs.

Griffin's generous offer. I thought of the poor old woman all alone in that big house, imprisoned by her luxuries and her memories, gradually being eaten away by her illness. Would it have been so terrible, I thought, to be with her as a comforting presence for the little time she had left? After all, it wasn't a matter of years. She was very ill—dying. Had I been too selfish?

As I drove, I imagined what her life would now be like without me as a daily distraction for her. I thought of her strolling over to the ballroom every now and then to look at my murals, and perhaps to think of me. I wondered if she'd continue to call me from time to time and ask me to visit her. I wondered how long she would live. I made up my mind to keep in touch with her. I felt that Mrs. Griffin's last display of affection toward me that afternoon could not have been easy for her. It had taken courage and kindness in the wake of a deep disappointment. It had made me realize that I was, indeed, fond of her after all. Not only that, I respected her more than anyone I knew, for it was she who had forced me to do my best work, setting me firmly on a path long obscured. Lastly, she was my only connection to Harry, whom I still loved and missed, despite all that I now knew about him.

I stayed up most of the night, throwing away all the old clippings about Cassandra, making a list of the clients I would call to say that I was back in business, as well as preparing my photography equipment for the next day. I packed up lights, a tripod, two cameras, and several rolls of film—color and black-and-white. I wanted to take great care in photographing the ballroom, especially my self-portrait.

I drove out to The Haven around noon the next day, when I had hoped the light would be strong and bright for my photographs. Unfortunately, the sun, which had been shining all morning, retreated under a veil of gray clouds just as I pulled in the driveway. The landscape glowed with an eerie silver light. I parked in the courtyard and began unloading my camera equipment to take to the ballroom.

Walking across the garden toward the ballroom, I wondered where Mrs. Griffin was, if she was going to come down and visit with me while I took my pictures, or if she was simply going to say good-bye to me at the very end. There didn't seem to be anyone around, not even Deane, who usually appeared somewhere whenever I arrived on the property. The increasing darkness of the day made me glad I'd brought along several lights, despite the inconvenience of having to carry them.

I trudged up the steps of the ballroom loaded down with equipment, feeling an impending sense of excitement at seeing my creation again—especially the self-portrait. Would it look as miraculous to me today, I wondered? Was Mrs. Griffin right? Was it the best thing I'd ever do in my entire life? I thanked God it was here, in this great house, where it would be preserved and properly cared for. If I couldn't keep it myself, what better home could I have provided for it?

Something—I'm not sure what—made me hesitate before I entered the ballroom. I put down my equipment and took a deep breath. I closed my eyes, swung open the doors, then walked inside, my eyes still closed. I wanted to snap them open, to take in my creation all at once. I stood poised for an instant, eyes shut . . . Then I opened them.

The horror I felt at the sight that greeted me was beyond measure. I clapped my hands over my mouth, stifling a scream that arose from the depths of my soul. The room was white! Not a clean, pristine white—but a terrible, haphazard white, the foam on a great ocean storm! Streaks of it, globs of it, raging over the walls like some ghastly hurricane of whitewash! Nothing was left of my creation but a few random patches of color where the paint had failed to cover the mural completely. Even the ceiling was covered with white swirls—the cherubs, the clouds, the moon—all gone.

The most frightening sight of all, however, was the figure in the center panel—my self-portrait, my masterpiece. Here, no simple whitewash had been used. A grisly impression of my face and body was left, eaten away in parts so that the flesh took on the aspect of rotting carrion. The dress looked as if it had been melted by a blowtorch.

At first, I could not imagine what force had created this sickening effect. I walked slowly toward it. One of my eyes, still in perfect order on that jigsawed face, stared at me as I crossed the room. I was less than three feet away when I realized what had happened, for I smelled an unmistakable stench emanating from the wall. For a moment I stood paralyzed. My self-portrait, my masterpiece—had been attacked with *acid!*

I felt dizzy and nauseous—reeling at both the smell and the sight of the picture. I fell against the wall, barely missing the still-damp, acid-soaked image, and sank to the ground as though I'd been stabbed. There, I began to weep.

Of all the things Frances Griffin could have done to me— this was unquestionably the cruelest. She had built me up, only to tear me down again. Having helped me give birth, she had destroyed the child!

I don't know how long I cowered there, sobbing away with a mixture of fear, anger, and self-pity. Gradually, however, my wails abated into intermittent whimpers. Finally, I was mute. Dragging myself up off the ground, I staggered outside, weak and distressed. I gathered up my camera equipment. It was all I could do to get myself across that godforsaken garden.

I reached my car and threw the gear inside. As I was about to get in, I felt a tap on my shoulder. I turned around with a start. It was Deane, looking grave. I couldn't help it—I threw myself at him and began beating on his chest!

"YOU LET HER!" I screamed. "YOU LET HER DE-STROY IT! YOU BASTARD! YOU BASTARD!"

Deane stood his ground, taking my pathetic blows without flinching. When I finally calmed down, he pulled out a hand-kerchief from his pocket and handed it to me. I took it and wiped my eyes.

"Oh, Deane, I'm sorry," I said, shaking my head. "I know it's not your fault. But why, *why* did she do it?"

"I don't know, Miss," he replied with a pained expression on his face.

"Who did it? Who helped her?" I said. "You?"

"She did everything herself, even the ceiling. I brought the ladder, that's all. She was up the whole night."

"She used acid on my portrait, didn't she?"

Deane hung his head and nodded.

"She's insane," I sighed, expecting no response.

None was given. Deane extracted an envelope from his jacket and handed it to me. I recognized Mrs. Griffin's pale blue stationery.

"Mrs. Griffin has asked me to give you this. It's your last payment," he said softly.

I opened the envelope. It was a check for more money than I'd ever seen. So much, in fact, that it looked like a bit of trompe l'oeil itself.

"This check isn't my last payment, Deane," I said, astonished. "It's about ten times my entire fee."

"I wouldn't know," Deane replied.

"She didn't leave me any other message?"

"No."

"Well . . . I suppose this is meant to be some sort of consolation. Wouldn't you say, Deane? She kills my baby and then she gives me a small fortune for my efforts. Everything has a price, right? Right, Deane?" I swallowed hard.

Deane hesitated. I could see this was a difficult moment for him. He bit his lip.

"Miss," he began, looking around furtively as if to make sure no one could overhear.

"Yes, Deane? What is it?"

"We all thought it was a beautiful thing, your work."

He so touched me at this moment that I blinked back new tears.

"Did you, Deane? Did you really? You have no idea how much that means to me," I said.

"We did," he said shyly.

"Thank you so much."

I looked at the check again, then carefully tore it in half and handed the pieces back to Deane.

"Do me a favor," I said. "Please tell Mrs. Griffin her final payment isn't necessary. She's already given it to me—*in full.*"

Deane nodded sympathetically, the flicker of a smile on his lips.

"I'll tell her," he said.

Just as I was about to get into my car, I stopped.

"Deane?" I said, suddenly wondering something.

"Yes, Miss Crowell?"

"How the hell did she do it?" I said.

"What, Miss?"

"How did she whitewash that entire room? That's a lot of work!"

Deane hesitated for a moment. I sensed he was on the verge of telling me something.

"Deane?" I said, pressing him. "Deane, what is it?"

Once again, he checked around to see if anyone could possibly be watching or listening. Then he drew close and put his lips against my ear.

"She's not sick," he whispered.

"What?"

"She doesn't have cancer," he went on. "She's not dying. It was all a show for sympathy, and God knows what else. She's as healthy as a horse. She'll outlive us all, the old bitch."

My eyes widened. I couldn't believe it.

"What are you *saying?* Why on earth would she make something like that up? Why would she want me to think she was terminally ill with only a short time—?"

I hardly got the question out before I knew the answer myself.

Looking at me with a stony, knowing expression, Deane said: "You tell me."

We nodded to one another in mutual comprehension. Deane turned around and started heading for the house. I got into my car and drove slowly down the driveway, glancing back at the great estate in my rearview mirror. I saw Deane go inside and close the front door behind him.

Then I caught a glimpse of someone watching me from a

window on the second floor. Slamming on the brakes, I jumped out of the car and faced the house, looking up at the window. I saw Frances Griffin glaring down at me, rocking back and forth, her demented laughter ringing out in the winter air.

I stretched out my arm and aimed it at her, pointing an accusatory finger. As I did so, her ghastly laughter stopped. Her face froze. She stepped back from the window into the shadows. With that, the curtain fell.

EPILOGUE

I sold the painting Harry had left me at auction. It fetched a remarkable price, partially on account of its provenance. The expert at Sotheby's found it had once been in the collection of Mr. and Mrs. Holt Griffin, a fact that was included in large black type in the sale catalogue. The money from the painting, as well as Frances Griffin's first two payments, has allowed me to take some time off.

The sign on my door no longer reads TROMPE L'OEIL, INC. I've closed up shop for a while. I am traveling.